GIVE MY LOVE
to the
Chestnut Trees

"Beverly Varnado spins a wonderful and touching tale, weighted with the folklore and beauty of St. Simons Island. The reader is moved to recall the trials of youth and the profound triumph of discovering great wisdom in our 'odd' elders."

-RUSTY WHITENER,
author of *A Season of Miracles,* Christy Award Finalist

"Beverly Varnado writes with the passion of a bygone era. Her characters leap from the page!"

-ELIZABETH LUDWIG,
author of *Love Finds You in Calico, California*

"This sentimental journey pulled me back to my own childhood. Purely enchanting. Picturesque. A tender, yet tenacious tale of growing up one memorable summer."

-MARION BOND WEST,
author of *Praying for My Life*

GIVE MY LOVE
to the
Chestnut Trees

To Beth,
  many thanks for your support
and encouragement.
        Blessings,
          Beverly Varnado

Beverly Varnado

Jane Kilburn May 2012
Judy Whitaker June 2012

WestBow
P R E S S
A DIVISION OF THOMAS NELSON

WestBow Press books may be ordered through booksellers or by contacting:

WestBow Press
A Division of Thomas Nelson
1663 Liberty Drive
Bloomington, IN 47403
www.westbowpress.com
1-(866) 928-1240

ISBN: 978-1-4497-2360-6 (sc)
ISBN: 978-1-4497-2361-3 (hc)
ISBN: 978-1-4497-2359-0 (e)

Library of Congress Control Number: 2011914733

Printed in the United States of America

WestBow Press rev. date: 09/15/2011

Contents

For Jerry

Thank you for believing in the story and for believing in me.

Chapter One

A Big Loss

Seeing the world takes more than just physical eyesight. Your heart also has to see.

As I sit at the marsh border, I take the pen from my backpack to ink the Southern-flavored utterances of the character cast in my head. From a cloudless cerulean sky, the calls of two herring gulls distract me, interrupting this otherwise tranquil June morning—a morning in many ways like the inaugural morning I spent here over two decades ago as a fourteen year old girl on St. Simons Island. The dark anxiety I felt then obscured my vision ... I never saw the gulls. Not for a long time.

Today, the gulls join a group of feathery comrades and soar out toward East Beach. A sultry breeze, pungent with the aroma of an ebbing tide, tosses my hair and meanders on to the expanse of golden marsh where I often still hear her voice when the grass ruffles in waves to the blue horizon: "Mary Helen, did I ever tell you the story about ... ?"

As I touch pen to paper, a scream from behind me splits the calm, and a painful smack sends me tumbling toward the marsh, where I end up on my back in tall, thick grass. The coolness of murky water seeps through my shorts and shirt. Out of the confusion, a woman's voice emerges.

"Are you all right? I'm so sorry."

Hands are on me, brushing debris away. I shake my head to re-orient, manage to rub the point of impact on my back, and look at my hand. No bleeding. I shake my head again. As I try to focus my eyes against the eastern sun, a figure hovers over me.

"You're a mess. Can I help you up?"

"What?" I manage to ask.

"I became distracted while looking at the egrets in the marsh, ran off the path, and hit you. I can't believe I was so careless," the young woman says, a bike helmet topping her long blond hair.

Still dazed, I push myself to a sitting position. A sleek new bicycle lies to my right on the creek bank. I gather my legs under me, and as I raise myself up, the mushy bottom of the marsh oozes between my fingers.

"Is anything broken?" She asks helping me to my feet.

"No, I'm fine. Just in shock. I was lost in thought and didn't hear the bicycle coming. It seemed like you descended from the sky." I rub my palms together, but can't get rid of the muck, so I wipe them on my shorts.

The cyclist moves to the marsh edge and bends over. "Is this yours?" She holds up my coffee-colored journal.

I nod, thankful.

"Great, it didn't go in the water. Good as new," she says. She wipes off the cover and hands it to me, and I welcome the feel of the smooth leather.

"Thanks. Do you see my pen anywhere?"

We cover the area, searching the bank and the edge of the water.

"It has to be here." Anxious, I retrace the path of my roll down the hill. "Do you see it?"

"No, I don't," she answers from over near the creek.

As I continue to search with no results, sickening tendrils of pain creep across my chest bearing the message of an inestimable loss. I sink down on the bank and put my head in my hands. A picture of the pen hitting the water during the accident rolls in my head like a YouTube video and troubles me with its twisted ending—the pen descending to the bottom, sucked into sticky goo, lost forever.

"It can't be gone." A sob tears at my throat.

The cyclist comes over to sit beside me and says, "I owe you a pen for the trouble I've caused. Even if it was a Montblanc, I'll buy you another."

My eyes mist. I can't say any words, but I rub my thumb and forefinger together imagining the comforting feel of the pen's fine wood grain.

She touches my arm. "Just tell me the pen you want, and I'll order it online within an hour. I'll get express shipping. It could be here tomorrow."

A tear rolls down my cheek, and then there is a long pause between us.

"We could have it here tonight."

I turn to the cyclist. "You don't understand. It's irreplaceable."

She takes her arm from my shoulders, skeptical. "Irreplaceable? What's it made of—gold?"

"Not gold. Chestnut. It's made of chestnut wood, but that's not the reason it's irreplaceable." I wipe my eyes with the back of my hand. "Someone I cared about gave it to me."

"Someone like a boyfriend?"

"No—a great aunt. I met her the summer my mama got cancer, the summer I first saw the marshes of Glynn."

Chapter Two

Asheville, North Carolina, April 1988

"Mary Helen, time to get up, sweetie. Your waffle's getting cold."

A light knock on the door and then Mama stuck her head into my room. "I ironed your new outfit last night. It's hanging in your closet."

I opened my eyes to Mama's soft, smiling face, the face that meant home to me. She was already dressed for her job at Franklin's Department Store. My friend Leslie said I had the prettiest, most stylish mama anywhere, and Leslie and I agreed about almost everything except who was the cutest boy in eighth grade. Mama was not only beautiful, but she was the center of my universe. Of course I was the center of hers.

Leslie said I was spoiled … maybe I was, but I liked it. I felt as if I lived in a snow-globe world in our house in Asheville, North Carolina. And if I did, Mama was its lone protector in a blue silk blouse. She crossed the room to my bed, leaned over, and gave me a kiss on the head.

"Up, up," she said, and then stepped out the door. I heard the delicate tap of her pumps descending the stairs and inhaled the lingering fragrance of roses in her cologne.

I sat up and stretched my hands high over my head, surrounded by the cozy cocoon of the bedroom I'd slept in since a baby. I smoothed the bedspread Mama had bought for me last week.

"Chintz," she'd called it.

I liked the word "chintz."

"The latest," Mama had said.

I studied the pattern of lavish pink flowers and leaves. "We're going to cover you in peonies," I remembered her saying. When I went to bed at night, I imagined I was sleeping on one of those rose floats in the New Year's Day parades. Instead of roses, I floated on peonies.

I reached to the nightstand for my journal. The night before, I'd recorded the tragedy of my eighth-grade year: Leslie had been ill with mononucleosis for two weeks. She'd gotten sick the day after my fourteenth birthday, and the devastating event left me with no one to confide in, no one besides Mama, of course. Leslie seemed to be better at last, and her mother said she'd return to school in a couple of days. I'd almost reached the end of my endurance and found consolation in writing in my journal.

My teacher, Mrs. Harding, said I had a gift for writing. I didn't know what difference that made to anybody else, but writing did make me feel better. I put the journal under my pillow, crawled out of bed, brushed my teeth and hair, and put on my new jeans and pink shirt. I studied my reflection in the mirror on the back of the closet door. What a cute outfit. I was glad Mama received a great discount at Franklin's.

Later, as I ate my waffle, Mama perched at the kitchen desk sipping coffee and opening mail.

She looked up from her stack of envelopes. "Don't forget you have piano this afternoon. Please put your books in the car so we'll have them when you take your lesson." Mama pointed to my music lying on the table. I saw the dreaded Mozart book on top. The sonata I'd been practicing bored me. I longed for a more exciting and showy selection to play in the recital, maybe a piece like "Clair de Lune." I loved Debussy. His music seemed so romantic. "I don't like what I'm working on."

Mama put aside the letter she was reading. "Maybe we can talk to Mrs. Anderson about changing the music. I don't want you to be unhappy about it." She reached over and touched my sleeve reassuringly. "You look darling in your new outfit." Then she went back to opening mail.

The coffee—and syrup-scented morning seemed full of tomorrows, just like today, but something felt wrong, and I didn't know why. Mama was usually sunny and talkative in the morning, but this morning, she grew strangely quiet and still. I stole a glance her way, but she seemed to notice only the letter in her hand.

A strange uneasiness warned that my snow-globe world was in danger. That's the problem with snow globes—they don't fare too well if knocked off the shelf—and I felt a big shove coming.

Just when I was about to ask if something was wrong, Mama slid the letter into her pocket and told me I was going to be late for school.

Mama often said I didn't miss a thing and that I was going to have my own detective agency when I grew up.

Later that week, I'd left my algebra book downstairs and came down from my bedroom to find it. When I picked up the book, I heard Mama in the kitchen.

I'm not sure what made me stop and listen—the tone in her voice, I guess. I crept down the hallway so I could hear a little better.

"Amy, I'm scared. This waiting to hear more about the situation is horrible," Mama said.

What was she talking about with her friend Amy? "Waiting to hear more"—about what?

"Ever since I received the letter, I've been scared out of my wits."

Scared of what? Could it have been the letter at breakfast? I couldn't erase the picture out of my mind of her sitting so quietly.

"And Mary Helen … what will happen to Mary Helen?" A chill pressed in on me, making me queasy. Amy must've had to get off the phone because Mama hung up a few seconds later. I could hear her crying. I wanted to ask her about it, but she'd know I'd been snooping again, so I went back upstairs to my room. When I finally went to bed, sleep chased me all night.

"Crying?" Leslie asked the next day as she pushed her lunch tray away from her. "Does she cry much?"

"Hardly ever." As I thought about it, the only time I remembered Mama crying was that sad time long ago, and then it was only when I woke one night with a bad dream and slipped into her room in the wee hours. In the broken moonlight falling through her bedroom window, I saw her glistening face. "Mama, are you crying?"

Instead of answering my question, she asked one of her own, "Sweetie, did you have a bad dream?"

It was always about me.

What did her tears mean now?

"Beats me what's going on," Leslie said, and then drained her milk carton. "You could ask her."

"No way. If she wants me to know, she'll tell me. Plus, she'll know I was eavesdropping. She jokes with me already about being too nosy."

*

It all started with us sitting down to eat a regular dinner.

"Mary Helen, I need to speak with you," she said.

I was sure she was going to fuss about my leaving my music books at home again. She'd been late returning to work that day because she'd had to retrieve my books from home before I could go to my piano lesson.

But she didn't mention it. Oh, how I wish it had been that.

"I've had to have a few medical tests lately."

I chewed the bite of chicken in my mouth and swallowed. "You mean like looking in your throat and tapping your knee. Stuff like that?"

Mama glanced away for a moment. "No, not like that. These tests were …" Mama hesitated. "Were more extensive." She paused again.

Worried, I put my fork down and searched her face. "What, Mama?"

"Mary Helen, I don't know how to tell you this, but … I have cancer."

Chapter Three

The Marshes of Glynn

Dad was dead from the accident, and Mama had cancer. I could see a snow globe falling from a shelf, shattering as it made contact with an unforgiving surface, and splintering into a thousand tiny shards.

Mama found out about the cancer the morning that had seemed full of waffle syrup, coffee, cute outfits, and peonies—the morning I knew something was wrong.

"What kind of cancer?" I finally managed to ask.

"Breast cancer," Mama paused, "but the doctor thinks it's contained. I'm going to be fine. I just have to have the surgery … the mastectomy."

In seventh grade, the assistant principal, Mrs. Thornton, had that same surgery. I couldn't stand to think of my beautiful Mama having her breast removed. I flew over to the other side of the table and wrapped my arms around her.

After a few minutes, I finally pulled my arms from Mama's neck and tried to stop sobbing. I wiped my face with my napkin, straightened my pink shirt, and managed to sit back in my chair. Just as I started to pull myself together, she dropped another bombshell. She wanted me to go to my Aunt Laney's to stay while she had the surgery.

"Who's Aunt Laney?" I didn't have any aunts that I knew of.

"She's actually your great-aunt. We saw her at a funeral for one of your dad's great-uncles, and she was also at that wedding in Macon for the Wests' daughter."

"I don't remember Aunt Laney, and I don't want to go to her house. I want to stay here with you. I don't know her, I don't know her," I cried. A creeping loneliness filled my stomach, making me sick of my still-full plate of chicken and rice. I pushed the plate away and put my forehead on the table.

Mama kept talking like this was the most normal conversation in the world. "I'm sure you remember. How should I describe her?" She paused, I assumed, to choose her words with care. "She's very tall and talked about how much you resembled your grandmother."

I lifted my head off the table and blinked. "Wait a minute. Tall. I remember somebody tall—and weird. She had on clothing that resembled a housecoat without sleeves, a gypsy dress. You can't be talking about her." I waited for Mama to tell me no, but she didn't.

"Your dad always spoke highly of her," Mama said at last. "Aunt Laney is one of the last relatives we have left. She said she always wanted you to come and stay with her."

This couldn't be happening. She couldn't be sending me away.

Mama granted me a sad smile, "You'll love staying on St. Simons Island."

I braced my elbows on the table, "No, I won't. I'm fourteen. I'll be fine while you're in the hospital. I want to stay here with you."

Mama sighed. "Mary Helen …" She took a long sip of water. "I won't be able to take care of you because of the surgery. I won't be able to drive, cook or do much else for a while."

Her brow wrinkled when she extended her slender hands almost as if she was pleading with me. "If you could stay with Aunt Laney for six weeks, it would be a big help."

My heart ached at the thought of how much I'd miss her, and I hadn't even left. But it was what Mama wanted. I shifted in my seat and dried my face with my napkin. For Mama's sake, I tried to be brave. I bit my lip. "When do I have to go?"

"We'll leave the day after school's out next week, because the doctor has scheduled my surgery for two days later, on June third."

I rose from my chair, crossed over to Mama, knelt, and put my head in her lap. The aura of fragrant roses that always surrounded her encapsulated me. "We've never been apart so long. How will we survive without each other?"

Her fingers ran through my hair. "We'll both be fine."

I raised my head and gazed into her eyes. "Promise me you won't die?"

"I promise."

A sob pushed its way again to the back of my throat, and as it escaped, we both knew she had no idea whether she could keep that promise.

A couple of hours later I pulled my journal from my nightstand. I wanted to write something deep, but all I did was fill two pages with "I don't want to go to Aunt Laney's." Maybe if I wrote it in black ink enough times, I wouldn't have to go.

Cancer had always been one of those words I'd read about in books or seen on TV. It knocked on someone else's door—not mine—not Mama's. I looked down at my shirt. How could I find out my mama had cancer when I was wearing a pink shirt? Pink was for happy times and celebrations. I pulled the shirt over my head and threw it on the floor. I never wanted to see it again.

*

"Being away from Mama for six whole weeks makes having mononucleosis seem good," I told Leslie the next day at lunch. "I can't stand to think about what's happening to her."

Leslie handed me the napkin from her lunch box to dab my eyes.

Then I had the idea to drink from Leslie's soda can and lick the spoon she'd used to eat her pudding in case she had a few good mononucleosis germs still hanging around. I figured that if I was near death, Mama wouldn't send me away, and I could stay close to her.

Leslie's germs must have all died, because I didn't even catch the sniffles.

And when I thought matters couldn't get worse, I wound up playing the Mozart *Sonata* in the recital after all.

"Too late to change, don't you think?" Mrs. Anderson asked me at my next piano lesson.

"No, I think I could do it," I said, holding the Debussy piece open in my hand.

"I don't think you can."

Why had she asked me then? I exhaled sharply.

Mrs. Anderson took the music book and settled on the piano bench beside me. "Mary Helen, music is not only about playing the notes. Music is much more. We can learn lessons from music that will stay with us our whole life. One of them is discipline. It takes discipline to stick with a piece and perfect it."

"Why can't I learn discipline playing the Debussy?" I was sure I had her there.

"You've already started work on the Mozart." She paused and put her hand on mine. "Mary Helen," she said in a gentler voice, "we don't always get to do what we want."

She was sure right about that, I thought, as my trip to Aunt Laney's loomed before me.

*

"I'll write you," Leslie said on the last day of school as we waited for our moms to pick us up. Any other year, the last day of school would be a time of celebration. Not this year. "Here's my address at Camp Whitestone." She handed me a sheet of notebook paper with three lines of printing on it.

I took the paper, unable to speak.

"I wish I was going with you, instead of to camp," Leslie said earnestly, pushing the strap of her purse back on her shoulder.

"Me too," I whispered. I reached into my jeans pocket and pulled out the now-wrinkled piece of paper Mama had given me with Aunt Laney's address and pressed it into Leslie's hand.

She took it and threw her arms around my neck. "I'm sure going to miss you."

I hugged her with the embrace of somebody headed for the gallows.

The next day, the sun hadn't come up when I helped Mama pack my bags in our white Oldsmobile, and we pulled out of our driveway to make the long drive to the Georgia coast.

The world beyond my snow globe of Asheville was a mystery to me. Of course I'd seen pictures in magazines and books, but I'd never been much farther south than Greenville, South Carolina. We did go to Myrtle Beach one year, stayed in one of those big hotels on the beach, and played putt-putt golf at a place with a giant green concrete dinosaur. A lot of fun, but Mama said St. Simons Island was nothing like Myrtle Beach. Whether she meant that in a good way or a bad way, I didn't know. Either way it wouldn't change things now.

After we passed into Georgia, we exited the interstate at a sign marked Toccoa, Lavonia, Highway 17. We turned left when we came up the ramp, and it seemed we went through a hundred little towns before the rolling foothills started to flatten out.

"The land looks different here," I said.

"It's because we're below the fall line. Many, many years ago, all of this land used to be on the bottom of the ocean. I've heard stories about

11

people going out in their cow pastures here and unearthing fossils of sea creatures."

Scrub pine trees stretched out in either direction, and I tried to imagine exotic saltwater fish swimming there. I was good at imagining but couldn't come up with a picture for that.

Mama and I didn't talk about cancer. She talked about how sweet I was as a baby and my cute little girl antics—like the time she told me to clean my room when I was five. I told her I didn't have any energy left.

"Why don't you have any energy?" she'd asked.

"I used all my energy making the mess and don't have any left to clean it up."

I never did have much energy for cleaning.

It seemed Mama could remember about everything I ever did or said, and while we were on the way to St. Simons, she told me the stories. I could hardly think of any response, except, "Turn the car around and take me home," which, of course, I didn't say, because it would have made Mama feel worse. It seemed she wanted to live in the past during those hours in the car. I did too.

After traveling most of the day, we finally arrived at a red light in Brunswick with our left blinker on, waiting to turn on to the bridge that would take us to the island and Aunt Laney.

Mama gestured to her left. "There they are—the marshes of Glynn."

The anxiety of arrival rose in me. I forced myself to turn my eyes to the left and saw a field of ochre-yellow grass that stretched to where it met the sky. But I knew it wasn't a field. I knew, because Mama had told me earlier, the tall grass had its feet covered in seawater.

"What's the 'of Glynn' part about?" I asked.

"This is Glynn County. Also, I believe there's a poem called 'The Marshes of Glynn.'"

"Oh."

"After we cross over the causeway, you're going to feel like you're in another world."

I liked my old world.

After we turned left, I tried to take in what seemed a whole ocean of marsh grass. I opened my window, inhaled, and almost choked. "What's that smell?"

"That, my dear, is the smell of the marsh."

"You mean I'm going to have to smell that for the next six weeks?" I'd never smelled an odor like it before.

"You'll grow used to it. In fact, you may even come to like it. I remember your dad talking about how he loved the smell of the marsh."

I never knew what to say when Mama brought up Dad.

We crossed over the causeway bridge to a road called Demere. I started to understand what Mama meant by "another world."

"What are those trees?"

"Live oaks. Isn't it a pretty effect with the moss draped on them?"

I didn't think it was a pretty effect at all. The dripping webs of moss evoked an eerie feeling in me. A midnight-monster-movie shiver ran up my spine as we passed under a dark canopy of live oaks standing so close to the road, I thought one might stretch out a snaky limb and grab us. I leaned closer to Mama just in case.

"Where does she live?" Not that I cared that much, but I needed a distraction to take my mind from the creepy trees.

"We've already passed her street. We're going to meet her in the Village. She's crabbing down at the pier."

There seemed to be no end to the oddities of this island. "Crabbing?"

"Setting traps with bait out on the ocean floor. Periodically, she pulls them up by a string to take the crabs out. That's probably what she's having for dinner tonight."

I imagined Aunt Laney shoving crab claws into her mouth. I tried to push the scene out of my mind. "I'm not eating any crabs. They sound disgusting."

"I'm sure you won't have to. I told her you've never eaten much seafood, growing up in Asheville. She said that was fine. She'd have other items on the menu."

Mama turned on her right-turn signal light and pulled onto a road signed Ocean Boulevard. That must have meant we were almost there. Then she turned left onto Mallery Street, and I could tell we were in the Village. Some other time, the slate blue strip of ocean on the horizon in front of us might have seemed enticing. Not today.

There were quite a few cars in the Village, which slowed us down and gave me the opportunity to study the stores on my side of the car. I spotted an art gallery featuring large seascapes and a hardware store offering pieces of fence with some sort of mesh baskets and mailboxes in the window. We rolled a few feet past doll-house-sized Village Jewelers, which appeared as if you could stand in the middle and put your hands on both of the side walls. Next up was Dressner's Café, and then St. Simons Drug Company which displayed inflatable floats. There wasn't any sign of a bus station—

which was mandatory for my number-one plan for escaping this island—a one-way bus ticket back to Asheville. I brought my birthday money with me, and if it became necessary, I was prepared to spend it all.

A group of children, obviously ignorant of life's complications, blew bubbles with a gigantic plastic wand in front of a novelty store, which had cages bearing signs that read Hermit Crabs for Sale. And according to a poster in the window, St. Simons Island Bait and Tackle offered Free Tide Charts. As we neared the end of the street, the Sandcastle Restaurant sported picnic tables with sand buckets containing silverware. Still no bus station. I scanned the other side of the street and didn't see one either. I began to feel a lot like those caged crabs.

We parked in a space close to the pier, a giant concrete structure standing on spider like legs, which stuck into the ocean. The part nearest the parking lot had a roof over it. Big birds, which I assumed were seagulls, lined up as if in a queue on the rooftop. Along the sides of the pier, people huddled in groups holding fishing poles, talking, pulling on strings in the ocean.

Aunt Laney was easy to spot. "I see her. She's wearing a housecoat again," I said with dread.

"It's called a tunic."

Mama knew the names of clothing because she had worked at Franklin's for so long. Tunic or housecoat, no matter, it was still weird, and this one had stripes on it like a carnival tent—a real spectacle.

When I turned to Mama, her brow wrinkled again with that desperate look. "Mary Helen, please. I've tried to work out the best possible arrangements for you. Aunt Laney is a caring and interesting person. Be nice, okay?" Mama took her hand and placed it under my chin, "Okay?"

"Okay," I said, sighed, and then looked back over to Aunt Laney.

"Let's go." Mama used a stern tone of voice I hadn't often heard. She grabbed her purse from the floor of the car and reached for the door handle. There wasn't a thing to do but get out.

Chapter Four

Aunt Laney and Sidney Lanier

As we approached the pier, the sun's effect on the ocean caused it to shimmer as if illuminated by a million tiny bulbs. I felt strangely unaffected by it.

Aunt Laney had her back to us and gazed out at the ocean. Her straight, mid-length, almost completely gray hair blew in the sea breeze.

We walked on to the pier, and Mama touched her on the shoulder. "Aunt Laney."

She swung around. "Laura." When she turned to us, her tanned face was lined with deep wrinkles, her eyes pale blue. She vigorously grabbed Mama and about squeezed the living daylights out of her.

"Good to see you. It's been such a long time." Then she spotted me.

"And Mary Helen …" She let go of Mama and came after me. "Named after my sister and the spitting image of her too. My, how you've grown."

When she gave me the squeeze, I wiggled a little so she couldn't get a good grip on me.

"We're going to have such fun together." Aunt Laney pulled away, glanced back for a second, and then turned and faced us again. Her housecoat flew out behind her in the breeze like a superhero cape.

"I know you folks are tired after the nine-hour drive, so y'all hold on and let me check my trap to see if I have a catch. Then we'll go on over to the house." Aunt Laney turned away and began to tug on a string. After a few seconds, a wire basket with something disgusting in it came up out of the water.

I guessed that was what a crab trap looked like.

Aunt Laney peered into it. "No, the crabs must be taking the day off. They left the liver alone today." She shook the reddish brown meat lying in the basket bottom into the ocean, collapsed the mesh layers, and put it in a plastic bag at her feet along with another container. "We'll come back tomorrow; I have plenty of liver left. Most people use chicken backs"—a big smile spread across her face— "but I've always had a lot of success with the liver." She emphasized the word *liver*.

We all started back to the cars along a palm tree-lined walkway. An older man in a sport coat, crisp white shirt, and bow tie strode toward us, a black standard poodle on a leash at his side. With so many clothes on I expected he'd be perspiring when he reached us, but as he came closer, there was not even a bead of sweat on his upper lip.

He stopped when he reached Aunt Laney. "Laney, how are you? We're eagerly anticipating your show next week."

Aunt Laney stopped and hugged the man. "Thanks, Sylvester." She gestured toward us. "Wait, I want you to meet my nephew's family, Laura and Mary Helen." Aunt Laney wrapped her arm around Sylvester's shoulders. "Sylvester Myers—my good friend."

Sylvester extended his hand to us. "Pleased to meet you both," he said shaking our hands vigorously. Sylvester's bow tie bobbed up and down when he spoke. It must have been the placement of his Adam's apple.

I shook his hand, "I like your dog."

"Thanks. Harold does enjoy a stroll, because he always draws at least one person over to pet him. He's quite sociable." Sylvester leaned over and stroked the dog's head.

I stooped to study Harold's face. It seemed he should be wearing a bow tie too. I loved it that he didn't sport the typical poodle cut with the hair taken down to the skin in places, but he had only a little short black curly hair all over his body. I rubbed Harold's ears as Sylvester continued to talk.

"I hope you folks can make the show. Laney has quite a following in this part of the state, especially for her Lanier pieces."

Mama answered, "I'm sorry I can't make it, but I'm sure Mary Helen would love to come."

What was she committing me to? I glanced up at Mama but didn't say a word.

"I was going to call you today, Laney," Sylvester said. "Come over Wednesday and we'll hang your pieces."

"I'll see you then."

We all said our goodbyes and started again to our cars. Aunt Laney turned and said, "You folks just follow me. I'll take a short cut." Aunt Laney slid into a big yellow Cadillac convertible.

"What kind of show was Mr. Myers talking about?" I asked Mama once we were in the car.

She cranked the car and started to back out of the space. "Aunt Laney is an artist. I'd almost forgotten about that. Mr. Myers must be involved with a gallery somehow."

"What did he mean by Lanier pieces?"

"I have no idea." She turned back onto Ocean Boulevard.

We followed Aunt Laney for a short time and then turned in behind her on a gravel driveway. I couldn't believe my eyes. "Mama, you're leaving me with a woman who lives in a house the color of stomach medicine?" Nobody in North Carolina had pink houses.

I thought of the magnificent Biltmore House the Vanderbilt family had built in Asheville. Mama and I loved to tour it, especially at Christmas. Antiques and masterpieces filled every room. I especially loved Mrs. Vanderbilt's bedroom, with its yellow silk-covered walls and its purple and gold velvet upholstery.

I'd hate to think what the Vanderbilts would say about the color of Aunt Laney's house.

Her house had brilliant pink walls with lime-green shutters. Planters by the front door featured an assortment of ill-matched petunias, geraniums, and some sort of succulents. I'd learned the names of flowers when Mama bought her planter flowers in the spring. In addition, several yard ornaments, which seemed to have been handmade because I'd never seen any like them at Wal-Mart, stood in the yard. One, a giant sunflower, appeared to be staring right at me.

Mama raised her eyebrows. "Mary Helen, you promised."

And I had. "Okay, okay." I bit my lip.

Mama popped the trunk and went around back to retrieve her overnight case and my suitcase. She called, "Come on, honey," but I couldn't make my legs move. They felt heavy, like they were tied to concrete blocks. Mama came to my side of the car and put the bags down. She opened the car door and eased onto the edge of the seat with me. She whispered, "You know I wouldn't leave you in the care of someone I didn't trust."

"I know." I was in danger of biting clean through my lip. Somehow I managed to pick up my backpack, move my concrete-block legs, and drag myself out of the car.

The sunflower glared at me mockingly as I trudged to the front porch, up the steps, and followed Mama into Aunt Laney's house.

"Y'all come in. I'll just put this crab trap out on the back porch," Aunt Laney called to us from the back of the house. Mama deposited the bags on the floor.

I guess it should have occurred to me that somebody who had a bright pink house on the outside might have something equally as loud on the inside. The purple walls held several colorful paintings. A big blue piano occupied one corner opposite a worn red sofa. Over the sofa hung a huge, extra-bright painting of birds, eggs, and nests. Written among the birds, eggs, and nests were these words:

> As the marsh-hen secretly builds on the watery sod,
> Behold I will build me a nest on the greatness of God.
> —Sidney Lanier

As sad as I was to be here, I had to about choke to keep from laughing.

"Can't you see Aunt Laney sitting on top of a big old nest, her tent-striped housecoat flapping in the breeze?" I whispered to Mama.

Mama put her finger to her lips just before Aunt Laney came back into the room.

Aunt Laney pointed to the red sofa. "You folks have a seat." She eased into a green chair opposite.

I nestled close to Mama on the sofa.

"Aunt Laney, this house is as I remember it from when Stewart and I visited after we were married, except you've added a few more paintings." Mama pointed with one of her long slender fingers to a couple of paintings. "I'd forgotten what a gifted artist you are."

I stared hard at Mama. Was she telling the truth? I didn't know whether I liked these paintings or not. Nobody in North Carolina painted pictures like these.

"Thank you," Aunt Laney said. "Since I stopped teaching, I've had a lot more time to do what I want to do. I sell a good many paintings, but every once in a while, there's one I can't bear to part with." Aunt Laney pointed to the painting behind us. I'd already seen it and didn't turn around again for fear of letting loose a giggle.

"Is Sylvester Myers a gallery owner?" Mama asked.

"He is. He owns the gallery in the Village, and he's invited me to have a one-woman show next week. They've sent out thousands of invitations."

"How exciting. It sounds like you're quite famous."

"Now, I think that would be overstating the case, but I do enjoy the work."

Mama turned and peered at the painting above the sofa. I started to choke up and Mama nudged me.

"Aunt Laney, may I use the restroom?" I blurted, trying to think of an escape.

"Sure, Mary Helen, I don't know why I didn't offer when you folks first arrived." Aunt Laney pointed to a door visible down a hallway. "Right through that door. The switch is on the right."

I went into the bathroom, closed the door, flipped on the light, but then gasped and jumped back, disturbing my bladder so much as to almost make the trip to the bathroom unnecessary.

Chapter Five

Culture Shock

A menacing sea creature extended its enormous pointed pincers toward me. Surrounding it was other equally foreboding marine life, all painted on the bathroom door.

I read the words inscribed around them along the doorframe:

> And I would I could know what swimmeth below when the tide comes in
> On the length and the breadth of the marvelous marshes of Glynn.
> —Sidney Lanier.

That name again. Nobody I'd ever known in North Carolina painted weird pictures on the back of their bathroom doors. Mama was leaving me with a crazy woman.

After I finished in the bathroom, I came out and heard a clatter. I followed Aunt Laney and Mama's voices to the kitchen. Mama perched in a metal chair at a table with a green Formica top, which I'd heard Mama call a dinette table. Aunt Laney held a spoon in her hand and stood in front of a white stove, the only normal-colored furnishing in the house. The walls in the kitchen were orange and white stripes, the floor a multicolored checkerboard.

"There you are. I'm about to put supper on the table." Aunt Laney waved the spoon in the air. "I made cornbread earlier, and I have cabbage, green beans, and fried squash." She started to turn to the stove but then she spun back around. "Oh, and I used canola oil to fry the squash and cook the cabbage. Dr. Gunn said I have to stop using fatback because it's not good for my heart."

Fat back? I turned to Mama and mouthed the words in disgust as Aunt Laney stirred a pot on the stove. I tried to tell Mama about the bathroom door, but Aunt Laney turned back around.

"This is a real treat for you all to visit. I'm sorry it has to be under these circumstances." She focused her eyes on me. "Mary Helen, you know your dad used to come and stay a week with me every summer when he was growing up."

"I don't remember much about my dad."

Aunt Laney continued as she placed bowls of vegetables on the table. "I have a lot of stories to tell you." She paused a moment, and her eyes took on a dreamy haze. "I remember your dad used to build sandcastles with moats. Why, one time he made a moat that came up to his waist. It took us the better part of an afternoon to fill it in before we left, so somebody walking on the beach wouldn't fall in it and disappear. Maybe we can dig one."

I couldn't see myself digging a moat, but I could see myself digging a tunnel out of this place.

Aunt Laney went on, not waiting for me to respond. "Yes, we did have some fine times together. He loved to crab too. It sure was a shock when he died in the car accident."

"It's been hard, but we've managed," Mama said quickly, almost rudely, very un-Mama-like. She leaned forward in her chair. "Aunt Laney, I want to thank you for letting Mary Helen spend her summer vacation with you. This will be much more enjoyable for her than staying in Asheville."

I couldn't think of any reason this would be enjoyable.

"I'm mighty glad to have her." Aunt Laney put her hands on her hips. "Now, I think all the food is on the table. I'll ask the blessing." She sat down and reached for our hands. "Lord, thank you for this circle of family. Thank you for sending Mary Helen to spend these weeks with me. Bless her, and bless this provision to our bodies. In Jesus' name. Amen."

After dinner, we helped Aunt Laney clear the table and then went into the purple room.

"Aunt Laney, why don't you play a selection for us? I remember you being talented at the piano," Mama said.

"I'd be happy to," she said. She took a seat at the blue piano and opened a book in front of her.

From the moment her hands made contact with the ivory, the keys seemed to take on a life of their own. I knew she had to be making up some of it, because there was no way there were that many notes on the page in front of her.

I'd never heard anyone play as loudly and strongly as she did—a piece she called "Dwelling in Beulah Land." The piano almost seemed to bounce while she played it, and she bounced along with it. After a few moments, her fingers stopped and she eased from the piano bench.

"Your mama tells me you're quite the pianist too," Aunt Laney said. "Why don't you play for us?"

I hesitated for a moment but then moved to the piano and began the Mozart *Sonata*. Beside the intensity of Aunt Laney's playing, the notes I played sounded like music on a distant AM Chicago radio station that Mama and I sometimes listened to.

"Mary Helen, I do believe you have the family gift," Aunt Laney said when I finished.

I didn't care about having the family gift. I wanted to go home.

Mama and Aunt Laney talked late into the night, even though Mama had that long drive back to North Carolina ahead of her the next morning. They mostly talked about my dad and Aunt Laney's family. I didn't have anything to contribute, so I just answered their occasional questions. I drifted off a little but shook it off, because I didn't want Mama to think I was sleepy and send me to bed. When they said goodnight, Mama held on to Aunt Laney's hand a long time, and though neither of them spoke, it seemed a wordless message passed between them—or at least something for which I didn't have words.

After getting sleepy earlier, it was strange that when I finally dropped into bed, I stayed awake a long time listening to Mama breathe. I wanted to memorize the way those soft exhalations of Mama-scented air sounded, so I could think about them when I was alone. I turned on my side, put my hand on her chest, watched it rise and fall, and then snuggled close and finally dozed off.

The next morning Mama rose early, even before the sun. When I heard her moving around I dragged myself out too, and dressed in shorts and a T-shirt. Always in fashion, she was wearing walking shorts and a light knit top.

I smelled bacon cooking as I tied my tennis shoes, and when Mama and I came out of our room, Aunt Laney already had breakfast on the table. I plopped on one of the dinette chairs. There was no way I was going to be able to eat eggs and bacon. When Mama took her seat, my eyes pleaded with her. She knew I couldn't stand eggs, and right now greasy bacon made me feel sick.

"Eat your toast," she whispered.

I choked down the dry toast and tried not to think about Mama leaving in a few minutes.

Later, after we'd put her overnight case on the back seat of the car, I clung to her. "Mama, what am I going to do without you?"

"The time will fly. You'll see, sweetie. You'll be busy with Aunt Laney going all over this island. You'll make new friends and have new adventures."

"But I won't have you." Biting my lip didn't work anymore, and I could feel the hot tears on my face. I was tired of having to be brave, and I was tired of Mama being brave.

"We'll talk on the telephone. I'll call you." Mama took my arms from around her neck and held my hands between hers. "And you can write me. I can't think of anything that would bring me more joy than to receive a letter from you." She stroked my face with her hand. "I love you with all my heart." She kissed me on the head, let my hands go, and turned to get in the car.

"Call us when you arrive in Asheville, Laura," I heard Aunt Laney say as she moved up behind me and gave Mama a hug.

"I will, I will." Mama closed the car door. She waved and then blew me one last kiss.

I perched on the front steps and watched her car until it disappeared from sight. I heard Aunt Laney close the front door when she went inside, but I languished there a long time hoping, wishing Mama would change her mind and return to take me back.

She didn't. After what seemed like hours had passed, I stood up, wiped my eyes using the back of my hand, and entered the pink house.

I heard Aunt Laney clamoring in the kitchen, so I slid into the bedroom. I lay on the bed and examined the room that was to be mine for the next few weeks. I smoothed out a wrinkle Mama had left that morning when she'd straightened the bed cover—a quilt, which seemed to have been pieced without a pattern, just one shape sewn onto another.

This room was the most ordinary one in the house, but even it had its strange elements. I actually liked the bright yellow walls, but once more Aunt Laney, who must be crazy in love with this Sidney Lanier fellow, had hung one of her marsh paintings bordered by what was bound to be some of his writing on the frame. I crossed over to read the words:

> Ye marshes, how candid and simple and nothing-withholding and free
> Ye publish yourselves to the sky and offer yourselves to the sea!

Sure enough right at the end of the last sentence was the name Sidney Lanier.

I turned from the painting and saw a desk in the corner. I moved across the room, picked up a little book lying on the desk, and found its pages blank. Beside the book lay a pen—an unusual pen made of wood. I held it in my hands and felt the tiny grain lines as my fingers folded around the barrel.

"I see you found the chestnut pen and the journal I left for you." Aunt Laney had slipped into the room. "The pen's kind of special to me. I wondered if you might like to use it while you're here."

"Thanks."

"Your mama told me you liked to write."

After a silence fell on the room, Aunt Laney turned and left.

I returned the pen and journal to the desk, rummaged through my backpack, retrieved the journal Mama had given me, as well as a pad for letter writing. I found a pen in a side pocket and slid them all under my pillow.

Aunt Laney returned later with a cooler in one hand and a crab trap under her arm. "Let's go crabbing, and I think I'll take my paints, too. I packed a lunch for us." She pointed to an olive green tackle box on the floor using the toe of her shoe. "If you would, please grab this box by the door."

She didn't seem to be asking if I wanted to go but telling me we were going. I wasn't sure I liked someone I didn't know bossing me around. "Why do we need a tackle box if we're going crabbing? Don't you just throw those baskets in the water?"

"That tackle box is not for tackle, it's for paints and brushes. My canvas and easel are already in the car."

I bent down and grabbed my sunglasses out of my backpack, put them on, picked up the tackle box, and followed Aunt Laney. She'd definitely be easy to spot in a crowd today. She wore orange stretch pants and a housecoat composed of large blocks of colorful fabric sewn together.

"Are we going to the Village?" I said.

Aunt Laney stopped as she put her crab trap hand on the front doorknob and turned to me. She smiled. "No, today we're going to the marsh."

Chapter Six

Grass

We took a different route to the marsh than the one Mama and I had followed coming in. Instead of heading back toward the mainland, this road seemed to lead to the ocean but instead crossed the marsh before it reached the shore. In order to reach the area Aunt Laney wanted to paint, she said she'd have to turn around and come back, which she did. She pulled off the road and steered the big Cadillac as much out of the road as she could without driving into the marsh.

After she parked, we unloaded her car. As we started trudging over a little path back and forth lugging her paints, easel, and canvases, I began to feel trickles of perspiration sliding down my face, back, and legs. How I missed our mountain breezes in Asheville.

When we placed her painting supplies where they needed to be, and Aunt Laney had set up her easel. To my shock she took the gross liver bait out of the same cooler she'd put our lunch in. The toast I'd eaten earlier started to rise. I didn't think I could ever eat anything that had touched liver, or anything that had touched anything liver was in.

"Is that our lunch in the cooler?" I asked, to make sure.

"Sure is." Liver obviously didn't bother Aunt Laney. She popped the lid off the container, dug into it, pulled out that raw red stuff and slung it into the crab trap.

"How long are we going to stay here?" I plopped down on the prickly grass bank trying to keep my breakfast from reappearing.

"I don't know. When I'm at the marsh I don't look at my watch."

No watch. We could be here for hours.

Aunt Laney put the trap in a little stream that meandered through the marsh. Then she returned to her easel and began painting.

What did she expect me to do while she painted and the crabs searched for liver? Sit in the sun and bake, I guessed. I adjusted my sunglasses, stared at the marsh, and tried to figure out what the big attraction was. This must have been where she painted the marsh painting in my bedroom.

"Who's Sidney Lanier?"

Aunt Laney stopped painting. She turned around and stared at me like I'd turned blue. You would have thought I'd asked, "Who's President Reagan?"

"You've never heard of Sidney Lanier?"

"Not until I saw your paintings and the bathroom door."

Aunt Laney laughed, turned back around, and started dabbing her canvas again. "You've grown up in North Carolina, and he's a native Georgian. But still, I would've believed you'd have come across him somewhere in your education by now." She shook her head, changed brushes, and then dipped the new brush in green paint and applied the color to the canvas. "Sidney Lanier is called the 'Marsh Poet.'"

"That's a weird name to call somebody." I scratched my leg where the grass had pricked it.

Aunt Laney laughed again. "I guess it is. His best work is the poem 'The Marshes of Glynn' and is, in the opinion of many, including me, one of the few great American poems."

"Is that why you like him so much?"

She dipped her brush and splashed turquoise blue across the upper part of her canvas. "My grandmother loved Sidney Lanier."

"Did she know him?" I slapped at stings on my leg, and not waiting for her to answer, I said, "What are these things biting me?"

"Sand gnats. No, but she knew people who did, like the Johnston family over in Brunswick. They passed along stories to her. I used to tell those same stories to your dad."

I still didn't get it. "You like him because of your grandmother?"

Aunt Laney changed brushes again and put sunshine yellow on her canvas. She stopped and faced me. "Yes, and for so many other reasons— like when I come here I feel like I know what he felt."

"What?"

Aunt Laney turned back to the marsh.

"Oh, what is abroad in the marsh and the terminal sea?

"Somehow my soul seems suddenly free

"From the weighing of fate and the sad discussion of sin,

"By the length and the breadth and the sweep of the marshes of Glynn."

When she started her dramatic recitation, I noticed a couple of sticky barbs on my shorts. I pulled them off. "What are these prickly things?" I asked when she finished.

I heard her sigh as she shot a glance my way. "Probably sand spurs."

I wiped my forehead with the back of my hand and took off my sunglasses, "I'm roasting."

Aunt Laney turned around and peered at me. "Your face is red. Didn't you put on sunscreen?"

"I didn't think about it."

"I left a tube in your room on the dresser. You need to put on sunscreen every time you're going to be outside here. You'll burn up, especially with your fair skin. Look in this tackle box and grab my tube."

I rummaged around in the tackle box, pulled out the sunscreen, took off my sunglasses, applied it to my face, and put my sunglasses back on. Laney kept painting as I applied the sunscreen to my legs and arms.

I stared out at the marsh and detected activity near the horizon. "I see movement out there," I said.

"Kayakers," Aunt Laney said as she dotted little bits of orange near the bottom of the canvas. "They often put in here at the creek. You can see their car beyond the bridge there." Aunt Laney pointed to a blue car pulled to the side of the road beyond the creek bridge.

"What do they do out there?"

"They navigate the marsh. There's a lot to see." Aunt Laney paused from her painting for a minute and glanced toward the kayakers. "The marsh is always fascinating." She smiled and then returned to her painting.

I looked hard at the marsh. Grass. More grass. What could possibly be so fascinating? My stomach started growling, and I began to believe I might be able to get past the liver.

"You say lunch is in the cooler?"

Another sigh from her direction. "Open the cooler and help yourself."

I stood, pulled up the lid, and tried not to see the liver container. I took out a sandwich wrapped in plastic, unwrapped it, and took a bite.

I spit the bite out into my hand. "What is this?"

Aunt Laney stopped painting again and turned around to see what I was eating. "Shrimp salad. I just knew you'd like it. It was your dad's favorite."

I threw the bite out into the marsh, rewrapped the sandwich, and put it back in the cooler. I took out a bag of chips and then plopped back down on the bank.

She returned to her painting. "Do you like to read?" she asked me.

"I guess." The truth was I read all the time, but I didn't want to sound too enthusiastic about anything Aunt Laney suggested. I sure didn't want her to get any idea I liked being on this island.

"I thought we'd go to the library this afternoon for you to pick out a few books." She put her paintbrush and palette aside. "I guess I'd better check those traps." As she moved to the stream, I could see the canvas she'd been working on more clearly. I was glad I wore sunglasses when I saw it.

When she brought up those disgusting wiggly crabs, I didn't want to think about what she was going to do with them. I stood and inspected my grass-prickled, bug-bitten legs and trekked up the bank toward the direction of what seemed to be the beach. Moms and dads towing children in carts, folks with dogs on leashes, and people my age with bodyboards under their arms streamed toward a line of sand dunes. They all appeared to be people who came here with their families to have fun—people who chose to come here, unlike me, who had it chosen for her.

Chapter Seven

Old Friends

The exterior of the library, a one-story red brick building in the Village, seemed inviting enough, but after we traipsed up the front steps and opened the doors, we seemed to enter a time warp. The dark antique tables and chairs, wooden bookcases, and even the librarian evoked another era. I could almost smell ink from first editions printed in 1952 and the accompanying dust and mold.

"You go on and have a look around," Aunt Laney said. "I'll visit a while until you find what you're looking for. Fiction's over there." She pointed to the left and then took off toward what I thought might be the circulation desk.

The woman standing behind it had reading glasses perched on her nose and a brown cardigan sweater wrapped around her shoulders with only the top button fastened. Her hair was not quite as gray as Aunt Laney's, and she was much thinner. I longed for our young librarian, Laura Vandyke, in Asheville. She always seemed able to help me find a book I enjoyed.

Aunt Laney and the librarian carried on a conversation the entire time I was searching for books. It wasn't too hard to figure out they were talking about me, because they'd stop and glance in my direction and then start talking again. Out of the corner of my eye, I saw the librarian take her hand and pat Aunt Laney's. I could imagine what she was saying. "Poor thing, stuck with a teenager all summer. Don't despair."

Even an old library like this one helped me feel I could travel far away. The pages of a book opened limitless possibilities. I only needed to decide where to go. Today, I wanted to go home. And if home were a book, it would be *Little Women*. I had to admit I was a little curious about Sidney

Lanier, so I thought I might try to find a book of his poetry, too. I flipped through the card catalog and found several volumes on a shelf next to the front windows. I scanned a few and decided on one bearing a navy blue cover. I picked up my other book and took them to the circulation desk.

Aunt Laney focused in my direction as I approached them. "It appears you had some success." Then she gestured toward the brown-sweater lady and said, "Mary Helen, I want you to meet Mavis Trueblood. She and I have known each other for longer than we want to talk about. Mavis, this is Mary Helen."

I put my books on the counter. "Nice to meet you."

The library lady twisted her mouth to one side as she picked up the books. "Laney has told me all about you."

Like I couldn't figure that one out.

"I hear you're visiting for the summer. We'll need you to fill out information for a library card." She handed me a lined index-sized card. "Fill in the blanks and we'll be in business." While I wrote my name and address, she continued to talk. "We're glad you're here. Please feel free to come by any time." She stamped the date-due cards and put them in the back of the books. I pushed the card I was filling out back to her, and she handed me my books.

"Thanks." I slid my books off the counter.

We said our goodbyes, and as we cleared the library, Aunt Laney said, "While we're here in town, let's pick up a hamburger from Dressner's Café. I know you don't want to eat those crabs I caught today."

She was right about that.

"Plus it'll give you a chance to meet another friend of mine."

When we reached the car, Aunt Laney said, "Let's leave the car here and walk instead of trying to find another space. It's only a couple of blocks to the café."

Along the way we passed an antique store, and Aunt Laney waved at someone inside. She must know everybody on the island. She even smiled at a young man in a real estate office we passed. Aunt Laney didn't seem like she'd know a cottage from a condo. We crossed over Mallery Street and went into the café in the middle of the block. As we pushed open the door, I heard the jangle of a bell.

The smell of grilled onions hit my nose, followed closely by the scent of pickle juice. Tables of four were decked in blue-checkered tablecloths. An older woman in an apron approached us at the counter. "Laney, here for more shrimp salad?"

"Not today, Florence. I just need a burger to go."

"With cheese or without?" Florence took a pencil from behind her ear and began to jot our order on a light-green pad lying beside the cash register.

Aunt Laney turned to me.

"With," I said.

"Who's your friend?" Florence nodded at me.

"This is my niece, Mary Helen."

"I thought so. Pleased to meet you, Mary Helen. Laney's been excited about you coming to stay with her. You gonna be staying long?"

"A few weeks."

"You'll love it."

I didn't want to start an argument with her right there in the restaurant, so I kept my mouth shut.

"You all have a seat while I put this order in. Can I bring you something to drink?"

"Water would be great for me," Aunt Laney said.

"Coke," I said.

"Be right back." Florence turned on her heel and headed back toward the kitchen.

We took a seat beside the front windows as a steady flow of tourists passed by. Florence came back carrying our drinks on a tray and put them on the table. I took a sip of the Coke and let the foaming cold liquid slide down my throat. At least some things didn't change.

"Florence and I have known each other a long time. We met before your dad was born."

There she went again. Why couldn't she leave my dad out of the conversation? I felt that familiar tightness in my throat whenever someone mentioned Dad. And there was something else too. Something hard to place ... maybe loneliness.

"It's comforting to have old friends," Aunt Laney said as she cast her eyes toward Florence, who was taking an order at another table. She appeared to be about the same age as Aunt Laney, and it made me wonder how she stood on her feet all day at her age.

Old friends. The oldest friend I had was Leslie. For some reason, I had started getting sick a lot in first grade. The relationship between Leslie and me had been forever cemented that first day my stomach turned upside down.

31

Mrs. Lawson, our teacher, had said, "Leslie, would you go with Mary Helen to the office and wait with her until her mother comes?"

"Sure," Leslie said. It surprised me because waiting with someone who might throw up any minute wouldn't appeal to many kids.

I'd never had to go to the office before, and it was a little scary, so I was glad Leslie was with me.

Mr. Akins, the principal, put a gunmetal-gray trashcan in front of me, and it clanked on the linoleum floor. "Now, if you need to throw up, please use this receptacle," he said. Leslie and I had been so tickled over the word "receptacle," I had almost forgotten I was sick.

"I'm sure you left friends back in Asheville," Aunt Laney chimed in.

I pulled away from the first-grade story in my mind. "Yes, my best friend, Leslie."

"You'll miss her, I know, but maybe you'll make new friends."

We'll see, I thought.

"You folks need any condiments to go with this burger?" Florence called from the counter.

"My, that was fast. No, we have all that at home." Aunt Laney traipsed to the cash register and paid Florence for the burger. I picked up my Coke cup to take with me so I could finish it off on the drive. The bell rang again as the café door closed behind us.

Aunt Laney stopped for a minute on the sidewalk. "I believe I'll make one more stop, but we'll need to take the car to get there. I think I'd like fresh tomatoes to eat with the crabs tonight."

I couldn't imagine a more unsavory combination of foods, but because I'd promised Mama to be nice, once more I checked my tongue.

"Ralph is due to have some big ones. We'll check and see."

"Who's Ralph?"

"Ralph Tullos—owns a produce stand. He has the best fruits and vegetables on the island. I've been trading there for a long time."

When Aunt Laney pulled onto the road, it appeared she was taking the route back to her house, but instead she turned onto Demere. I knew, even without checking the street sign because of the oak trees so close to the road. In Aunt Laney's big car, it felt like we'd sideswipe one. In a minute or two, we pulled into a roadside market. The sign read Ralph's Fresh Produce. It didn't look like much—a few boards nailed together with boxes of produce raised at an angle so you could see their homely contents. You would've thought we'd pulled into the Taj Mahal though, Aunt Laney was so excited.

"Is that him?" I asked, pointing to a man in a pair of blue overalls, a red plaid shirt, and a dark blue ball cap emblazoned with the words Niagara Falls.

"That's Ralph." She sprang from the car like a woman half her age.

As soon as she opened the car door, he started calling to her. "Laney, I hoped you'd stop by today." He fanned himself with a paper sack.

"Hot, isn't it?" she asked.

"I'll say. I'm sweatin' like a mule eatin' briars. You won't believe what I got for you today." Ralph stepped over to a mound of red vegetable balls. "A farmer from over in Valdosta brought in tomaters this mornin' that'll bring tears to your eyes."

I couldn't have said it better myself. When I got out of the car, a big, almost-white mutt with a few spots sprinkled across her back, loped over to me and gave me a lick on the knee.

"Molly, I told you about lickin' the customers. Folks don't like you spreadin' your germs around like that. Sorry, Missy. You must be Laney's niece." Ralph looped a thumb under the left suspender on his overalls.

"My niece, Mary Helen," Aunt Laney said.

"Oh, yeah, I remember, from Asheville." Ralph picked a tomato out of a bin and handed it to Aunt Laney. Aunt Laney turned it around in her hand.

I stooped to pet Molly, and she licked me on the nose.

"Molly," Ralph snapped at her.

"It's all right," I said, "I like dogs."

"Likin' 'em is one thing—kissin' 'em is another." Ralph held up another tomato for Aunt Laney to inspect. "Brandywine. Heirloom. Makes the best tomater sandwiches you can imagine."

Aunt Laney held it up. "You're right, Ralph. These are beauties. I'll take two pounds."

As I stroked Molly's fluffy fur, the tomato sandwich thing kept floating through my mind. Surely she didn't think I would eat something like that.

"Those boiled peanuts smell good too. Why don't you give me a bag of those, as well?" Aunt Laney reached into her purse for more money and paused, "Is that a new hat?"

"Sure is." Ralph took it off, revealing a shock of unkempt gray hair, and handed the hat to Aunt Laney. "One of the snowbirds on the island brought it to me. Told me if I couldn't get to Niagara Falls, he'd bring a little of Niagara to me. Mighty nice of 'im."

Aunt Laney gave the hat a once over and handed it back to Ralph.

"Me and Gladys always did want to go there. Heard them Falls was somethin' to behold."

Gladys? I waited for an explanation, but none was forthcoming. I didn't want to sink in too deep here, so I didn't ask.

Ralph finished putting the tomatoes in the sack and sauntered over to a huge boiling pot. It looked like it might hold a witch's brew. He picked up a ladle, plunged it into the vat, and drew it out full of slimy dark peanuts that bore a striking resemblance to wet bugs.

I shuddered.

He drained the water off the peanuts, dumped the contents of the ladle into the paper sack he'd been using to fan himself, and handed it to Aunt Laney.

"You're the best," Aunt Laney said, as she handed him her money.

"I aim to please," Ralph said. "Check back first of the week, I'll have fresh cantaloupes." He picked up another sack and started fanning again.

I said goodbye to Molly, and we got in the car.

When we reached Aunt Laney's we unloaded the Cadillac, and then she went straight to the kitchen with her haul of produce and crabs. I put my hamburger in the kitchen and then slipped into my room with my two library books and closed the door. I lounged cross-legged on the bed, opened the book of poems I'd gotten at the library, and found "The Marshes of Glynn" in the index. I turned to the page listed. It read:

> Glooms of the live oaks, beautiful-braided and woven
> Intricate shades of the vines that myriad-cloven
> Clamber the forks of the multiform boughs,
> Emerald twilights—
> Virginal Shy lights ...

I closed the book and threw it to the foot of the bed. I reached under my pillow, took out my journal, and began to write:

> After Mama left today, Aunt Laney and I went to the marsh. I don't see what all the fuss is about. We're talking about grass and water. And she goes on and on about somebody her grandmother loved. The only thing I like about this island is the dogs.

Chapter Eight

Crab Cakes

I put my journal down, picked up *Little Women*, leaned up against the headboard, and began to read the familiar words. After a while I started to smell something … something fishy. I got up and went into the kitchen.

Aunt Laney was taking fritters from a pan that resembled fried brown biscuits and putting them on a platter.

"What's that smell?" I asked.

She held out a tray of food to me. "That, my dear, is the smell of one of the greatest delicacies known to humankind: crab cakes. Maybe while you're here, you'll be willing to try them sometime."

I scrutinized the crab cakes and decided that would not be a possibility. I couldn't erase the picture of the wiggly crab main ingredient out of my mind. Aunt Laney put the platter of crab cakes on the table and wiped her hands on the striped apron she was wearing.

"Since you're going to be living here, I might as well show you where the tableware is stored, so you can find your way around." Aunt Laney began to open the cabinets and drawers, showing me the china, flatware, and glasses. "Here's where I keep the napkins. Why don't you set the table? We're about ready to eat, and I know you're hungry since you didn't have much lunch."

I put out the napkins and silverware but didn't pay much attention to whether or not I'd done it right. When I took out the plates, I noticed that every single one of them was a different color, and they were heavy. She must have seen me examining them.

"You like my plates? A local potter made them for me. He does such unique work."

"Unique" was a word I could certainly put to use around here. I grabbed my hamburger off the counter, retrieved the ketchup from the refrigerator, and pulled up to the table.

As I unwrapped my burger, Aunt Laney said, "I'll say the blessing." Then she grabbed my hand. "Lord, thank you for your wonderful provision from the marsh. Thank you for all the food we're about to receive. Use it we pray to strengthen us for your service. And Lord, please bring healing to Laura. Amen."

I had to bite my lip when she prayed for my mama. "Can I call her after dinner?"

"Yes, you may. I know you're concerned about her surgery tomorrow." She took a big bite of crab cake.

"In the morning at eight ... her friend Amy said she'll call us tomorrow afternoon and let us know how Mom's getting along."

"She told me Amy's going to stay with her after the surgery."

I nodded and took a sip of tea. I should have been the one with Mama. The hurt of disappointment sliced through my heart.

"We'll try to make a point of being here tomorrow afternoon so we don't miss the call," Aunt Laney said as she finished off one of the crab cakes.

I took another bite of my hamburger, and my eyes fell on a book lying on the kitchen table. I could barely read the faded words Holy Bible lettered on the tattered black cover. The edges of the pages were worn and watermarked. It must have been old, because all the gold on the pages was gone.

"You go to church?" I asked Aunt Laney.

"Sure do," she said.

Sitting in that kooky-colored kitchen, I let my mind wander to what kind of church Aunt Laney might attend. I'd never been to church much, but I didn't remember anybody who looked like her in any of the churches I'd been to. I couldn't stand it. I had to ask. "What church do you go to?"

"Glynn Fellowship."

That sure didn't tell me anything. Usually you could tell a little bit if it was First something or other. "What kind of church is that?"

Aunt Laney ceremoniously popped the final bite of her last crab cake in her mouth, chewed, and swallowed. She took a big sip of iced tea. "It's the kind where people gather together to worship God."

This was going nowhere. I decided to change the subject. "What are we doing in the morning?"

She raised her eyebrows and acted as if I'd slapped her. "We're crabbing, of course," She picked up her plate and carried it to the sink.

Of course. How silly of me. Let's see now. How long was I going to be here? Six weeks. Six weeks times seven days equaled forty-two days of misery. Forty-two days of Mama-less, grass-prickled, gnat-buzzing, sun-scorched, crab-wiggling, liver-filled, housecoat-wearing, Lanier-marsh, lunatic-painted agony.

Chapter Nine

Ben

I melted on a bench outside St. Simons Island Bait and Tackle the next morning and waited on Aunt Laney, who was inside gabbing. The sky was cloudless, and Aunt Laney told me on the way to the Village that the weatherman had forecast a record high temperature today. I fanned myself with a piece of the *Brunswick Times* someone had left lying on the bench. Crabbers and fishermen in assorted shapes and sizes unloaded coolers, tackle boxes, traps, and fishing poles from their cars, and then lugged them to the pier. Some stopped with their gear after a few steps while they were still under the big canopy and flung their traps or fishing lines in the water. Others traveled all the way to the end of the pier where the big boats came in. Some found a fishing spot somewhere in-between along the extensive stretch of the pier. I could hear Aunt Laney droning on and on inside the bait shop, and then finally she and a boy about my age came out. He was dressed in a green Dillard's Atlantic Charters T-shirt, khaki shorts, and worn-out deck shoes. His blond hair didn't appear it had been combed that day, and freckles covered the bridge of his nose.

Aunt Laney gestured toward him. "Mary Helen, I want you to meet Ben Dillard. His dad is a friend of mine and owns the fishing charter service just down the way."

I nodded.

Aunt Laney went on with her introduction. "Ben, this is Mary Helen. She's visiting me for the summer. I'll let you two get acquainted. I'm going to go on over and set out my trap."

I watched Aunt Laney sashay over to the pier in her yellow pants and purple housecoat. I couldn't bring myself to call it a tunic.

"Laney's something else," Ben said, and it sounded like he meant it in a good way.

"She's something else weird." I adjusted my sunglasses.

"What do you mean?" His shoulders stiffened.

"Look at what she's wearing." I pointed to her standing over at the pier. "You don't call that weird? And have you seen her house? It looks like it was decorated by Dr. Seuss." I stared at Ben, waiting for an answer. Nothing. He was getting a little white around the mouth. "Plus, she's obsessed with Sidney Lanier and crabbing. Have you read Lanier? I can't understand a word he says."

Ben relaxed a little and then laughed and gazed back over at Aunt Laney. "Almost every kid in Georgia has read Sidney Lanier."

"Why's that?"

"Four words: Georgia history. Fifth grade."

"What torture."

"It's not so bad. I even memorized part of 'Song of the Chattahoochee':

"Out of the hills of Habersham,
"Down the valleys of Hall,
"I hurry amain to reach the plain,
"Run the rapid and leap the fall . . ."

My mouth hung open. "You sound just like her." I heard noise in the bait shop and turned around to see what it was. I couldn't see anyone, but it sounded like talking.

I continued: "What about this ... this crabbing? You'd think crab cakes fell out of heaven."

"Some people think they do. I heard you were from the mountains."

I sat up straight. "Asheville, North Carolina." Then I heard that noise again from inside the bait shop.

Ben settled on the bench beside me.

"The mountains—I'll bet they're pretty. I've never been to Asheville, but we had a kid in our school that'd lived up there. He talked about snow."

"Every winter, we do get a little." I remembered the few inches that fell back home each year.

"I've lived on this island my whole life. I'll bet I haven't seen three flakes since I was born."

"That's sad."

"Sometimes in the winter I imagine the sand on the beach is snow." Ben was quiet for a minute. "But I don't think I could live anywhere else. I don't know what I'd do if I had to give up the marsh."

I took off my sunglasses and peered at him. "The marsh? What's wrong with you people? She talks about the marsh all the time. I don't get it."

"Maybe you have to live here for a while to get it."

"I don't think I ever will."

"I heard your mama was sick."

I guessed Aunt Laney had told everybody on St. Simons why I was here. Why did Ben Dillard care if my mama was sick?

I put my sunglasses back on. "My mama has cancer. She's having surgery right this minute. She wanted me to stay here while she recuperates." I bit my lip again. A trickle of perspiration streamed down my leg. I fanned harder.

"Is your dad going to stay with her?" Ben swatted at a flying insect.

"My dad died when I was six."

"I'm sorry. Why aren't you staying to help your mama?"

He probably thought I was some kind of selfish, spoiled brat kid.

"That's what Mama wanted." What else could I say? "Her friend Amy is there with her." I heard a sort of squawking sound. "What is that noise I keep hearing? At first it sounded like people talking, but then it sounded like a squawk."

Ben laughed and stood up. "It is a squawk. That's a parrot, Wallace. Do you want to see him?"

I stood up. "Sure." I followed him into the bait shop, and there in the corner was a big gray parrot with a red tail.

"I've heard he used to belong to a sea captain. He's an African Grey and can live as long as a human can. He's quite a character."

"So he talks?"

"Pretty girl, pretty girl," Wallace said.

I laughed. "He does talk."

Wallace let go of an ear-splitting catcall whistle.

I put my hands to my ears. "Is he always like this?"

"Only in the company of a beautiful lady." Ben walked over to Wallace. He held up his hand and Wallace stepped out on to it. "He'll stand on your head. Would you like that?"

"On my head? I don't know."

"He won't hurt you. You need to live a little."

"I guess." I cringed as I waited for Wallace to use me as a human perch. The toes on his feet gripped my scalp.

"Pretty girl, pretty girl," he said again.

"Would you like to take a picture?" the man behind the counter said and handed Ben a Polaroid camera.

Ben took the camera. "Mr. Kendall, this is Mary Helen, she's visiting Aunt Laney."

"Pleased to meet you, stop in any time," Mr. Kendall said in an amiable way.

I nodded. "Nice to meet you."

"Smile," Ben said as he pointed the camera at me. He clicked the picture, and placed it on the counter for it to develop. "Okay, boy, enough flirting for one day." Ben reached up for Wallace, and his feet left my head.

"I've never seen a parrot in person before." I searched around on the top of my head to see if Wallace had left anything behind.

"Your hair's fine." He smiled at me and put Wallace back on his perch.

"I guess I'd better go on over to the pier to see what Aunt Laney's doing."

"I'll see you around then. Hey, are you going to Laney's show next week?"

"I don't guess I have a choice." Like much in my life lately.

Ben picked up the Polaroid and handed it to me. "Charming," he said. "It looks like you have a parrot growing out of your head."

"Thanks," I said, "just the effect I was going for," and accepted the picture.

*

I couldn't believe it when Aunt Laney set a platter of tomato sandwiches on the table for lunch. I gave her my best, "You don't expect me to eat those?" looks.

"You don't like tomato sandwiches?" She acted as if I'd turned down a million dollars.

"I've never had them before."

"Would you like to try one?'

I guess she figured the answer was "no," because she turned around and reached for the peanut butter and grape jelly in the cabinet to make a sandwich. She was right. The answer was "no." She handed me the jars, and I smoothed the peanut butter over my bread and tried to spread the jelly evenly.

"Did you and Ben get acquainted?" Aunt Laney asked as I slid a slice of bread on top of the jelly.

Nobody my age "got acquainted." We usually just hung out together. "We talked."

"That's good. You'll probably run into each other quite a bit this summer. He's a fine boy."

As I took a bite of the sandwich, my leg bounced up and down, something I did when I was nervous. Laney must have noticed.

"Mary Helen, don't worry. Your mama is in good hands, and Amy will let us know what's happening as soon as she can."

I nodded and chewed. But as she kept talking, her voice sounded kind of like those voices the adults have in the Charlie Brown movies. "Blah, blah, blah, blah."

Later that afternoon, the phone finally rang. I heard it from my bedroom and bolted out, but Aunt Laney had already answered.

"Yes," she said as she nodded. "I see. Please keep in touch. I'll tell Mary Helen." She hung up the phone and turned to me.

"What is it? How's Mama?'

"She's out of surgery."

"And?"

"The surgery went well …" She paused only a moment, but it seemed a week. "But Amy said the doctor thought the cancer appeared to be more extensive than he anticipated at first. They won't know for sure until they get the pathology report."

The life drained out of my body. Aunt Laney tried to put her arm around me, but I resisted. An ache for Mama swelled in my chest.

"I know you'd like to be there, but staying here is what your mother worked out for you. It's what she wanted."

"It's not what I want." I shuffled off to "my" room, slammed the door, and threw myself across the bed. The tears spilled on to the scrambled-up-looking quilt. I sat up, reached for my journal under my pillow, and searched for my pen but couldn't find it. I wiped my eyes with my hand and scrounged under the bed. Did I put in a drawer? I rifled through each one, but it wasn't there. I was desperate to write. I saw the chestnut pen on the desk and grabbed it.

I opened my journal and wrote:

> Mama's surgery is over, but we don't know how she is. I wish
> I could be with her. I don't know why she sent me here. I hate
> it. I want to go home.

Chapter Ten

On the Island

Saturday morning I woke to the pattering of rain on the window. I rolled over and saw the heavy gray skies through a split in the draperies. Since finding out Mama had cancer, I'd woken every morning hoping my circumstances weren't actually happening. But something about hearing those drops of rain hitting the roof made it all real. Mama did have cancer. I was on this island. Mama could, in fact, die. The rain was the soundtrack to my hurting heart. I groaned.

A knock sounded on my bedroom door, and I sat up in bed. "Come in."

The door opened and Aunt Laney stepped into the room dressed in her usual ensemble. This time it took the form of purple knit pants and some sort of African print—I tried to think of the word tunic. "Did you hear the rain?"

"Yes," I mumbled

"We need it, but of course it means we can't get out as usual today."

I knew what "as usual" meant. It meant sitting at the marsh baking in the sun, or sitting at the pier swatting gnats.

"Why don't we go eat breakfast at the Sandcastle? We can sit on the porch and watch the ships come in to the pier while we eat."

I couldn't think of anything more boring, but it beat being cooped up here all day, so I nodded, crawled out of bed and dressed.

As we left our umbrellas outside the Sandcastle, pushed the door open, and felt the cool blast of blueberry-pancake-scented air, we discovered that the tourists had the same idea as Aunt Laney. We had to sit on a little bench to wait for a table. While we waited, I noticed a world map on the wall with colorful pins in it, and I moved to examine it. I discovered that the pins represented the homes of tourists who'd visited from all over the world.

Pins in Ghana and Ethiopia begged the question of what might bring people from Africa to this tiny island. A person could drive from one end of St. Simons to the other in only a few minutes. How would someone from a giant continent like Africa feel on such a small piece of the earth's crust as this island? A pin in Paris, France, reminded me of my geography book picture of the Eiffel Tower.

I scanned the map for other faraway pins: five in Australia, three in the Philippines, one in China, three in Spain. I supposed they'd willingly come to this place from all over the world. Why?

I took a green pin from the container on the counter and added it to the two already placed on Asheville. Green was for mountains, magnificent white pines, and grass that didn't grow in water.

"Laney," I heard a waitress call. I turned around to see Aunt Laney rise and follow a girl with a blue T-shirt out to the porch. She seated us in a corner and gave us menus.

"Their Belgian waffles are the best," Aunt Laney said to me, and turned to the waitress. "Heather, this is my niece, Mary Helen."

"Nice to meet ya," Heather said, smacking her gum while simultaneously twirling a lock of red hair with a finger that held a pencil. "What are y'all having to drink?" She quit twirling and wrote our order on a pad she held in the other hand.

After taking our drink orders, she left to retrieve them, promising to be back "in a flash."

Behind Aunt Laney's back, a group of dark birds watched us from the porch rail.

"What are those birds doing?"

Aunt Laney turned around. "Oh, them. They're beggar birds, and they make their living off the food they find on unattended plates."

"They make me feel weird, like they're staring at me."

"They are."

I tried to focus my attention on the menu but kept an eye on the vulture-like birds lining the rail. When Heather came back, I ordered pancakes, and Aunt Laney asked for egg whites and whole-wheat toast.

"Keep the doctor happy," she said when I gave her a questioning look.

"She doesn't do that too often," Heather said, smacking as she took the menus.

At times the rain came down so hard we considered moving inside, but after a while the drenching subsided to a steady drizzle. Emerging from the rainy mist, a ship made its way down the channel.

Aunt Laney scrutinized it. "Appears to be a freighter." As it drew nearer, I saw unfamiliar writing on the side and knew it must have crossed the Atlantic.

"Going into the port at Brunswick, I guess," Aunt Laney observed.

Just as I had when I stood before the map, I began wondering. Wondering about the people onboard the ship. About where they'd come from, and what they'd brought with them in the belly of the great ship. Not a pretty ship, mostly gray, but I guess a freighter was like a transfer truck on the water. It didn't have to be pretty, just servicable.

"We can go down the street to Rob's Charter Service and visit Ben after we've finished. He works there a good bit during the summer," Aunt Laney said as the waitress put our food before us.

"Okay," I said as I drenched my pancakes in syrup.

After Aunt Laney paid the bill, we left the table and the beggar birds immediately descended on our plates. "Scoot," Heather said, swatting at them with her cleaning rag.

As we passed the fishy-smelling bait shop, Wallace whistled, and I gave Aunt Laney a "Can we go in?" look. She nodded and we moved inside.

I crossed over to Wallace. "Remember me?"

"Pretty girl, pretty girl."

"He does remember me." I glanced at Mr. Kendall behind the counter, who nodded.

I stroked Wallace's red tail feathers. "I've never seen a bird with such a beautiful tail." His feathers contrasted sharply with the dullness of the beggar birds' feathers.

"He's a beauty all right. What are you all doing on a rainy day?" Mr. Kendall asked.

"We just ate breakfast, and I thought we'd go over and visit Mavis at the library for a few minutes."

I didn't know if I could stand the excitement.

Behind us, the door opened, and a loud whistle pierced my ear.

Wallace immediately responded with an equally ear shocking whistle.

"Good morning to you too, Wallace," the mailman said as he shook himself off and reached into his bag. His wet rain gear dripped onto the floor. Even with a raincoat on over his shorts, I could see he had suntanned skin and muscular legs and arms which made him seem like someone who might have been a lifeguard when he was younger. He took out a stack of mail, handed it to Mr. Kendall, tipped his hat to Aunt Laney and me, said, "Pleased to see you ladies this morning," and exited.

"He's pretty cheerful on such a gray day," Aunt Laney said. "Does he always whistle like that when he comes in?"

"Always," Mr. Kendall said. "He gets a charge out of Wallace answering him."

"I don't believe I've met him before," she said.

"Moved here about three months ago," Mr. Kendall said. "Name's Archie Campbell. He delivers downtown."

"I guess that explains why I haven't met him. Mavis probably knows him."

We said our goodbyes, left the bait shop and walked a few doors down to Dillard's Atlantic Charters.

Ben rested behind the counter reading *Fishing Today* magazine. "Hi," he said.

"Business slow?" Aunt Laney asked.

"Yeah, the people going out today launched early this morning. Only the die-hards will go out in this kind of rain."

"I guess your dad is aboard this morning's launch." Aunt Laney put her bag down on the counter.

"Left around five o'clock."

A funny expression formed on Ben's face, kind of like he was wondering whether to say the next thing that was on his mind. "How's your mama?" he asked me as he put the magazine aside.

"She came through the surgery fine." I didn't want to go into all the stuff about "more cancer." It might not even be true.

"I'm glad," Ben said.

Later, as we stepped across the threshold into the street, the rain began to come down in torrents. Aunt Laney and I sloshed our way to the car, struggled with collapsing our umbrellas, and got in.

After Aunt Laney pulled herself into the car, she said, "Maybe visiting Mavis is not such a good idea right now. We'll likely get even more drenched."

For once I agreed with her.

So we went straight back to the pink palace. Yawn. A few more days like this and my brain could atrophy. I consoled myself by settling down to read. I'd only been at it a few minutes when the phone rang. Mama. I raced from my room and almost ripped the phone from the wall.

"Hello."

"Mary Helen, sweetie. How are you?"

Everything in me melted at the sound of her voice. "Mama, it's you. How are you? I miss you so much."

Aunt Laney came out of the bathroom and saw me talking. She must have guessed who it was, because she went into her bedroom and shut the door, I suppose to give me privacy.

"I miss you too. I'm doing pretty well. Amy's been a great nurse, and the doctor said I can go home in a few days."

"Amy told me the doctor thought there was more cancer than they originally believed." I didn't mean to blurt it out that way. Too late now.

"He said he wouldn't know for sure until he gets the pathology report back."

I bit my lip. "What does that mean?"

"It means I'll probably have to have treatment—chemotherapy or radiation. Maybe both."

"I'm sorry. I love you, Mama." I wanted to reach through the phone and pull her close.

"I love you, Mary Helen."

We talked a little bit longer, and I tried not to let Mama know I was crying. I kept making small talk, anything that would keep her on the phone. Mama finally said something about how much the call was going to cost. When we hung up, my heart ached so badly I could hardly breathe. I went back into my room, retrieved my writing pad, tore a couple of sheets of paper out of it, and started a letter using the pen Aunt Laney had loaned me.

"Dear Mama,"

I stared at the words. Dear Mama. What could I say? Please stay here with me. Please don't let this cancer take you away. The words seemed to echo in the pattering rain … take you away … take you away.

I grabbed the paper, crunched it into a tight little ball, and threw it on the floor. I couldn't do this now.

I looked at the other piece of paper. I hadn't written Leslie since I'd been on the island. That would be an easier message to write, so as the rain continued to pour outside, it helped me pour out to Leslie everything that was going on with Mama and how much I hated staying on this island.

And how scared I was. The only good subjects I had to write about were Wallace and the two dogs I'd met. Leslie loved dogs as much as I did.

After I finished the letter, I grabbed an envelope from my backpack and addressed it to Leslie at Camp Whitestone in Decatur, Tennessee.

In bed that night, I tried to hold on to the image of Mama breathing in and out, in and out. I put my head on the pillow where she'd put her head that last night we were together, and I sobbed.

*

Aunt Laney knocked on my door early Sunday morning.

"Mary Helen, you need to get up. We need to be at church in a little while."

Was there no mercy? I rested more when I was in school than I did living on this island. And church? I had a hopeful thought and then tumbled out of bed to find Aunt Laney.

"I don't have any dress-up clothes for church," I announced, wishing for an excuse to stay away.

She lounged at the kitchen table drinking coffee. Her Bible lay open in front of her. She never even looked up. "That's good, because we don't dress up at my church." She smiled and then took another sip of coffee.

Was she wearing what she had on? I found out later she did, indeed, wear the red and orange striped tunic over green pants to church. She looked like a traffic light.

When we pulled into a parking place at a shopping area, I got confused.

"Aren't we going to church?"

"We are," she said, and stepped out of the car.

I followed her around to a building that I was pretty sure used to be some sort of store. The windows were bricked up and there was an artistically lettered sign over the door that read Glynn Fellowship.

We entered a small room lined with paintings.

"This resembles an art gallery," I said.

"These are paintings done by a few of the church members." Aunt Laney straightened the shoulders of her tunic.

An attractive woman whose nametag read "Rachel" ran straight for Aunt Laney and struck up a conversation. After Aunt Laney introduced me, I wandered around and inspected the paintings. Psalm 30:5 was the title of a painting of an orange-red sunrise. The next picture, one of little children playing on the beach, hung beside a plaque that read Matthew

19:14. I came to a painting I thought Aunt Laney had done, and when I read the signature, sure enough, I was right. She'd painted an older man sitting alone on a park bench. The picture was painted from a point of view behind the bench and the title was Psalm 130:5.

Aunt Laney approached me. "Are you ready to go in?"

"Yes, but what's the deal with these paintings? I mean, why do they have Matthew and Psalms, things like that written beside all of them?"

"These are paintings done to illustrate a particular scripture. Each artist has given his or her interpretation of the scripture in a visual way."

"Oh." I thought I understood, but maybe not.

I'd never been to a church where they played the guitar, but they sure did at this one. They didn't play one guitar, they played three, and all at one time. Maybe they feared one of the people playing them would suddenly forget the music or something. The few times I'd been to church, there'd always been an organ—big, loud organ music. Not in this church. Hardly anything in the building resembled a church. We didn't sit in pews but on blue cushioned chairs, and everybody dressed as if they were going to a picnic afterward. I should have guessed Aunt Laney wouldn't go anywhere normal.

Aunt Laney and I eased in beside Mavis, and across the aisle I spotted Ben and a man with him who must have been his dad. After the music, the preacher, whose name Aunt Laney told me was Pastor Ray Warren, talked a little about verses in the Bible and prayed. He asked if there were any prayer requests, and Aunt Laney raised her hand and told them about Mama. I could feel my face get red. Thankfully the service didn't last long.

As we were leaving the church that morning, I caught a whiff of a familiar scent—Mama's scent. I scanned the crowd around me, and had no idea who might be wearing it. But it was enough to send my heart back to Asheville for the rest of the day.

*

Aunt Laney about broke her neck getting back over to Ralph's early on Monday morning to check and see if he'd received the new cantaloupe shipment.

As we pulled up in the car, I saw a section of his stand piled high with the balls of fruit.

"Do you see that?" She pointed to the produce and slammed on the brakes, jerking the car to a stop. Aunt Laney could make more out of nothing than anybody I'd ever seen. My only consolation was that at least

I'd see Molly. As I moved from the car, I didn't spot her at first, but then she came out from the back of the stand, wagging her tail.

While Aunt Laney picked over the cantaloupes to select a ripe one, I roosted on a fruit crate and rubbed Molly's ears.

"I heard from a customer you got a big art show startin' this week." Ralph took the two cantaloupes Aunt Laney had selected and put them in a bag.

"That's right. Why don't you come over and take a look?"

"I don't know much about art. All I know is fruit and vegetables."

"I think you might be surprised by what you see."

She was right about that.

"You might find you're an art connoisseur," Aunt Laney said.

Ralph chuckled. "That'd be a mighty big revelation if I did," he said as he handed her the bag of melons.

Molly lay at my feet and rolled over on her back. I scratched her stomach, and her left leg involuntarily moved up and down.

"I believe that dog's taken a likin' to you, missy," Ralph said, laughing at Molly. "She don't generally warm up to strangers like that."

It felt good to be liked. I stroked Molly's head and then stood up.

"We'll see you later, Ralph," Aunt Laney said. "Remember, come on over to the show. Wait, I even have an invitation to the reception in my purse." She dug around in the big satchel she always lugged around and pulled an ivory card from her purse. "Yes, here it is. It has the time and everything on it. You come, okay?"

Ralph took the card and waved at Aunt Laney as we strolled away.

"Do you think he'll come?" I said after we were seated in the car.

Aunt Laney glanced back toward Ralph before she pulled out on to the road. "Not a chance."

Chapter Eleven

The Big Event

I perched in a chair behind Sylvester's desk, watching Aunt Laney and Sylvester hang her eye-popping pictures on the wall of Sylvester's gallery. It appeared she'd hauled several of her Lanier series paintings down here. Where had she stored all these creations? She must have kept them under her bed.

"What do you think, Sylvester? Does this one hang better here or on the back wall?" Aunt Laney said as she studiously cocked her head to the left and then to the right in front of a painting, acting as if she was making a decision that likened in importance to whether or not to have elective surgery.

"Oh, definitely where you have it now," Sylvester said, with an equal air of significance.

I studied the painting, inspected the front and back wall, and couldn't for the life of me know why they thought the way they did. What difference could it possibly make?

"You know, Laney, I think this is going to be one of the best shows we've ever had. We've already had folks calling from Atlanta."

"All I can say is I hope they're not disappointed, or you either." Aunt Laney turned around to pick up another painting.

"Let me help you with that," Sylvester said. He lifted the other side of the painting Aunt Laney was reaching for.

After they placed the painting on the wall, she glanced back at the front window and said, "Oh, look. Ben's face is pressed against the glass. I didn't even hear him knock. Let's open the door."

Sylvester took a key from the desk and unlocked the front door.

"Hi, everybody. Are you ready for the big day, Laney?" Ben said as he sauntered in. Ben's blond hair was more tousled than usual, and he carried a book under one arm.

Sylvester had already crossed back across the room to help Aunt Laney with one last painting she was trying to lift by herself. They finally managed to hang it on the wall. "I think we are," Laney said, exhaling.

Ben marched around the room taking in the paintings. "One day I'm going to have a Laney original."

Living on this island must dull the senses. The next thing I knew, Ben would be telling me he ate tomato sandwiches for lunch.

"What are you reading, Ben?" Sylvester asked, pointing to the book under Ben's arm.

"Oh, another book about dogs," Ben said.

As if on cue, Harold appeared out of nowhere, prancing around the gallery.

"Come here, boy," I said as I knelt to pet him. "Where did you come from?"

"He's been asleep on his pillow in the back room and is probably hungry. Mary Helen, do you and Ben mind feeding him?" Sylvester pointed to the back. "His food's in a bin just through the door there, and his bowl is beside his bed."

"Come on, boy," I called to Harold, who obediently trotted behind me. Ben trailed behind Harold. I found the bin Sylvester was talking about and opened the lid.

"I'll get the bowl," Ben said, brushing past me.

Harold wagged his stump of a tail, anticipating his supper. I took the bowl from Ben, filled it, and then set it on the floor. As the dog crunched the food, his whole body started to move in pleasure along with his tail.

"He's a great dog," Ben said, stroking Harold's head.

"Yes." I reached for Harold as I heard Aunt Laney call my name.

I returned to the gallery and found Aunt Laney collapsed in the desk chair. "Mary Helen, I think we're through here. I'm a bit worn from moving all these paintings. Do you mind if we go home?"

Just as I had someone to talk to and a dog to pet, she decides to go.

Sylvester put a hammer on a chair. "Laney, listen, you do seem tired. Try to rest as much as you can so you'll be ready for your big night. If you could be here around five tomorrow evening, that'd be great. It would give us time to make any last-minute changes before the show." Sylvester turned to me. "Did you find the food?"

"Yes, Harold sure was hungry. He dove into it."

"That dog does have an appetite. I'll see you folks tomorrow night."

*

I sipped my Seven-Up while Georgia art connoisseurs fawned over Aunt Laney's paintings. When I scanned the guest registry, I noticed that many of them had driven several hours to attend this event. As I wandered through the crowd, I overheard them speaking about the Lanier pieces. I knew now what they meant by that term, but I still didn't understand the attraction.

"I positively must have one," one woman wearing several gold necklaces said.

"Me too, but they're all wonderful, how does one choose?" another said.

Sylvester seemed to be in his element as he escorted prospective clients from one painting to another. He chatted and laughed, never at a loss for words, his bow tie bobbing up and down as he spoke.

Dressed in black pants and her signature tunic—a silver fabric I'd heard Mama call organza, Aunt Laney somehow seemed subdued. I couldn't quite put my finger on it. In fact, she seemed less excited about the art reception than she had been about the cantaloupes yesterday morning. It seemed odd to me. She talked to anyone who wanted her attention, but she was holding part of herself back. After about an hour of people milling around, coming and going, Aunt Laney came toward me like she was ready to go, but then a lady in a leopard-print jacket intercepted her.

Not long after that, the front door opened, and Ralph, decked out in a yellow-and-black-plaid sport coat left over from the seventies stepped into the gallery. Molly's slicked back ears indicated she was highly suspicious of this new place, and she followed closely behind him.

"Who in the world is that?" I heard the leopard-print jacket woman whisper to the man standing by her.

I scrambled through the crowd to get to Ralph. "Hi."

"Missy, it's good to see a familiar face. I ain't never been in no art gallery before." Ralph nervously put his hands in his pants' pockets and rattled his change.

I leaned over and gave Molly a pat. "I'll show you around. Follow me."

I accompanied Ralph from painting to painting. At each one he stood for a moment, but for the life of me I couldn't figure out what he might be thinking. Occasionally he'd say, "Uh, huh," or "Mmm," but that was it. After we viewed the last painting, he simply said, "Got to go now." He turned to Molly, "Come on, girl." Then they headed for the door.

"Don't you want refreshments?" I called as he proceeded to leave.

"No, thank you, missy."

I watched them exit and amble down the sidewalk outside.

"Was that Ralph?" Aunt Laney said as she came up behind me.

"It was."

"What did he say?"

"Nothing. He didn't utter a word. He just viewed the paintings and left."

"Imagine that." She navigated around me to the door and stood a moment still gazing through it, as if she'd seen an apparition. Then she was gone, swept along with a group of women who were raving about one of the canvases. Mavis, who I hadn't seen until then, joined them.

A hand touched my arm. "Are you having any fun yet?"

I spun around to see Ben smiling from ear to ear wearing a navy jacket. Until that moment, I hadn't thought of Ben being nice looking, but he was.

"What do you think?" I whispered.

"You want to go see Harold in the back room?" he asked.

"Is he back there?"

"Yeah, I already checked. He seems bored too. Hey, wasn't that Ralph and Molly?" Ben pointed toward the front door.

"Sure was." I found it hard to believe they'd actually come.

"I never thought I'd see Ralph in an art gallery."

"I guess that's Aunt Laney's influence." I nodded my head toward Aunt Laney whose organza frock was barely visible in a crowd of what seemed to be her most avid fans. I'd been overhearing their comments, "Outstanding, Breathtaking, Your best work," for several minutes.

She was speaking now with a woman attired in the weird kind of tunic Laney always wore. Birds of a feather.

Ben and I slipped through the crowd and found the poodle lying on his bed. "Hello, Harold." I plopped beside him, and Harold lifted his head and I scratched him under his chin. "You're much better company than that boring art crowd." I could still hear the murmurings of conversations in the gallery.

"You know poodles are one of the most intelligent breeds. They were bred as hunting dogs." Ben dropped beside me and stroked Harold's back.

"How do you know? Do you have one?"

"I read about it. No, I don't have a dog, but I wish I had one. We live in an apartment complex, and the owners don't allow dogs." He started rubbing Harold's stomach, and the dog rolled over on his back.

"That's too bad. I don't have one either. I guess Mama's had all she could do working and taking care of me. She never wanted to have a pet."

"Do you know they can retrieve?" Ben reached over and picked up a stuffed bone lying on the floor. "Watch this." He waved the bone at Harold. "Come on, boy, fetch." When he threw the bone, Harold lunged off his cushion, flew across the floor, gripped the bone with his teeth, and brought it back to Ben.

"Good boy." Ben stroked the dog on the head with one hand as he picked up the bone dropped in front of him with the other. Ben threw the toy even further the next time. Harold retrieved again.

"Can I try?"

"Sure." He handed the toy to me.

I wanted to send the bone, so I threw it hard, too hard. It hit boxes stacked against the wall, and Harold went after it, crashing into the boxes as well. What happened next is kind of a blur, but a whole lot of cardboard went in different directions. Boxes tumbled and made a loud thud as they hit the floor. Out of one of them spilled what appeared to be a bubble-wrapped piece of pottery, and it rolled like a bowling ball across the floor. There were other pieces I couldn't identify but were probably breakable. It fell silent in the gallery. Ben gaped wide-eyed at me.

Sylvester came running into the back room. He flung his hands out in excitement and then put them on his hips. "What's going on?"

Ben started explaining, and when he reached the part about me throwing the bone, he didn't say it was me, which I found chivalrous of him. He said we threw the ball. Not exactly the truth, but not exactly a lie either. I noticed other people had gathered behind Sylvester, including Aunt Laney. Sylvester moved across the room, knelt down, picked up the bowling ball, and then opened each box that had fallen and examined its contents.

"It doesn't appear any harm was done, but you kids have to know I've procured some rare, and expensive 'objet d'art' which are stored back here."

Sylvester stood up and strode over to Ben and me. "If you want to throw the ball, take Harold to the park sometime. He'd love to have a chance to run and exercise outside."

Ben stood straight up. "Yes, sir. We're sorry about the crash, but we'd love to take Harold out."

I heard a voice from the crowd standing in the doorway. "Ben, let's go. I have a group coming in for a charter early in the morning."

"See you later," Ben said to me and left with the man I'd seen in church, who I assumed was his dad, Rob.

Laney stood there for a few minutes staring at me as if she didn't know what to say.

I went back in the gallery, and positioned myself behind the desk until the crowd thinned. The clock on the desk said nine and there were still a few people milling around. Finally around nine thirty the last one left, and Aunt Laney came over and picked up her purse.

"Are you ready?" she said.

"Yes, ma'am."

She didn't say much on the way—probably still mad at me about the crash in the backroom.

She didn't say much when we arrived at her house either, just went into her bedroom.

The phone rang a few minutes later. I hoped it was Mama, and it was.

"Mama, I'm so glad you called."

"How was Aunt Laney's show?" Mama asked in a weak, tired voice.

"Fine," I lied.

"Did many people come?"

"A million," I said.

"Glad to hear it. Listen, Mary Helen, dear, I received the pathology report today, and as the doctor predicted, the cancer was more serious than he originally believed." I detected a slight tremble in her voice, but as always, it also carried the tenor of courage.

"How much worse?"

"I'm definitely going to have to have chemotherapy. But I'll be fine. No problem, but I've been thinking. Could you possibly stay at Aunt Laney's a couple of more weeks past the original agreement so I can acclimate to the treatment?"

I bit my lip as a tear slid down my cheek. The air diffused from me like one of those inflatable rafts in the windows of St. Simons Drug

Company when stuck with a pin. "Sure, Mama, sure." I slid to the floor. "I'm sorry."

"Don't worry, dear. We have to stay positive."

"I know."

"I thought it would be better for you to stay on with Laney. I'll speak with you later. I love you so."

I stood to hang up the phone, collapsed back on the floor, and put my head in my hands. A strange ache surged in me. I'd never known distress like it before. I heard Aunt Laney come out of the bedroom, but I didn't look up.

"Mary Helen, what's wrong?" Aunt Laney pulled a chair over to where I was sitting. "Is there something I can do?"

I tried to get out the words about this crushing turn of events. "The pathology report said her cancer was worse than they thought, and Mama has to have treatment—chemotherapy. She wants me to stay here two weeks longer than we originally planned."

"Of course that's fine, but I know you're sad. I'm sorry for your mama too. I wish she didn't have to go through all this."

Aunt Laney put her hand on my shoulder. I pulled away, stood up, and went into my bedroom. I lifted my journal out from under my pillow, picked up the wooden pen, and began to write.

> Poor, poor Mama. I hate cancer. I hate what's it's doing to Mama, and I hate what it's doing to me. It's a mean thief that steals, and stabs, and rips people's lives apart. Mama can't die. She can't. I want to go home. I don't feel like I'm ever going to leave this island. I'm marooned.

I wished I could talk to Leslie.

I heard a loud crash from the back of the house. I dropped my journal and flew toward the noise.

When I stepped into the kitchen, a pot, a lid, one spoon, and an upturned chair were scattered like loose change across the kitchen floor. Aunt Laney lay in the middle of them all, her eyes closed, blood pooling around her head.

Chapter Twelve

A Blessing

In the emergency waiting room of the hospital on the mainland, Ben occupied the seat beside me and was reading *National Geographic* magazine. Mavis flanked my other side with her arm wrapped around me. Ben's dad, Rob, sat beside Ben.

Rob Dillard wore a fishing vest and smelled as I thought a fisherman would smell, a cross between saltwater and the seafood counter at Winn-Dixie. "After I left Laney's party, I started cleaning a few fish I caught this morning and didn't have time to change," he had said apologetically when he first rushed into the emergency waiting room. He didn't say much else but just took a seat and stared at the floor.

Sylvester, situated in the chair opposite me, still had on his bow tie. I was beginning to wonder if his pajamas had bow ties.

In my mind, I kept seeing blood, but the blood I saw was not on Aunt Laney's kitchen floor but on my own clothes. Why did I see blood on my clothes? I rubbed my eyes to try to erase the picture and squirmed in my chair.

To wash the blood out of my mind, I pretended that instead of being here in a hospital waiting to find out if Aunt Laney was dead or alive, I was actually in an airport terminal, about to board a jet to Asheville, and when I deplaned, Mama would be waiting. She would have been miraculously cured of cancer, and I would have never found Aunt Laney like I did, sprawled on the kitchen floor.

I didn't know what to do when I first found her, so I dialed the operator. When I told her what was going on, she took my address and said she'd call the ambulance. Then I found Mavis's number in Aunt Laney's address book by the phone, and she called Sylvester and Rob. She came by and picked me up, and we came to the hospital after the ambulance left.

Absorbed in our own thoughts, nobody breathed a word for a long time, but finally Mavis spoke. "I've known Laney almost my whole life. I can't even imagine not having her as my friend." She took her arm from around me, picked her purse up off the floor, dug around in it for a minute, and then pulled out a tissue and dabbed her eyes.

"I shouldn't have let her lift all those heavy paintings. It was too much. I knew she had a heart condition." Sylvester's shoulders drooped. "She always seems so vibrant and alive. It's easy to forget she suffers from a health problem."

Ben laid aside his *National Geographic*. "I guess I believed Laney was going to live forever."

Sylvester turned to Mavis. "She had such a fabulous reception. Everyone was excited about her work."

"I know. I didn't talk to one person all night who wasn't wild over it," Mavis said.

Ben peered up at his dad. "Do you think she's going to be all right?"

Rob set his eyes on Ben. "I sure hope so. Nobody could ever take her place, that's for sure. Laney's one of a kind."

I saw a familiar figure burst through the side door and go to the information desk. The young woman at the desk pointed in our direction, and Pastor Ray Warren strode toward us.

"Thanks for calling me, Rob," he said, reaching to shake Rob's hand, and then went down the line shaking all of our hands.

"Do you know everybody?" Mavis asked.

"Oh, yes. Sylvester and I have known each other a long time. The new artists he features in his gallery always intrigue me, and of course, Mary Helen and I met the first time she accompanied Laney to the church."

"Now can someone tell me what's going on?" Worry lined Pastor Warren's tanned face.

"Mary Helen found Laney on the kitchen floor. Looks like she hit her head on something when she fell, but we don't know exactly what caused the fall," Mavis said as she put her hand to her heart. "We have our suspicions though."

"Hard to imagine Laney being sick." Pastor Warren took a seat beside Rob and took the Bible from under his arm. His fingers rubbed the smooth leather almost as if it felt comforting to him.

"That's what we were just talking about." Sylvester extended his hands in a helpless way.

"She's always been such an encouragement to us," Pastor Warren said. "I sure hope she's going to be all right." I had the idea that when Pastor Warren used the word *us* it meant he was talking about himself. I had a principal who used pronouns that way. He'd say, "We're going to study hard this year, and be the best we can be," or "We're going to have to stay after school if we throw food in the lunchroom." I knew exactly what part of the *we* he was talking about, and he wasn't talking about himself. I guess it was hard for Pastor Warren to admit he needed Aunt Laney, too.

I heard a door open behind us, and we collectively turned around at the same time.

"Hanberry family?" The nurse looked up from her clipboard.

"We're with Laney Hanberry." Mavis stood, and we followed her lead.

"The doctor would like to see you." The nurse turned, and we followed her white-laced shoes as she padded through one door and then another into a small conference room.

"Please sit, the doctor will see you shortly," she said, and closed the door.

Sylvester pointed to the chairs for Mavis and me. Rob, Ben, Sylvester, and Pastor Warren leaned against the wall. In a few minutes, the door opened and we all jumped.

"Hello, I'm Doctor Miller, the cardiologist on call." He extended his hand to each of us. We held our breath.

"Miss Hanberry is stable at the moment." We exhaled in relief. I saw Mavis wipe her eyes again.

The doctor continued. "We've stitched up the cut on her head." He turned to Mavis. "From what you told us when you came in, it seems she must have hit her head on a table or chair when she fell, but thankfully she doesn't have a concussion."

He turned and faced the rest of us again. "We won't know what happened to Miss Hanberry until after we've run more tests. We're fairly certain her fall was caused by a heart event."

"When will you do these tests?" Mavis reached into her purse for another tissue.

"We're doing some right now, and we'll perform more tomorrow. She's going to be in intensive care tonight. Any more questions?"

"Is she going to make it?" Rob asked, his brow furrowed with worry.

"As I said before, I believe she's stable. We'll know more after we gather the tests results."

"May we visit her?" Mavis asked.

"Are you family?" Dr. Miller asked surveying the crowd.

"We're the only family she has," Mavis said with firmness in her voice I'd never heard before.

"Well, I suppose you could slip in, but no more than five minutes."

"If you have any more questions, please call." The doctor nodded and left the room.

"Thank God," Sylvester said.

We all got up to leave the conference room. As Rob held the door for us, Mavis eased her arm around me. "Mary Helen, you've been tossed about so much in this past month and since you're just getting settled, I hate to make you move again and stay with me. I'll just pick up a few things, come over and stay at Laney's tonight so you won't be by yourself. In fact, I'll stay on until Laney gets home from the hospital, longer if you folks need me. I'm thankful Laney is being taken care of here."

Everything seemed such a whirl. Just then a nurse raced past the door.

"Could we see Miss Hanberry?" Mavis called after her.

The nurse stepped back. "Yes, the doctor said you could visit her, but only a few minutes. He wants her to rest. She'll be moved to ICU for the night in just a few minutes."

We followed the nurse into a cubicle where Aunt Laney lay hooked up to several monitors and an IV. A big white bandage covered the left side of her head. She attempted a weak smile. "I can't believe all of you have been here all this time. You need to go on home. It's late." Aunt Laney reached out to me. "Mary Helen, I'm so sorry. You've just received that bad news about your mama and now this, but I'll be up on my feet soon."

"You forget about that 'on your feet' business. You need to rest. Mary Helen is in good hands. I'm with her," Mavis said.

Aunt Laney scanned all of our faces. "You're the best friends anyone could have."

"Laney, could we pray together?" Pastor Warren asked.

Aunt Laney didn't answer but extended her hands. Since Mavis and I were on each side of Aunt Laney, we took her hands.

"Lord, thank you for protecting Laney through this ordeal. Thank you for the blessing that Mary Helen has been by being there to get help for Laney at just the right time. Please encourage her and bring healing. In Jesus' name, we pray. Amen."

Mavis patted Aunt Laney on the shoulder. The nurse reappeared, and we knew it was time to go by the frown she gave us, so we said our goodbyes.

As Mavis and I hiked to the car, I noticed Mavis was twisting her mouth. "You know Mary Helen, I hadn't thought of it before until I heard Pastor Warren pray, but if you hadn't been at Laney's, she might have lain there all night. She might not have made it."

I opened Mavis's car door. I hadn't thought of that either. I guessed it was the one and only good thing that had come from my being sent here.

Then she said, "Mary Helen, what did Laney mean when she said 'bad news about your mother'?"

"We found out that Mama has to have chemotherapy. She wants me to stay here two extra weeks."

All Mavis said was, "Oh" and then shook her head.

Chapter Thirteen

Gentle Surprises

We stopped by Mavis's house so she could pack her overnight case to take to Aunt Laney's. As soon as we went through her front door, one of Aunt Laney's paintings met me in Mavis's foyer. A lone figure stood on the beach gazing toward the marsh. A brilliant sunrise colored the picture with warmth. It evidently was one of Aunt Laney's Lanier pieces, as it had a quote by him written on the frame:

> Bending your beauty aside, with a step I stand
> On the firm-packed sand,
> Free
> By a world of marsh that borders a world of sea.
> —Sidney Lanier

As usual I wasn't sure exactly what it meant, but I had the oddest feeling I might want to spend time pondering what it did mean. I actually liked the words "a world of marsh that borders a world of sea." It reminded me of Mama when she said I was coming to "another world."

When Mavis came out from the back of the house with a blue overnight case in tow, she found me still standing in front of Aunt Laney's painting.

"Do you like it?" she asked.

I guessed I did, so I nodded.

"Laney did that one especially for me."

I took in the way Aunt Laney had blended the colors in the sea.

"Did she go to art school?"

"No, she's primarily self-taught, though she has studied with several well-known artists in the area. More of a primitive style, but her work is winsome, don't you think?"

I didn't know what "winsome" meant, although I vaguely remembered reading the word before, so I just smiled at Mavis.

"I guess I have everything I need." Mavis glanced around her house as if to see if she'd forgotten anything. "Oh, the fish." She moved over to an aquarium in her bookcase-lined living room, picked up a small container, and sprinkled a few flakes from it into the aquarium. She peered into the water. "You fellas behave while I'm gone."

Fish didn't seem like real pets, but I guess if that's all you had, they'd do. If I ever got a pet, I wanted something big and lovable.

Mavis picked up her overnight case, and we headed out to her car.

At two in the morning, we finally dropped into bed. I tossed and turned, trying to get the picture of blood on my clothes out of my mind. I hadn't been asleep any length of time when I heard a knock on the door.

Mavis said, "Mary Helen, do you want to come with me to work this morning?"

I didn't want to get up, but I didn't want to stay by myself either, at least not yet. I'd also been thinking it didn't seem I was going to be able to escape this Sidney Lanier thing. Ben said that kids here have to take Georgia history, so maybe if I found a Georgia history book it would help me.

Mavis went straight to work behind the circulation desk because there was a lot of coming and going that morning, especially little kids. Summer reading programs, so I tried to stay out of her way. I found what I needed in the card catalog, located the book, and chose a chair near a window to read.

The first book I examined had a lot more than I ever wanted to know about Georgia government and leaders and hardly anything but a mention of Sidney Lanier. I looked up and saw movement out the window—a ship in the channel heading out to sea. It appeared much like the one Aunt Laney and I saw the morning we ate at the Sandcastle. The water was shining like diamonds again today, as if nothing bad could ever happen, like Mama having cancer, Aunt Laney crashing to the floor like a broken doll, and blood staining my clothes.

I went back to the shelf, found a couple more books, and was in the process of going through them when Mavis approached.

"I called the hospital, and Laney's been moved to a private room. When I have my lunch break, we'll pick something up from Florence at the café and then head to the hospital."

I nodded, and then Mavis took the book I was reading and scanned the spine.

"*Georgia History*, huh?"

I closed the book and set it aside. "When is your lunch break?"

Mavis checked her watch necklace. "About fifteen minutes."

I gathered up my books, took them to a cart for re-shelving, and then went to the fiction area to get a book I'd seen earlier, *From the Mixed-up Files of Mrs. Basil E. Frankweiler.* I'd finished *Little Women* and this book seemed a good choice, mainly because I felt mixed up. Plus, it was about a girl who ran away and decided she'd live in an art museum. I was with her on the running away part. Didn't know about picking a museum as her escape destination, though. I checked it out, and then Mavis and I started for the hospital.

*

"How're y'all doing today?" Florence called as soon as Mavis and I rang the bell on the front door of the café.

"We're fine. We need an order to go." Mavis plopped her handbag on the counter by the cash register.

Florence stared hard at me over the top of her glasses. "Aren't you Laney's niece?"

"Yes, ma'am," I said.

"What's she up to today?"

"Oh, Florence, I thought you'd heard by now. Laney had to go to the hospital last night. She collapsed at home." Mavis touched my arm. "Poor Mary Helen here found her on the kitchen floor."

Florence put her hand to her chest. "The hospital? I hate to hear that. Is she still there?"

"They're doing tests. It's probably her heart, you know."

"I know. She doesn't take care of herself like she should—painting out there in the baking sun, running all over this island like somebody on the sunny side of fifty." Florence stopped and rang up an order for a customer. The door jangled, and we all turned to see a young couple holding hands come through the door.

Florence continued. "The Lord knows I've tried to talk to her, to get her to slow down. She doesn't listen to me."

"Me neither," Mavis said.

"Well, when she gets home, I'll bring her shrimp salad. Heavy on the celery, low-fat mayonnaise, and light on shrimp. Shrimp's high in cholesterol, you know."

Mavis nodded. "I guess we'd better order. We're on our way to see her, and I'm tight on time. Mary Helen, what would you like?"

"A cheeseburger plain, please, ketchup only."

"Chicken salad sandwich on whole wheat for me," Mavis said. Florence took our orders and in no time brought back a brown paper bag and two iced teas.

"Tell Laney to get well soon." Florence handed us the bag. She rang our orders and we were on our way, eating our lunch in the car as Mavis drove to the hospital. When we arrived, we found ourselves in the parking lot of a construction zone.

"I forgot about them renovating the hospital. I'm glad we didn't have to deal with this last night when Laney came in. I guess they've already finished on the emergency room side," Mavis said.

It took us forever to find a parking space, and then it took us even longer to find her room.

"Finally, I think we're almost there," Mavis said, as she and I zigzagged through what felt like a rat's maze. "I haven't been to this part of the hospital since they started the remodeling. I think it's this way." Mavis pointed to her left; we turned and began scrutinizing the numbers on the doors. Mavis had picked up a plant at the florist in the Village that morning on the way to work, and I tried to juggle it in my arms and at the same time look at the room number on the notepaper the woman at the front desk had given us.

I came to the door that matched the number on the piece of notepaper but was puzzled by the name on the door. "This is the number they told us at the front desk, but the name says …"

I paused and searched Mavis's face as she moved toward me. "I thought her name was Laney." I pointed to the name on the door. "The name on the sign here is Grace Lanier Hanberry."

Chapter Fourteen

Into the Woods

Mavis's face lit up. "That's her name all right."

"So that's another reason she's wild for Sidney Lanier. She was named after him."

Mavis got a pensive expression, and twisted her mouth to the side. "I suppose that's one of the reasons she's drawn to him, but I would imagine not nearly as important as some of the other reasons." She knocked on the door.

We could hear a faint, "Come in."

We pushed open the door. Aunt Laney lay with monitors surrounding her. The many tubes coming and going from her body seemed overwhelming to me. Her eyes drooped, her face was grey, and her hair a mess. The Aunt Laney with a light blue gown draped over her contrasted sharply from the person I first saw standing at the pier, her flamboyant housecoat swinging in the breeze.

"Good to see your smiling faces and to know you haven't come to poke or prod around on this old body," she said managing a smile.

"You can count on that," Mavis laughed. "How are you doing today?" Not waiting for an answer Mavis continued. "You must be better because they've let you out of intensive care."

"I am better."

She didn't sound very convincing.

"The doctor says I can probably leave tomorrow, but I'm going to have to mind my manners. I have to stay home for two weeks. Can you imagine?"

"No, I can't, and I'd hate to be the one to enforce it, but I guess I'm going to be. Mary Helen can help police you." Mavis turned toward me.

I stepped toward Aunt Laney and extended the plant in my hands.

"A gloxinia. How I love them. I'll paint it when I return home. Thank you. Put it in the window, please."

I strolled over, deposited the plant on the windowsill and then turned in time to see Aunt Laney give Mavis a critical look. "Is painting allowed, boss?"

"I talked to your doctor this morning on the phone, and he says you can paint all you want as long as you don't go to the marsh to do it. He said painting would even be good for you."

Aunt Laney turned back to me. "I sure am sorry for this, Mary Helen. Your mama sent you here to avoid hospitals and sickness, and here you are right in the middle of it."

She was right. Mama would sure enough have had a fit if she'd known what was going on.

"Stop fretting, Laney. Mary Helen's made of strong stuff. She has some of you in her, doesn't she?"

Scary. That was a thought that hadn't occurred to me before. I wondered if I'd wake up one morning craving crab cakes and wanting to wear Aunt Laney's hand me down tunics. I shivered.

Mavis leaned over and kissed Aunt Laney on the head. "Take care, my friend. My lunch hour is almost over and I need to get back to the library."

"Feel better," I said and waved goodbye to Aunt Laney. Then Mavis and I moved out into the hallway.

"Do you want to come back to the library, or do you feel comfortable staying by yourself at Laney's?" Mavis asked as we once more navigated the twisted hospital hallways.

I waited a minute before I answered. "I think I'll be fine at Aunt Laney's. I can call if I need anything."

We found our car in the parking lot, and then made the trek back over to the island. When we passed over the causeway, I noticed the tide must be high because the water was edging up to the road in places along the marsh. A pelican flew over as we topped the bridge. I admired it as it flapped its big wings toward the ocean.

"Are you sure you want to go back to Laney's?" Mavis raised her eyebrows in question.

"I'm sure. I have to do it sometime. Might as well be now." Mavis dropped me off, and I found myself alone for the first time in Aunt Laney's pink cottage.

I had the same feelings I did the first time Mama and I ever came to this place. Two opposite feelings. The first feeling was that I wanted to run far away so I'd never see her pink house and purple walls and weird paintings again. The second feeling was I wanted to stay and touch everything, read every book, try to understand what brought this odd collection of items together, what made Aunt Laney choose them, and what made Aunt Laney, well ... Aunt Laney.

As the two feelings battled inside me now, I guess the second won, because I started walking around the purple room inspecting the paintings, searching for who the artists were. I picked up the pottery Aunt Laney had displayed and tried to read the signatures on the bottom. I had gained the morsel of knowledge from Aunt Laney that the potter always signed their pottery.

The blue piano had a book open on it. I hadn't played the piano since I left Asheville except for the night when Mama and I first arrived. I had to admit that I missed my piano lessons and Mrs. Anderson. I moved across the room, sat at the piano, and picked up the open book. The front cover said *Cokesbury Hymnal*.

I placed the book back on the piano and played a few lines of the song where the book was open. The hymn was set in a minor key. I didn't ever remember hearing it before. I stopped playing and peered at the print at the top of the page. "Into the Woods," Sidney Lanier.

He was everywhere. The words read:

> Into the woods my master went, clean forspent, forspent.
> Into the woods my master went, forspent with love and shame.

Forspent? I rose from the piano and went over to Aunt Laney's bookcase. Surely, Aunt Laney had a dictionary somewhere. I spotted it on the third shelf and pulled it off.

I found the word and right beside it the note "Archaic." I'd definitely agree there. Even without knowing what it meant it sounded archaic to me. I read that Mr. Webster said it meant "worn out."

I'd been to church just enough times to know that maybe the "Master" was Jesus and he was worn out.

I scanned the next lines:

The olive trees they were not blind to Him,
The little gray leaves were kind to Him,
The thorn tree had a mind to Him,
When into the woods He came.

It sounded like his friends were leaves and trees. There were times when Leslie had mono I felt like my only friends were leaves and trees. If she hadn't come back when she did, I don't know what I would have done. I turned to Aunt Laney's bird and nest painting and spoke aloud the words written on it:

"As the marsh-hen secretly builds on the watery sod,
"Behold I will build me a nest on the greatness of God."

The ring of the phone surprised me, and I stepped to the kitchen and picked it up.

"Mary Helen, is that you?"

"It's me. How do you feel, Mama?"

"I feel better, thank you. Are you having fun?"

"Oh sure." I hoped my voice didn't give away anything.

"Are you being nice to Aunt Laney?"

"I'm trying. When do you start the treatments?" I tried as much as I could to redirect this conversation back on the Asheville side of things.

"The doctors want me to heal some from the surgery before they begin."

"Oh." I slid to the floor and tried to think of something happy to say. My heart ached for home and Mama. "I've made friends with a dog named Molly at the produce stand Aunt Laney visits, and Sylvester says Ben and I can take Harold to the park some time. He fetches."

"Harold? Oh yes, the poodle. That's fine. I hope you're having fun." Mama said again and then paused. "Mary Helen, Amy said that Leslie's mother called today. Evidently, Leslie has had a relapse of the mono. They had to fetch her from Camp Whitestone."

Poor Leslie. "I just wrote her the other day."

"She probably didn't even receive the letter yet. They'll forward it to her from the camp. And you can write her at home. I'm sure her mother would be glad to read your letters to her. Amy said she's sick right now, though, so I wouldn't count on her writing back."

71

Mama's sick, Aunt Laney's sick, and now Leslie's sick. Was everybody I know going to fall prey to some malady?

"I'm feeling a little tired, Mary Helen, let's talk tomorrow."

"Fine, Mama." A knock sounded on the front door. "I love you." I reluctantly hung up the phone, moved to the window and peered through it. Ben stood there, a bag in his hand. I opened the door and stepped out on the front porch.

Ben's overturned bicycle lay abandoned on the grass behind him. He extended a rumpled paper sack toward me. "My dad sent me over here with these. They're frozen crab cakes. Put 'em in the freezer and then heat 'em up in the microwave when Laney wants one."

"Thanks." I took the sack, put it in the refrigerator, returned to the porch and sank down on the step. Ben settled beside me.

"I guess you're in charge now, having to take care of Laney. Are you okay with that? I know you don't like her that much." Ben took off his Braves baseball cap, readjusted it, and then put it back on again.

"I guess I don't have a choice. Mama called, and I didn't say a word about Aunt Laney being sick."

"Why not? You know she's going to find out."

"I told you she just had surgery. She'll worry. Her situation may be worse than we believed at first." I knocked a mosquito off my arm.

"What do you mean?"

I didn't want to answer all these questions. "It means that, in addition to surgery, she's going to have to have chemotherapy. The least I can do is not rock the boat." I swatted another mosquito. "Do you have to wear insect repellant all the time here?"

"Pretty much." Ben blew at the gnats buzzing his head. "But I always forget."

"How do you do that?"

"What? Forget?"

"No, silly. Blow kind of sideways and up to make the gnats go away."

"You grow up learning how to do it, or else the gnats drive you crazy. You put your lips together, make a little opening at the corner, and then force the air in the direction of the gnat."

I put my lips together, and blew, but the air went everywhere instead of in one spot.

"No, you've got to keep your lips tightly closed except for one little hole. Like this. See." Ben aimed his breath precisely at a gnat cruising by.

I tried it again and was a little better that time.

"See, it takes practice."

We stayed on the front steps a little while practicing our gnat blowing, and then Ben got up and set his bicycle upright.

"You want to go bike riding sometime?"

"I don't have a bike."

"Laney has one out back in a shed. I saw it one day when I was helping her mow the grass. She doesn't ride it anymore, but I think it's in pretty good shape. You could ask her. If you want to go, I'll check it out and pump up the tires for you. What about tomorrow?"

"I don't know. Aunt Laney's coming home from the hospital, tomorrow. Probably not a good day."

I'll call you. Maybe we can go early one morning before many people get out. It's a great time to ride on East beach and around to the marsh. See ya."

I stood up. "See ya."

I watched Ben peel off toward the Village and then went back inside the pink house.

Later when Mavis came by, she fixed hotdogs and coleslaw for supper. She said it wasn't a real supper, but we had things to do and needed to fix something quick.

"Let's straighten this house before Laney gets home. She probably hasn't dusted since she retired from teaching. You can mop the kitchen while I give the furniture a going over."

"Mop?" I said.

"Haven't you ever mopped before?"

I shook my head no.

Mavis twisted her mouth. "My, you have led a sheltered life. High time somebody educated you in these things. I'll show you."

Mavis went to the back-porch, and brought a bucket and a mop back in. "Ever seen anything like this before?"

I laughed. "Of course, I've seen them; I've just never used them."

"Come on over here then." Mavis proceeded to give me a crash course in mopping.

"This is kind of fun," I called to her as I swabbed the mop back and forth over the floor.

"You get over that fast," she called back from the other room.

I finished the kitchen and Mavis came in from the front room. She wiped her brow with the back of her hand. "Okay, now let's hit Laney's room. Empty the bucket, put it and the mop on the porch, and grab the carpet sweeper on your way back in."

I hadn't actually been in Aunt Laney's room, but I'd seen it through the door and decided I didn't know how she slept at night with so much going on in there.

First off, you hardly noticed the walls were green, because almost every square inch of space displayed artwork with shelves supporting pottery pieces and small wooden sculptures. The walls were lined with fabric weavings and paintings, which were not hers. Since coming here, I'd developed the eerie ability to spot her style. "There are a lot of things in here," I commented to Mavis.

"Laney's always said she likes to support her artist friends. And boy, does she ever support them." Mavis stopped and twisted her mouth again. "You know, I think that chair on this side of the bed is going to be in her way. She's going to need a clear shot to the bathroom. I don't want her falling. Let's move it to the other side."

After we moved the chair, I cleaned her nightstand and noticed a picture on it of a middle-aged man sporting hair slightly graying at the temples. I didn't recognize him as being any of the people I'd met. I picked up the picture for a minute and put it back beside Aunt Laney's Bible. I was not surprised to discover there was also a much-used copy of *The Poems of Sidney Lanier* lying on her nightstand, as well. She probably stayed up at night memorizing that stuff. I picked up the poem book, and underneath was yet another old book with Sidney Lanier's name on it—*A Biography of the Poet, Sidney Lanier* by Edward Mims. Riveting I was sure.

We'd almost finished cleaning in Aunt Laney's room when we heard the roar of an engine outside.

"Who could that be?" Mavis gave me a questioning look. She put her dusting rag aside, and I leaned my carpet sweeper up against the wall. We both trekked to the front door and saw an old blue panel truck sitting in the driveway. The driver's side door opened, and I recognized Molly as she jumped out of the truck followed by Ralph holding a big basket in his arms. We opened the front door.

"Ralph, what in the world do you have there?" Mavis called out to him. How did Mavis know Ralph?

"I knew somethin' was wrong this mornin' when Laney didn't show to pick up more tomaters. A customer told me she's in the hospital with her heart. Another customer told me she's a comin' home tomorrow. So I brought her a bushel basket of produce. Never seen a woman git so excited over a tomater in all my life."

As Mavis held the door open, Molly made herself at home and pranced right into the house.

"Hey, Girl, how are you today?" I stooped, rubbed Molly's head, and she gave me her usual lick in the face.

"Won't you come in?" I heard Mavis ask.

"I'll bring this produce in, and then I'll be on my way. Me and Molly got a couple of more deliveries to make." Ralph brought the basket into the house, deposited it onto the kitchen table and started unloading it. "Yeah, I brought squash, cucumbers, and another cantaloupe cause I didn't know if she ate up the ones she bought the other day. And of course there's some fine lookin' tomaters in here." He pointed to a separate paper sack. He finished unloading the vegetables on the kitchen table and picked up his basket. "Tell Laney I hope she's back in the pink purty soon."

"We will, Ralph."

Ralph headed for the front door. "Come on, Molly. We still got work to do."

Molly turned from me and obediently followed him. I watched them move to the truck, and when they reached it, the fluffy mutt leaped up and took her place on the passenger side.

"That was sure sweet of Ralph," Mavis said after they'd gone. She picked the tomatoes out of the sack and moved to the sink. "We'll put the tomatoes on the window sill here. You can't put them in the refrigerator because it makes them lose their flavor."

"I know. Aunt Laney told me."

"Laney is knowledgeable about all things tomato," Mavis said. "The rest of this can go in the bottom drawer of the refrigerator. How about you doing that while I finish my dusting?"

"I will, but how do you know Ralph?"

Mavis stopped in her tracks as she headed to the bedroom. "How do I know Ralph?" She laughed. "Hardly a person on St. Simons who doesn't know Ralph. He's been our pipeline for the freshest fruits and vegetables since forever."

She traipsed off mumbling under her breath, "How do I know Ralph … gracious …"

I shrugged. All I asked was an innocent question. I started loading all those vegetables into the refrigerator. We'd be eating squash for weeks. I remembered something I hadn't told Mavis, so I stepped to the doorway of Aunt Laney's room.

"Ben brought over frozen crab cakes today."

"Oh good, we can have a welcome home meal for Laney tomorrow. Won't she be excited?"

She probably would be thrilled about the crab cakes, but I was confident I'd be able to harness my excitement.

*

That night when I went to bed, I found the mysterious picture in my mind of blood on my clothes fainter, so I fell asleep more quickly than the night before. I did not know then that it was only a temporary reprieve.

Chapter Fifteen

Chestnut Trees and a Gift

"Take it slow," Mavis said as she assisted Aunt Laney up the front steps. I held the door for them until they made it inside. After a few feet into the house, Aunt Laney paused and sniffed the air.

"Mmm, that smells like crab cakes. Could it possibly be?"

"Yes," I said, "but you know I didn't cook them. Ben's dad sent them over."

"Wasn't that sweet of him?"

"They were already cooked; I just had to heat them up. Ralph brought tomatoes last night, so I cut those up for you, too. I knew you liked them together." For the life of me, I didn't know why.

Aunt Laney turned to Mavis. "Can you believe it? I feel like royalty. It's good to be home."

"Aunt Laney, come sit and eat. The food's ready. There's enough for you, too, Mavis."

"I'm going to run. We're short of help at the library today, and I can't be gone too long. There's much to do."

Mavis said her goodbyes and left. I tried to help Aunt Laney into a chair at the kitchen table. How strange to be doing this.

She waved me away. "I'm fine, just a little weak, that's all."

I reached for the refrigerator door handle. "Would you like iced tea?"

"I'd love some. It's good to be home, but I guess I've said that already."

I took the tea out of the refrigerator and poured it into the glasses I'd set on the table. I couldn't believe I'd actually made this meal. As I set the tea glass in front of her, she grabbed my hand and spontaneously erupted into prayer.

"Oh, Lord, thank you I'm finally home. Thank you for these delicious crab cakes. Thank you for Ben and Rob who brought them to me, and Mary Helen who's prepared them for me. Bless them all, Lord. And Lord, thank you for life. Amen"

Aunt Laney took a bite of the crab cakes. By the look on her face, you'd think she'd bitten into a big piece of chocolate cake. I pulled a chair up to the dinette table to eat the peanut butter and jelly sandwich I'd fixed for myself. She relished her food for a while, and then turned thoughtful.

"When I was lying up there in that hospital in intensive care I prayed hard I wouldn't have to die in a sterile place like that. No way to see outside." Aunt Laney fixed her eyes on the kitchen window where the afternoon light streamed in through the sheer curtains. "Yes, if I'm going to die, I want to do it like Sidney Lanier. He wanted to die looking out through an open window, and he did. When I go, I want to go gazing out over the marsh."

I swallowed the bite of sandwich in my mouth. "Aren't you afraid of dying?"

"No, ma'am, I'm not. The God I've known for all these years is one day going to sweep me up in his arms and take me to heaven when he's good and ready—and not one day before."

"How do you know that?"

Her hand moved over to her Bible still lying on the table where she'd left it before she went to the hospital, and she patted it. "I know it because it's right here, right here." She then took another bite of her crab cake.

I stopped chewing and studied the book under her hands. What was right there? The telephone rang and I got up to answer it. It was Ben.

"Mavis told me to give you a call and tell you I was coming over to get the grocery list. She's afraid she's going to have to work late and you'll need a few things before she gets there."

"How are you going to carry them?"

"On my bike. I have a basket I don't use much, because I look like an old lady. I guess this is an emergency."

After I'd hung up the phone, I reached for a pad by the refrigerator.

"Did I hear you mention Ben?" Aunt Laney asked.

"Yes, he's coming to get the grocery list then go to the store. By the way, Ben said you had a bike out in the shed. Do you mind if I ride it? He said he'd be happy to pump up the tires and do whatever repair work needs to be done. It won't cost you a penny to get it going again."

"Don't mind a bit." Aunt Laney put her napkin on the table. "This food was delicious, Mary Helen. Thank you."

"You're welcome. Is there anything special you'd like from the store?"

"I can't think of a thing."

I opened the refrigerator and saw we needed milk. I wondered if Ben could fit it in his basket. I couldn't find a pen in the kitchen to jot it down, so I went to my room to get one.

When I returned, Aunt Laney was trying to clear the table.

"I'll do that. You're supposed to rest." I placed the pen in my pocket and took the plates out of her hand.

Aunt Laney shook her head. "This is a fine mess I'm in. You're supposed to be my guest." She leaned back in her chair.

The bread was getting low, too. If I couldn't get a peanut butter sandwich, I'd be in bad shape around here. I pulled the pen from my pocket and wrote "loaf of bread."

"I see you're using the chestnut pen," Laney said observing it in my hand.

"I had to. I lost the pen I brought from Asheville." That probably didn't come out right, but it was the truth.

"You know, your dad used to use it."

Once more, words seemed to vanish from my brain.

"You don't like to talk about your dad much, do you?"

"I don't have much to talk about. I don't remember him."

Aunt Laney turned pensive a moment. "Your dad liked to write. In fact, I think I saved a letter he wrote to me. Let's go in the front room and see if we can find it."

Aunt Laney wouldn't let me help her in any way, and she was so weak it took her a while to make it to the front room. She lowered herself into the green chair. "Now then, check over in the top drawer there."

She pointed to a chest by the red sofa. I opened the drawer and started pulling out papers.

"There's a blue stationery box on the left hand side. Under it."

I lifted the box, and, when I did, I saw a yellowed envelope which I held up for Aunt Laney to see.

"You've found it."

I examined the handwriting. You could tell that a kid had written it. I'd seen a few things my dad had written as an adult, and I could recognize just a little bit of similarity in the handwriting.

"My dad wrote this?"

"He sure did, when he was about your age, too. You can have it."

"What about this pen. Where did you get it?"

Aunt Laney held her hand out. I placed the pen in her open palm, she took it, rolled it around in her hand, and admired it lovingly.

When she gazed up at me, tears filled her eyes. "Ben's grandfather, Marvin, gave me this pen."

"Oh." I'd never seen her quite so emotional.

She cocked her head to one side. "Do you even know what a chestnut tree looks like?"

"No." Flowers I knew because I went to the nurseries with Mama. But she never bought trees. I knew a few—like cedar, white pine—Christmas tree types, but not much else. Since I came to the island, I'd learned about live oaks.

"I have a book somewhere." Aunt Laney started to squint and stare at the bookshelf on the far wall. "I think I see it—brown, second row."

I moved over to the bookcase, pulled out the book she indicated and handed it to her. She laid the pen on a table, rifled through the pages and finally found what she wanted. She held the book up and pointed. "See here. This is an American chestnut tree. Well, what a chestnut tree used to look like."

She handed the book to me, and I studied the picture of the large spreading tree and nodded. "It's beautiful."

"That's one of the reasons why it was such a loss when the chestnut blight came along and killed all of them. Then, of course, we lost the chestnuts themselves. Chestnuts were great eating."

I handed the book back to Aunt Laney; she put it in her lap and leaned back in her chair. "Amazingly, the stumps are still alive after all these years and still produce shoots."

"Shoots?"

"Yes, little trees that grow up from the stump. The blight gets them, though, when they reach a certain size."

"No one's been able to stop the blight?"

"Not so far. Maybe someday. Anyway, Marvin heard me talking about a line I loved in one of Sidney Lanier's letters that referenced chestnut trees. He went out and did the most beautiful thing."

"What was that?"

"He went up on Blood Mountain in North Georgia and carved wood out of a chestnut stump in the National Forest, brought it back to his workshop on the island and made this pen for me." She picked up the pen again from the table. "The forest service lets you carry out a little bit of wood from the stumps."

"That's a long way to go just to get wood to make a pen."

"You're right. I couldn't believe he'd done it. When he gave it to me, he asked me to marry him. I, of course, said yes." A moment passed before Laney continued. "He died suddenly, though, before we ever made it to the altar."

Aunt Laney always seemed larger than life. I hadn't considered that she had this kind of heartache in her past. "That's sad."

She didn't speak, but only nodded. Strange to see Aunt Laney as a player in a love story. "What was the line about the chestnut trees?" I asked, but before she could answer, a loud knock sounded on the front door.

"I guess that's Ben. I need to give him this list."

"Maybe I can finish telling you about the pen another day. I believe I'm going to have to lie down right now."

Once more, she shooed me away from helping her, and crept slowly toward her bedroom. I couldn't believe one event could zap her strength like this one had. I followed her with my eyes until she closed her bedroom door, and I heard the creaky box springs of her bed as she lay down.

Ben continued to bang on the door and I turned to open it.

"I thought you'd never get to the door," he said as he stepped inside. "Do you have the list?"

I handed it to him, and he scanned down the list. "It's only a few things, so do you think you can fit the milk in your basket, too?"

"No problem. You want to go bicycle riding Monday morning?"

"I asked Aunt Laney about the bicycle and she said I could use it. Mavis said she only had to work a half day in the afternoon on Monday, and she's coming over here early, so I think I can go."

"Great. I'll check Laney's bike when I get back to make sure it's okay." He slammed the door behind him as he stepped out onto the porch.

I couldn't wait to read the letter from my dad. I picked it up off the bookshelf where I'd laid it when Ben came, went into my room, shut the door, and collapsed on the bed. I knew it'd been sent to Aunt Laney but somehow it seemed it'd been sent to me, too. I carefully opened the yellowed envelope and took out a piece of folded notebook paper. When I opened it up, the slightest smells of ink and mildew reached my nose. I read:

> Dear Aunt Laney,
> It's always hard to come back to Asheville after I've been on St. Simons with you. I dream about the marsh for days after I get back, and it's difficult to explain to anyone else why I love it so much.

I picked up the envelope and checked the postmark: Asheville, North Carolina, August 1, 1957. I read on.

> Thank you for the shrimp salad you sent back with me. I ate it for lunch and dinner for two days.

I smiled to think of my dad existing on nothing but shrimp salad for two days. He continued:

> Thanks for letting me use the chestnut pen while I was there.

I picked up the pen lying on the bed and wrapped my fingers around it.

> One day when I have kids, I want to bring them to St. Simons, I want you to teach them how to crab, and I want you to tell them about Sidney Lanier. I want them to love the marsh as much as you do, as much as I do.

> Your nephew,
> Stewart

I held the letter, and once more had two opposing feelings. I wished I could have known my dad, that he could have been with me at that very moment, told me about the marsh, and crabbing and why he loved it so much. Then I also had the feeling of wanting to put the letter back in Aunt Laney's chest and never, ever see it again.

Chapter Sixteen

Long Word, Good Food, Bad Joke, and Distant Mountain

The day after Aunt Laney returned from the hospital was Sunday.

"I'm sorry you can't go to church this morning," I said to her as we faced each other at the breakfast table. Not too sorry, though. I wasn't that crazy about guitars.

"Me, too," she said as she picked at her oatmeal.

"Would you like more coffee?"

"No thanks," she said.

"Maybe you could watch a church service on television."

"Not the same."

There were no words that would lift her out of this state. I finished my toast and jelly, and while I was clearing the table, I tried to come up with a plan that might change the way things were going. Aunt Laney had been quieter than usual since she'd left the hospital. Mavis told me that the doctor said that sometimes, when people go through what Aunt Laney was going through, they get down and have a few bad days. This must be one of them.

The phone rang. I raced to get it, glad for the interruption.

"Mary Helen, this is Pastor Warren. Is Laney available?"

Saved. "Yes, she's right here," I said as I turned to give the phone to Aunt Laney.

Aunt Laney took it, and I watched as her face brightened when she heard the voice. After a few minutes, she said goodbye. She pressed her napkin against her face, and I saw her eyes were red.

"That's kind of him. He was about to go in for the morning service, but he wanted to let me know how much they were going to miss me."

After that, Aunt Laney perked up a little and we played a game of Scrabble. Of course, she won because of all those years she spent teaching literature. She knew every weird word in the dictionary. There was no way to win a game of Scrabble against someone who could spell *sprachgefühl* off the top of her head.

I had just spelled *uh* and earned a double word score, which gave me ten points. That put me ahead by two.

Aunt Laney glanced over at me, and I saw the corner of her mouth turn up a little. I thought she was about to twist it like Mavis, but she didn't. Instead, she gathered up every letter on her rack and put them on the board connecting my *uh* with three other seemingly random letters. Was she kidding?

"That's not a word," I said as I crossed my arms.

"Oh yes, it is." She leaned back in her chair.

"If that's a word, what does it mean?" I had her—I knew she was trying to get away with something.

"I know what it means. You go look it up."

"I will." I was calling her bluff even if I did promise Mama I'd be nice. I remembered if she used all seven of her letters, she received a fifty-point bonus in addition to the tally of her letters. I'd never seen anyone do that before.

I found her Webster's dictionary, and sure enough, there it was. "Sprachgefühl: An ear for the idiomatically correct or appropriate language." Whatever that was.

"Okay, it's a word." I went back to the table in the kitchen and dropped in my chair. "How many points?" I put my head in my hands.

"Let me see," she said as if she didn't already know when she dropped that train of a word on the board. "Twenty-six for the word, and then add the double word score which gives me fifty-two." She scribbled numbers on the score pad. "I believe there's a fifty point bonus for using all seven letters which brings the total to one hundred and two. Yes, that's it. One hundred and two points." She smiled. "I guess I win."

She had a morbid sense of humor for a sick person. "Do you have Monopoly," I asked. I was a whiz at Monopoly.

"I do, but I'm getting pretty tired," she said as she rose from her chair. "I think I'll lie down for a while."

That's right. Quit while you're winning. Oh, well. I picked up the game pieces and put them back in the box as Aunt Laney headed off to her bedroom. I had a lot on my mind to do in my room anyway, so I headed back there.

Just before lunchtime, a knock sounded.

I put the chestnut pen on the bed and went to the front door. When I opened it, I was surprised to see Mavis trying to hold a cardboard box the size of Aunt Laney's Cadillac in her hands.

"Folks at Glynn Fellowship brought food for Laney, but when I told them I'd deliver it, I didn't know they had enough for the entire island."

"Can I help you?" I tried getting my hands around one of the ends of the box.

"Much appreciated," Mavis said then together we stumbled through the house and dropped the box on the kitchen table. Mavis shook her hands at her side, "Wow, that was heavy."

I peered into the box as Mavis started pulling out casserole dishes, bowls wrapped in plastic, and a large chocolate sheet cake. Mmm, chocolate. I held the cake to my face and the scent of the strong cocoa in the dark confection nearly made me dizzy with joy. Finally, a dish I could eat.

"Mary Helen, why don't you set the table while I get the food ready, and get a tray out for Laney. We can serve her food in the bedroom if she's tired."

Anything for chocolate cake. "I was going to fix a couple of sandwiches, but Aunt Laney will be excited to see this spread."

Aunt Laney absolutely refused our offer to serve her lunch in bed, and insisted on joining us in the kitchen. "I'm not an invalid," she said.

"That new mailman, Archie Campbell, was at church today," Mavis said as she spooned creamed corn onto each of our plates. "Have you met him, Laney?"

"Mary Helen and I met him at the bait shop last Saturday. Cheerful sort and good looking. Seems he only delivers in the downtown area. Have you had a chance to get to know him?"

"Yes. Every day when he brings the mail into the library, he has a new joke. You won't believe the one he told me Friday."

"Try me," Aunt Laney said, "I could use a little humor right now."

And you're not even the one who lost the Scrabble game by a hundred points, I thought.

"He comes up to me and says, 'I've been reading an interesting book about anti-gravity.' I couldn't remember checking a book like that out to him, but I didn't say anything. Then he says, 'Yeah, it was so interesting, I couldn't put it down.'"

Mavis laughed, "Couldn't put it down. You get it?"

I got it. Just hysterical. However, Aunt Laney laughed so hard, she scared me. I sure didn't want to have to call the ambulance again.

"That's pretty good, Mavis. Do you remember any more?" Aunt Laney asked.

"Do I remember any more? I told you, he tells me a new one every day. I don't know where he gets all this stuff. Now did you hear the one about the gas station attendant who …"

I zoned out the comedy. I wanted to get back to the pen, the letter, and the chestnut trees.

"May I be excused?" I asked as I squirmed in my chair.

Aunt Laney managed to catch her breath long enough to say, "Sure, Mary Helen, although I don't know why. I haven't laughed this much since Marvin was alive. He always could tell a good joke."

I took my plate to the sink, and then retreated to my bedroom. I spent most of the afternoon recording in my journal the story Aunt Laney told me about the chestnut pen, and how she gave me my dad's letter. I even wrote Mama about it. I was glad to have a bit of information to put in a message to Mama that didn't feel like I was editing the truth. I was sorry to keep so much from Mama these days, but how I could tell her this trouble with Aunt Laney? She'd just worry.

I went out to the purple room and found a book I remembered about Georgia and looked up Blood Mountain. Creepy name. I found that at 4,458 feet, it was the highest peak in Georgia on the Appalachian Trail. A picture from the top of the mountain showed a vista of rolling blue peaks. It made me homesick, because it seemed so much like Asheville.

The book said no one knew for sure how Blood Mountain got its name. The Creek and Cherokee Indians fought a battle for it in the late 1600s, and that might be how it came to have the word *blood* in its name. The explanation I liked best was that it was named for the color of the lichen and rhododendron that grew on its slopes. I examined the pen in my hand once more.

It seemed strange to hold a piece of that distant place in my hand. However, as I spent more and more time on this island, I was getting used to these strange experiences being the norm.

Chapter Seventeen

What Swimmeth Below

I put *From the Mixed-up Files of Mrs. Basil E. Frankweiler* in my lap as I reclined in the front room. I couldn't concentrate, because I'd had a question bobbing around in my brain ever since I went to the marsh for the first time, but kept forgetting to ask Aunt Laney. The question would disappear and then resurface, but always at a time when Aunt Laney was asleep. Aunt Laney rested across from me reading a magazine called *The Artist's World*. "What's a marsh hen?" I asked.

Aunt Laney looked up from her reading, peered at me and squinted.

"Marsh hen … you know like in the painting?" I pointed to the canvas above me.

Aunt Laney shook her head and laughed. "Now, I'm with you. I think all that medicine they gave me in the hospital has clouded my thinking."

She shifted her weight in the green chair, and laid her magazine on the end table. "A marsh hen is a clapper rail."

Now that was helpful. "What's a clapper rail?"

"It's a hen-like bird that lives in the marsh." Aunt Laney turned pensive. "I don't see near as many of them as I used to even though the clapper rail is a saltwater marsh bird and the marshes in Georgia account for one-third of all the East Coast tidal salt marshes. Sadly, their numbers are down because of the loss of so much coastal land to development."

"That's too bad."

"Indeed. But, still, when we're out at the marsh let's keep an eye out for one."

I knew Aunt Laney would follow through on helping me to sight the bird. She was wild about anything that had to do with the marsh.

Later that day, after Mavis came to stay with Aunt Laney, Ben and I went bike riding. I'd actually looked forward to wheeling around on a bike, but I hadn't anticipated how I might feel when I did it. It seemed that every group of people we met was a family—a mom, a dad, kids. If Dad had lived, and Mama hadn't gotten cancer, they'd be the ones showing me around the island. I glanced ahead of me at Ben who already was flying so fast on his bike, I couldn't keep up with him. He came to a cross street, hit his brakes and turned around to see where I was.

As I pulled up beside him, he said, "We'll go to the Village first, circle around the lighthouse, and then get on the beach at Massengale Park."

Asheville is hilly. I'd never been able to ride easily there as I did on the wide flat bike paths on St. Simons. Since it was early, it hadn't gotten too hot yet, and the breeze cooled my skin as we whizzed along. Ben seemed to slow a little, though; I was sure for my sake.

Aunt Laney had said something last week about visiting the lighthouse, but now that she was housebound, we'd have to put it off. I was glad Ben and I could at least go by there. After cruising down Mallery through the Village, we turned left on the bike path to the lighthouse and passed the pier. The crabbers were out in force today. I could see their multiple lines hanging over the railings. I felt sorry for Aunt Laney who I knew would be here, too, if she hadn't had this heart ailment.

Ben, riding ahead of me, stopped when he reached the lighthouse.

"How do you like it?" he asked. "It's more than eighty feet tall."

The tower of white painted brick rose above what most likely had been the lighthouse keeper's residence. "Aunt Laney said they let you climb to the top."

"Yeah, I've been up a bunch of times. About twice a week, somebody comes over from the Coast Guard station and lets folks go up in the tower. From up there, you can see over the ocean to Jekyll Island and way back toward the north end of the island. You can even see the mainland from up there."

From growing up in the mountains, I loved being on something tall and gazing out in the distance. It made you feel like you knew what a bird experienced—flying around getting a view of everything. "Maybe when Aunt Laney gets better I'll get to go up."

"Yeah, maybe."

We got back on our bikes, went by the Methodist Church, turned right on Ocean Boulevard, and then made another right into Massengale

Park. I followed Ben over the wooden bridge that crossed the dunes and deposited us onto East Beach.

Ben turned and yelled, "It's low tide."

We rode to the water's edge and pedaled through the surf. The sun hovering over the horizon to our right began to radiate my body. Most of the tourists and sunbathers wouldn't come for another hour Ben had said, but I still had to pay attention that I didn't run into any early morning shell-seekers or walkers.

The wind was behind us and almost pushed us up the beach, making the peddling easy. After a few minutes, Ben stopped.

"Are you okay?"

"I'm fine," I said. "This is so much fun."

"If you're not too tired, we can ride up to the point and then come back along the marsh road."

I pulled my windblown hair out of my mouth. "I'm not too tired. Let's do it."

Ben took off again and I tried to keep up. This time he stepped up his speed, and I pedaled to match his pace. As we wound around the coast, we reached a point where I could begin to see the marsh, and then Ben stopped.

"We'll have to get off and walk our bikes across the public access path. The beach pretty much plays out into the marsh here."

I dismounted and followed Ben over a tree-shaded path through a residential area. I could see into the back yards of the lovely large houses we passed. As we passed one of them, I heard running water and couldn't resist peeking through the hedge along the path into the back yard. Water bubbled out of a fountain into a bowl surrounded by white flowers. It felt like something in *The Secret Garden*, and I wanted to stay a bit longer, but Ben called to me to join him. We crossed over a couple of streets and then emerged onto a lane, which lined a wide expanse of wetland.

Along the marsh, several egrets stood sentry. "Look," I cried. They began to step lightly among the reeds, their snowy white bodies contrasting with the murky waters. We mounted our bikes again and followed the path along the border.

Ben stopped, turned to me, and put his finger to his lips. He then pointed at something up ahead, down the bank. At first, I had no idea what he was pointing toward. Then I saw them. Around a dozen bunnies grazed lazily along the marsh. They hopped in and out of the water appearing to forage for food.

"Oh, they're cute," I whispered.

He smiled. "I wanted you to see them, because even if we cross over to the other side of the road they're probably going to hop off. They're marsh rabbits," he said softly.

As we moved across the lane, we could still see the rabbits, and amazingly, they didn't hop away. After we passed them, we crossed back over to the bike trail and continued toward Aunt Laney's.

When we pulled up into the yard, I took my helmet off. My back ached, but still I'd had fun. "Thanks for taking me," I said to Ben.

"You're welcome."

"I have a question. Where do those rabbits actually live?"

"They live in the marsh. They're strong swimmers because of their webbed feet and can hide in the water with just their noses sticking out for air."

That night as I was undressing for a bath, I stopped and read again the words of Sidney Lanier which Aunt Laney had painted on the bathroom doorframe.

> And I would I could know what swimmeth below when the tide comes in
> On the length and the breadth of the marvelous marshes of Glynn.

Had Sidney Lanier seen the rabbits and the egrets? Maybe that's what got him thinking about what else might be down there.

After I'd had my bath, I stopped by Aunt Laney's room. Mavis had come by for a while earlier and then left me in charge for the night. I rapped on the open door then entered.

"I'm going to my room. Do you need anything?"

"No, I'm fine. Mary Helen, thanks for staying with me. You didn't sign up to be my caregiver."

Aunt Laney laid a book she'd been reading in her lap. "If you want to come and sit here a little while, though, that'd be great. I'm tired of this book."

"Sure." I went in and took a seat in the chair we'd moved to the other side of the bed. It felt funny just to sit there. I searched my brain for something to talk about. I scanned the array on the walls, and finally came back to the man's picture on her nightstand. "Who's this?" I said as

I held up the picture. "I saw it the other day when we were cleaning. Is he a relative?"

"That's Ben's grandfather, Marvin."

"The one who made the pen for you?"

"That's right." Aunt Laney grew silent. It didn't seem she wanted to talk about Marvin tonight. Maybe she missed him.

I studied the picture. I could see the slightest resemblance to Ben around the crinkling eyes. I put the picture back. I tried to think of another subject that might get her talking. "Oh, when you were in the hospital, I picked up that songbook on the piano and saw Sidney Lanier had written one of the songs in it." She always wanted to talk about Sidney Lanier.

"Yes, he wrote the words to the hymn 'Into the Woods,' but have I told you what a wonderful musician he was?"

Now we were getting somewhere. "No."

"Your dad used to love this story." She stopped and folded one arm across her chest and put the other hand on her cheek. "Now let me think. Where do I want to start?" She paused again. "Why not the beginning?" she said and smiled.

Chapter Eighteen

Beautiful Music

"Sidney Lanier started to play the flute when he was only a little boy. He made his first flute out of a reed he cut from a riverbank in Macon, Georgia, where he grew up. He stopped the ends with cork and then cut finger—and mouth-holes."

"Could he really play it?" I asked, suspecting Aunt Laney might be given to stretching things for the sake of a story. I couldn't imagine making music out of a stick. Why, when I first started taking piano lessons it took me forever to remember which key was which. I shifted in my chair.

"Sure he could. In fact, his mom and dad were so impressed they gave him a real flute when he was just nine years old." Aunt Laney punched the air with her right index finger to give emphasis to the word nine.

"I bet he was excited."

"So excited that he rounded up all his friends and formed a little orchestra that he played in and directed."

"A lot of kids get tired of music lessons as they grow older. Did he keep playing?"

"By the time he was eighteen, folks said there wasn't anyone in Georgia who could play the flute like Sidney Lanier." Aunt Laney leaned forward in her bed giving weight to her words. Her pillows fell down behind her and I tried to help her rearrange them. I plumped them and she settled back again.

"He must have been good," I said using my best "I'm really interested" voice.

"Good? I'll say. One of his friends said he played on the flute 'like one inspired.' His friends loved it when he regaled them with his songs. He even carried his flute into the war."

"Which war?" I said dreading the answer. I'd never been much on history, but I eased back in my chair to wait for the answer.

"The War Between the States—the one that tore our country apart." Aunt Laney's eyes clouded. "Sidney Lanier fought on the side of the Confederacy, but he later grieved over how wrong he'd been before the war started and talked about how glad he was that slavery was overturned."

"He used to play his flute for his comrades in the army as they gathered around the campfire at night. He and his brother wound up being scouts together along the James River in Virginia. I read somewhere that Sidney Lanier turned down multiple promotions so he could stay with his brother. Before the circumstances became grim, he and his brother had a lot of fun together. But that didn't last. The war's gruesome reality finally descended upon him."

Aunt Laney paused a moment as if dreading what she was about to say. "Soon, he was sent to serve on a blockade runner. A federal cruiser captured them and took him prisoner."

"What's a blockade runner?"

Aunt Laney gave me the same look she'd given me when I didn't know who Sidney Lanier was. She sighed what I'd come to know as her patient sigh. "A blockade runner is a ship used to get supplies through to a city that's been closed off at its port by an enemy navy. It's a dangerous assignment requiring much skill, so usually only the best crews are assigned to them."

"But he was captured?" This was sure enough getting interesting. I didn't even have to use my special voice.

"Yes, taken prisoner."

"How awful."

"It was awful. He spent months in prison under harrowing conditions. Still, one of his comrades said that he 'was an angel imprisoned with us to cheer and console us'."

Aunt Laney reflected another moment. She began again quietly. "He played the flute for all the men imprisoned alongside him. Can you imagine making music under those circumstances?"

My piano lessons had often seemed tedious to me. "I have trouble making music under great circumstances, sometimes," I confessed.

"Me, too," Aunt Laney said.

I was not sure whether I believed her or not. Aunt Laney played as if she could go on through a tornado.

"Sidney Lanier had a pure heart. A fellow prisoner said he couldn't recall a 'word of his that an angel might not have uttered ... '"

I leaned forward in my chair. "Did he die in prison?"

"No, he didn't. He became emaciated and probably would have died there had a friend not smuggled him some gold."

"How did that help?"

"It purchased his release. His friend brought it into the prison in his mouth and then took it out when no one was looking and gave it to Lanier. But the worst was still ahead."

"How could anything be worse than being in prison and almost dying?"

"His health had been broken through his imprisonment." Again, Aunt Laney stopped, and it appeared she had tears in her eyes. "He traveled to Fort Monroe, Virginia, in the hold of a ship, and slept in a cattle stall. An old dirty blanket covered him. He was sick, really sick. The others around him weren't much better." Aunt Laney looked me directly in the eye as if she didn't want me to miss this next part. "Then a miracle happened. Without it, he would have surely died and we'd have never had the beautiful poetry he later wrote."

"What?" I said sitting near the edge of my seat. "What happened?"

"An old friend was traveling from New York to Richmond on the same ship and happened to hear that Sidney Lanier was aboard. Imagine how upset she was when she found him dying in such horrible conditions."

"What'd she do?"

"She went to him and began pouring brandy down his throat to revive him. Then she solicited the colonel in charge to help her get him to her cabin. He was so weak he could hardly move so in order to get him out of the hold, the men around him passed Lanier over their heads. When she got him to her room, she warmed him up and continued to pour fluids into him. And you know what happened?"

She was torturing me now. "No, tell me ... tell me ... ?"

"After a few hours had passed, he asked for his flute. When he played the first notes on that flute, a great cheer went up from the hold, because the men knew that their friend, their comrade, Sidney Lanier, was alive and not dead."

Aunt Laney looked a little blurry. I couldn't believe my eyes were misting. "That's a good story."

"Yes, it is, and because he made it through that terrible ordeal, we have our beautiful marsh poems."

She adjusted her pillows again. "He always believed that it was during this time in his life that his health was broken in such a way that the stage was set for tuberculosis to come in ... the dark thing he would fight for the rest of his life."

I leaned back in my chair. "What's tuberculosis?"

"We have immunizations now for tuberculosis. That's why we don't hear of it much. It's a terrible lung disease."

She sank deeper into her pillows and yawned. "I guess we'd better get some sleep now. I'll tell you about him playing the flute with the Peabody Orchestra in Baltimore another time."

"Sure." I stood up, stretched, and shuffled in the direction of my room. Then I turned back. "Thanks."

She smiled, and I turned out the light and closed the door.

*

I went to my room, changed into my pajamas, and got in bed. I reached for my dad's letter lying on the nightstand. I reread it again, folded it carefully, and then took my journal out from under my pillow and put the letter between a couple of blank pages. The chestnut pen was also underneath my pillow, and with it I wrote a few lines before I turned out the light.

For the first time, tonight, as Aunt Laney told a story about Sidney Lanier, I started to realize just a little bit why my dad loved the stories, and why Aunt Laney admires Sidney Lanier.

I looked around the room and studied the paintings Aunt Laney had hung there. As I'd listened to her tell one of her Lanier stories tonight, it seemed she bore a responsibility to pass on what she knew. It was her passion to tell the stories and to paint the marsh. I wanted to have that passion about something.

I put my journal back under my pillow and turned off the light.

Somewhere in the night, I saw a man in my dreams whom I was sure looked exactly like Sidney Lanier might have looked, and he waved at me from across a golden marsh set against a blue sky. I remember ... I waved back.

*

Early the next morning, a loud roar in the front yard almost made me jump out of bed. I heard the crunch of gravel then a creaky car door slam. A dog barked.

Ralph and Molly. I jumped up, put on my robe and peeked out my curtain. Sure enough, I saw Ralph lugging another basket of produce up the walkway. He lowered it to the porch and started pounding the front door. I raced to the door to open it while pulling my terry cloth bathrobe around me.

"How you doin' this fine mornin', missy?" Ralph said, tipping his "See Rock City" ball cap to me.

"I'm fine."

"Hope I didn't wake you all. I figured you'd be runnin' low on produce about now, so I brought you a fresh supply."

He pointed to the bushel basket at his feet which seemed to explode with squash, cucumbers, and okra. Who was going to cook all this stuff? We hadn't used all the produce from his last haul.

"And here's a sack of tomaters. I didn't want to put 'em in the basket, afraid they'd bruise, you know."

As I took the bag, Molly shot into the house.

"You come back here, Girl," Ralph shouted.

I quickly put the tomatoes down, turned around to chase her, and followed her straight to Aunt Laney's bedroom where, just as she raised up in the bed, the dog jumped and licked her in the face.

"Good morning to you, too, Molly," she said laughing, and then stroked the dog's flanks. The fluffy animal reigned on the bed as if she owned it.

Ralph continued to stand on the front porch yelling for his companion. "Girl, you get back out here." He always sounded stern with her, yet Molly felt comfortable sitting on the bed. Had she done it at home?

I pulled Molly off, although I knew Aunt Laney would have gladly let her stay.

"Ralph has brought a lot of produce by again," I told her.

"Please tell him how much we appreciate it." She pulled her robe to her from the foot of the bed and put it on. "On second thought, I'll tell him myself." She got out of bed and headed toward the front room, as I followed leading Molly by the collar.

"Ralph, you're too much," she said when she saw the big basket of produce.

"He brought these, too." I picked up the tomato sack and opened it up for Aunt Laney to see.

She pulled one out and held it up to the light streaming through the front door. "These are lovely. Some of your best."

A little color came into Ralph's face. "Thank you, ma'am. I do try to get good ones."

I didn't understand any of this, why Aunt Laney gushed over produce, and why Ralph hauled all of it over here.

"Oh, one more thing. I almost forgot," he said as he dashed to the truck. He came back bearing another sack in his hands. "Peanuts."

Ugh. Those slimy things.

"You're too kind,' Aunt Laney said as she took the sack extended to her then gave it to me. I could feel the wet slime seeping through the bag onto my hands. I turned around, rushed the bag into the kitchen, put it by the kitchen sink, turned the water on and scrubbed my hands.

When I returned to the front room, Ralph had gone leaving Aunt Laney going through the vegetables. "These look delicious," she said. "Wouldn't it be wonderful to have stewed squash for lunch?"

She had to be kidding. No, it would not be wonderful. Liking a story she told was one thing, but I sure wasn't going to get tangled up in the quagmire of her food obsessions.

She kept picking up the vegetables, examining them, and then she turned to me. "I could teach you how to cook the squash and fry the okra," she said.

No way—no how.

A couple of hours later I stood in the kitchen before the stove stirring mushy yellow vegetables. Then I shook cut okra into a cornmeal-filled paper bag to get it ready to fry.

Aunt Laney sat at the table cutting the rest of the okra into little pieces. "Let's call Mavis to come over and help us eat all of this good food."

Help you eat all of this food, not me. I put the sack aside holding the okra and strode over to the phone. Oh, what I wouldn't give for a cheeseburger and fries right now.

"I was wondering what I was going to have for lunch," Mavis said when I called her.

Later as we gathered at the table and I ate yet another peanut butter sandwich, Mavis noticed my lack of interest in the lunch bounty.

"You should have told me you didn't like vegetables, and I would have picked up something from the Dressner's for you," she said.

Now she tells me. I took another bite of my sandwich, and Aunt Laney helped herself to another serving of okra.

"Cooked in canola oil," she said defensively.

"I don't care what they're cooked in, they're still fried," Mavis said. "You'd better back off those things."

Aunt Laney glared at her and then took a big bite of the fried okra.

Mavis's shoulders dropped. She sighed. "You're hopeless."

*

"It's boiling outside. It never gets this hot in Asheville," I said holding an icy canned drink against my flaming face. Ben and I had been riding bikes for a while, and then decided to stop under the live oaks at the pier. We bought two Pepsis from drink machines under a picnic shelter there, and collapsed at one of the tables.

"How's your mama?"

"I guess she's all right. I just hope the treatment goes well. I've heard bad things about what chemo can do to you."

"Yeah, a friend of mine's dad had to have it. He said it was pretty rough."

I changed the subject. I didn't want to hear any bad medical reports right now. "Aunt Laney told me a Sidney Lanier story last night. Pretty amazing."

Ben's mouth dropped open. "So you liked it?"

"Well, yes, who wouldn't?" I wished he wouldn't make such a big deal out of it.

As if reading my mind, Ben shrugged, and then stepped over and picked up a brown paper bag out of his bike basket. He opened it and offered the contents to me. "Have some."

"What is it?" I said suspecting the answer.

"Boiled peanuts."

"You've got to be kidding. You like them?"

"Love them. Why don't you try a few?"

I hesitated and then tentatively stuck my hand in the bag and took out a few pieces of its slimy contents. I hated the way the peanuts felt in my hands. "Now what do I do with them?"

"You open the shells and eat the nuts, silly," Ben said demonstrating how it was done.

I bit down into an un-peanutty texture, but the flavor was not bad. In fact I kind of liked the saltiness.

"So," Ben said. "Do you like them?"

"They're okay." Not wanting to seem too impressed. I threw the shells on the ground, and a few seagulls that'd been lurking about dashed over to see if there was anything salvageable in my discards.

Movement out in the ocean caught my eye. "Oh, my goodness—look—dolphins." I raced to the edge of the water. The sleek gray forms arced in and out of the water a short distance beyond the pier. Ben stood beside me for a few minutes watching what seemed to be playful antics, though I later learned they were just breathing.

"I've never seen dolphins before. How many are there? One—two—three. Wait, one more over by the pier," I said.

"I love to watch them," Ben said. "Sometimes, when I'm out on the boat with Dad, we'll be surrounded by them. I've heard about folks who swim with them. I'd like to try that sometime."

We stood for a long time watching, waiting for the dolphins to appear, submerge, and reappear again. The dolphins eventually drifted out to sea. I threw my can in the trash bin next to the picnic table. Ben took the last swig from his can and tossed it in the trash, too.

"Are you ready to go? I have to get back to the charter service. My dad has a dentist appointment this afternoon, but I'll ride with you back to Laney's."

"You don't have to. I know the way. You go on over to the shop." I put my hands on the handlebars of my bike, and released the kickstand.

"Are you sure?"

"Of course. I'll see you tomorrow."

"I'll call you tonight. Oh, and I talked to Sylvester. He said we could take Harold out tomorrow if we wanted to."

"Sure, that'd be fun."

Ben mounted his bike and rode the short distance to the charter service. I watched him a moment and then hopped on my bike and pedaled away.

Since it was only me, I could choose any route back I wanted to. I decided to circle by the lighthouse again. Mavis had said that on Saturday if it didn't rain, we'd all come down to the Village, and she'd go with me to the top.

Of course, the other reason we were coming is there was a big art festival in the Village, which Aunt Laney didn't want to miss, because several of her friends were going to have booths. I stopped at the lighthouse and tried to guess how many steps there were to the top. I soon gave up on that and headed to Massengale Park. I loved to circle around under the oak trees at the park because there was hardly any traffic, and it was cool. I drove along Ocean Boulevard then turned onto the Marsh Road.

I stopped for a moment at the little creek watching two kayakers coming in from the marsh. They laughed and talked as they brought their bright red and yellow kayaks, still glistening with marsh water, up the bank. Also on the bank were three older men, who I guessed were crabbers, sitting patiently waiting for their supper. They talked in muffled tones and fanned themselves against the still heat of the late afternoon. A chocolate Labrador loped toward me running alongside his master on the bike path. She stopped to let me pet her, but I soon heard, "Lucy," from the biker, "Lucy, come on." The dog peeled off toward the bike just as three seagulls flew low over my head.

Almost without realizing it, I had spent several minutes studying the happenings at the marsh. I remounted my bike and turned toward home.

When I came through the front door, I found Aunt Laney sitting in a chair, a canvas on an easel in front of her. The gloxinia I'd given her in the hospital was on a nearby chair. Her eyes were fixed on the plant, studying it intensely.

"Did you have a good ride?" she said seeming never to lose her concentration. She picked up her paintbrush.

"I did. I see you decided to paint."

She touched her brush to the canvas. "I'm feeling good enough to be bored now, so I spent a little time at the piano, and then I saw the gloxinia sitting on top of it. I just had to paint a little." I wondered if painting for Aunt Laney was a little like words were for me. Sometimes I felt like words piled up inside of me like floodwaters behind a dam. If I didn't get them out I'd explode. Maybe Aunt Laney had brush strokes, colors, and shapes in her that cried out to be put on canvas.

Mavis came out of the kitchen. "She's getting tired of my company." She dried the pan she held in her hands.

"You people are overprotective. What I'd like to do is go to the pier and throw my traps in the water." Aunt Laney pointed a paintbrush menacingly at Mavis.

Mavis looked at me, raised her eyebrows, and shook her head. "What are we going to do with her?"

I had no idea, so I turned and went into my bedroom, but as I did, the phone rang in the kitchen. It might be Mama, so I flew out to answer it, but Mavis had beaten me to it. I waited to see who the caller was.

"Oh, hi, Sylvester. Yes, she can talk." She stepped into the front room and motioned for Aunt Laney.

"Me?" Aunt Laney said pointing to herself. She seemed pleased that someone was asking for her. "How wonderful—contact with the outside world."

"Don't be smart," Mavis said as she handed the phone to her. "It's Sylvester."

I started to go back into my room, but for some reason I stopped and pretended to study a cookbook on the shelf in the kitchen.

Aunt Laney took the phone. "Hi, Sylvester. Oh, that's great." A big smile spread across her face. She grinned at us in an almost naughty kind of way. "Really. Well, I don't know how long it would take. Let me think about it and get back to you." She hung up the phone.

"What was that all about?" Mavis said as she put a pan in a cabinet.

"Sylvester said I sold several paintings at the show, but he also has several clients who want to commission paintings." Aunt Laney's eyes were gleaming. "They want them as soon as possible. You know what that means, don't you?"

Mavis put one hand on her hip. "I'm afraid to ask."

"It means I have to return to the marsh, and soon. I have a lot of work to do."

Mavis turned her back to Aunt Laney and leaned against the sink. "I don't guess there's anything I could do to stop you."

"Not a thing."

"Thanks a lot, Sylvester," I heard Mavis mutter under her breath.

Aunt Laney almost pranced back into the front room. She seated herself once more in front of the canvas and began to paint with new vigor all the while humming loudly.

"Pssst," Mavis said, and motioned for me to come into the kitchen.

I proceeded over to the sink where she was still standing.

"You know she's going to head out to the marsh first chance she gets."

"I know." I could feel my insides tighten a little. If Mavis thought I could control what Aunt Laney did, she'd been spending too much time at the library.

"You need to stay with her. In a twinkle of an eye, she could get too hot." Mavis folded a dishtowel and put it by the sink.

"What should I do?"

"Make sure you take a cooler filled with plenty of water, and force it on her. Watch her for signs she's getting overheated. Surely, she has enough sense to go early in the morning before the sun gets too hot."

"What if she doesn't?"

Mavis picked up her purse to go home.

"Call me. I'll have to come over and heavy hand her. Remember, stay on her."

Aunt Laney called from the front room. "I hear you two in there. What are you whispering about?"

Mavis and I went into the front room.

"We're whispering about you," Mavis said.

"I thought so." She smiled, stopped painting, and directed her eyes to us. "You two are just wearing yourself out for nothing." She started painting again.

Mavis and I exchanged looks, helpless to stop Aunt Laney from anything she determined she was going to do.

Chapter Nineteen

Assembling the Pieces

"Aren't you tired of the way things are looking in this bedroom?" Mavis waved her hands at the array in Aunt Laney's bedroom. We'd washed and dried all the dishes after dinner and were trying to help Aunt Laney settle in before Mavis went home.

"I hadn't considered it," Aunt Laney eyed Mavis a little suspiciously, "but yes, I guess things could be spiffed up a bit. What did you have in mind?" I knew Aunt Laney well enough by that time to know it'd be hard to pull anything over on her.

Aunt Laney put aside the book she'd been reading in bed. I knew Mavis was trying to create a diversion to keep her beloved artist friend from venturing out to the marsh. It seemed Aunt Laney knew something, too, but she couldn't figure out what. This could get rough.

"I'm off a couple of days and I thought we might spend time sprucing things up a bit. You know, rearranging, that sort of thing. When I was dusting the other day, it looked like your belongings had been sitting in the same place since the Flood. It might rain anyway; it'd be a good way to pass the time."

"That's fine, but Sylvester ..."

"Sylvester can wait. Giving this place a good going-over is what we need to do now while Mary Helen and I are still here." Mavis turned and winked at me. Aunt Laney studied Mavis closely as she left the room.

The next day Mavis and I stripped everything from Aunt Laney's bedroom walls and shelves. We dusted, and then spent most of the afternoon trying to decide how to put everything back.

"I kind of liked it the way I had it before," Aunt Laney said when Mavis tried to move her favorite seashore painting to another wall.

"You're in a rut. It's time for a change," Mavis said.

Aunt Laney threw up her hands. "Maybe I should just go to the marsh and get a little painting done."

"Oh, no. You can't do that—we need your input." Mavis blew dust off a tiny wooden sculpture of a bird in flight.

"Need my input. That's a joke. You haven't listened to a word I've said."

"That's not true," Mavis said defensively. "We needed to know what order to hang those copper enameled plates in. You're the only one who knows things like that."

"Big deal," Aunt Laney said and collapsed against the headboard.

Before we even finished that project, Mavis decided we needed to organize the bookshelves in the front room "library" style.

We tore all the books off the shelves, and then Mavis started sorting them into piles.

"Now I can go," Aunt Laney said as she stood surveying the mess in the floor.

"We need you now more than ever. We might want to thin out these books, and we wouldn't want to dispose of anything that has sentimental value." Mavis put a copy of *Pride and Prejudice* in the keeper pile.

"Give them all away—just let me go to the marsh," Aunt Laney said.

"Nonsense," Mavis said.

Aunt Laney plodded back to her bedroom with her tunic sagging off her shoulders, looking sad.

Mavis waited until Aunt Laney closed her bedroom door. "Wow that was close. Now, we'll pull all the fiction titles out, and then you can alphabetize them by author," she said to me. "While you're alphabetizing, I'll work on the non-fiction."

As she slid the books to me, I stacked them. I couldn't help but notice the wide assortment of fiction Aunt Laney kept around the place, everything from *To Kill a Mockingbird* to *Moby Dick*. Her black and silver copy of *Moby Dick* appeared to have been around a while. I thumbed through the yellowed pages to see when it was published. Ooh, 1930. An antique. As I flipped the pages, I came across several intriguing illustrations. One of a giant tail tossing a boatload of men in the air sent chill bumps up my spine. Another of an old-fashioned sailing ship looked different from the freighters and yachts that passed through the channel off the pier. When

I had more time, I might come back and examine this book again. As I started to close it, a folded pink piece of paper drifted from the pages to my lap.

I picked it up, and started to put it back in the book, but a faint hint of fragrance wafted from the letter. The snoopiness Mama always talked about almost forced me to open it and see what it was. I glanced over at Mavis, who was absorbed in her book organization, and then I opened the letter, which turned out to be written in elegant penmanship. It began "Dear Stewart." My dad? From who?

> Thank you for remembering to write a mother who is missing you very much. Things in Asheville have not been the same since you left for Aunt Laney's. I'm glad you are enjoying yourself and have found a friend.
>
> Remember your manners while you are at Aunt Laney's. It's kind of her to have you there. Tubby often sits at your door. I think he's missing you as much as everyone else. We can't wait for you to come home in a couple of weeks.
>
> I'm sure Aunt Laney has filled your head with all of the stories about Sidney Lanier. Since Grandmamma died when I was little, I never had a chance to hear the Lanier stories straight from her like Laney did. Aunt Laney is a living depository of all Grandmamma passed on. Listen well, for there is much wisdom in the words she shares.
>
> I love you much and look forward to your return.
> Mama

Mama—this had to be Mary Helen, the woman I was named after. I sprang to my feet and strode toward Aunt Laney's room.

"What are you doing?" Mavis said as I pushed past her almost knocking a stack of her books over.

"Look what I found," I said as I burst into Aunt Laney's room and waved the letter in front of her face as she rested in bed reading.

"And what is this?" She took the paper from my hands. "Well, I'll declare. A letter from Mary Helen." She read the letter then looked up at me. "Where did you find this?"

"It floated out of *Moby Dick*."

"*Moby Dick*. Oh, yes. That makes sense. Your dad used to read *Moby Dick* every year when he came. He must have used the letter as a bookmark. How about that! This letter is quite a treasure. I don't recall her ever being much of a letter writer." Aunt Laney handed the paper back to me.

A letter from my grandmother. "Can I keep it?"

"Of course. Take *Moby Dick* too. It's not read much around here anymore. In fact, if you see any other books you want to keep, feel free to take them too, please."

"What's going on in here that almost caused me to get my head knocked off?" Mavis said as she appeared in the doorway, her hands on her hips.

"A letter from my grandmother," I said as I showed the letter to her.

"Oh, my." She read the letter, and then she pointed a finger at Aunt Laney. "See, I told you this was a good idea. Mary Helen would have never found this if I hadn't insisted we do some rearranging."

"Okay, okay, you've made your point," Aunt Laney said, waving us out of her room.

I took the letter to my bedroom, put it in the back of my journal next to the one from my dad, and then returned to the front room to finish my alphabetizing job. Strange, how that letter had been stuck in *Moby Dick* for so many years.

Mavis kept thinking of projects, but eventually Aunt Laney figured out what was happening.

"You people are keeping me prisoner using home improvement jobs," she said on Friday at lunch.

"Us?" Mavis said innocently.

"Both of you, and I want you to know I'm going to the marsh first thing Monday morning. You can turn this house upside down and inside out if you want to, but you'll do it without me because I'm going to be painting."

"We're only trying to be helpful," Mavis said and gave me a "What are we going to do?" expression. "I didn't think it'd hurt to have a few more days of recuperation before you head back out into the blazing sun."

"Fine. I've had it. Now …" She paused and made direct eye contact with Mavis. "Now I'm going."

Chapter Twenty

A Different Perspective

For once, I agreed with Aunt Laney. I was tired of these house projects, too. Saturday couldn't come fast enough for me. I wanted to climb to the top of the lighthouse, and write down everything I saw, so I could tell Leslie about it when I returned home. As soon as I rolled out of bed that morning, I put my sketchbook and the chestnut pen in a backpack so I wouldn't forget them. Then I dressed in a white knit top and denim shorts, put the backpack in the front room, perched on the red sofa, and waited for Aunt Laney to dress and for Mavis to pick us up.

When Aunt Laney came out, she sported her signature look, wearing a tunic I'd never seen before. How many of these things did she have? As she passed by me, I saw a huge butterfly design on the back of the flowing fabric. Somehow she knew I was staring.

"My friend Margaret made it for me." She held out the sides and spun around. "She's going to be at the festival today, and I wanted to do a little free advertising for her. It's made with a batik process. This is silk." She lifted the wispy material for me to examine, obviously proud of her friend's work.

Mavis arrived a few minutes later, and we loaded into her blue Volvo and headed for the Village. It took us a while to find a parking place because of all the people.

The festival booths were set up in front of the library under the big oaks. People were swarming for treasures everywhere you looked. I knew Aunt Laney was going straight to find her friends at the festival, but I wanted to go to the lighthouse first. I looked at Mavis with pleading eyes.

"I know, I know. We'll leave Laney here and walk on over," she said acknowledging my wish. "She should be alright by herself for a little while."

I clapped my hands for joy. When we arrived, we discovered there was a short wait. I didn't much mind, though, because it gave me a chance to explore the outside of the lighthouse keeper's house. I rambled around examining the grounds and poked around in the oil house that was now a gift shop. This lighthouse, built during the Victorian period in 1872, was not the first lighthouse here, I learned. Actually, the first one built in 1807 had been torn down during the War Between the States.

In the gift shop, a book on display, *Lighthouse*, by Eugenia Price, intrigued me. When I read the back cover, I discovered this was the first novel of what was called the St. Simons Trilogy. It said she was a *New York Times* best-selling author. How had I missed this? Sidney Lanier and now Eugenia Price. Two people in the literary world I'd never even heard of before. I checked the price, and found I'd brought just enough to cover it. I made my purchase and stowed it in my backpack.

When it was finally our turn to go, I noticed Mavis took a deep breath before she started. It didn't take me but a few minutes to know why.

It was a long way to the top. Mavis grew out of breath a couple of times, and we had to stop on one of the landings and let others go by. Once she even collapsed on the steps, she was huffing and puffing so much.

"Go on ahead," she said, "I'll catch up later."

"I'm not leaving you here. It's no big deal. I'll wait until you catch your breath."

"The last time I scaled these steps, I was ten years younger. Didn't realize my age was affecting me this much," she said between puffs.

After much longer than I imagined it would take, we finally emerged onto the platform around the light. The ocean vista rolled out directly in front of us. One hundred twenty-nine steps to the top. My, was it high.

"Magnificent, isn't it?" Mavis said gasping.

"I had no idea it would be this great." I covered the three hundred sixty degrees around the top of the lighthouse, took my journal and pen out of the backpack and tried to describe everything I saw.

Signs on the handrail showed which way was north, south, east and west. I looked over the edge that said southeast and could see the top of the lighthouse keeper's house, a gazebo roof, and a flagpole with a flag undulating in the sea breeze.

As I moved to the east, I could see along the coast toward Sea Island. Ben had told me where it was, though I'd never been over there. To the north—trees as far as I could see. The gnarled branches of the old live oaks stuck their arms up into the air declaring their endurance. As I turned northwest, there was Brunswick with the billowing smokestacks of the paper mills, and then to the west, the bridge over the river, the pier, the rooftops of the Village businesses, the library, and the park filled to overflowing with the art festival bunch.

To the southwest, Jekyll Island. Ben had pointed out the island one day on a bike ride. It was easy to see from the pier, and even easier from way up here. As I walked left, the rolling sea lapped against the giant rocks set along the shore—the sea to the horizon, and on the horizon a shrimp boat.

Ben was right. It seemed from the top of the lighthouse I could see forever. The map at the Sandcastle came to mind. From the whole world people came and went from this island—France, Africa, China, Brazil. Strangely, a phrase from the nest painting came to mind, "The greatness of God."

Mavis was patient and didn't try to hurry me. I knew if I didn't get everything down right then, I'd never remember. After I'd finished, I reread what I'd written to make sure I'd gotten it all. Because the trees were so tall, I couldn't see the marsh from the lighthouse. That didn't seem possible, because every time I saw the marsh it seemed to stretch on forever.

"Are you ready to go back down?" Mavis asked. "I don't want to hurry you, but I think we need to see what Laney's up to."

"I'm ready."

Descending from the top was easier and took a lot less time than going up. We trekked back over to the art festival, searched a little while, and finally found Aunt Laney visiting a man who did paintings that all resembled the human eye in some way. Aunt Laney was holding a blue-eyed painting admiring it.

"There you folks are," she said as she spotted us. She turned the painting to us. "What do you think? I'm thinking of getting it and hanging it in the kitchen."

She didn't want to know what was going through my mind. I couldn't imagine being stared down every morning while I ate my cereal.

"Lovely," Mavis said. I turned to see if she said it with a straight face. She did.

"That's what I thought," Aunt Laney said as she wheeled back to the man that I assumed was the artist. "I'll take it."

I almost choked when he told her how much it cost. She, on the other hand, seemed to be pleased.

"Excellent," she said as she pulled her wallet out of her purse. "I'll think of you often and pray your work finds homes with people who truly appreciate it. Oh, and here's my card if I can ever help you in any way." Aunt Laney produced business cards out of her giant satchel and handed it to the man. While she finished her transaction, Mavis and I drifted over to a booth displaying jewelry.

"Did you like that painting?" I asked Mavis.

"Quite interesting," she said as she picked up a turquoise bracelet. "I guess Laney has influenced me over the years. She's broadened the way I view things, helped me learn to appreciate artistic expressions I might have been closed to years ago. Laney says that if someone is trying their best to use the talent God has given to them, they ought to be encouraged never to give up. Of course, they should try to work on their craft, and study and all that … but, she says we should always find something encouraging to say about their work. One of the things I love about Laney is how she's always encouraging other artists. There are a great many artists here today at the festival that have found success because of Laney's encouragement."

Although I had already done what I'd come for, I soon found that Aunt Laney was just getting started. No one would have guessed she'd gotten out of the hospital a few days before. She bounced around from booth to booth meeting and greeting as if she had all the energy in the world.

"I'm about worn out," I told Mavis as we finally landed in some Adirondack chairs. "How does Aunt Laney keep going in this heat?"

"It's her passion," Mavis said. "Not a thing we can do about it. At least she's not sitting in the hot sun at the marsh, which I guarantee is where she'd be if she wasn't here."

"I guess you're right."

"We're going to need a wheelbarrow to lug all her stuff to the car. She's stacking it up in Margaret's booth right now."

Aunt Laney came striding toward us holding high a pottery vase. "Look at this treasure I just picked up."

Not very Aunt Laney like because the color was subtle—a sea blue glaze.

"I like it," I said.

"Good, it's yours." She handed it to me.

I took it from her, felt the cool fired clay in my hands. "Thanks," I said. I turned the vase around in my hands and admired its beauty. Its mouth was small and it reminded me of choirboys singing. I imagined it making an "ooh" sound. I wrapped it in a rain jacket I carried in my backpack and nestled it in a zippered compartment, making sure I secured the zipper.

"I had several people ask about who made my tunic. Margaret has sold several scarves today because people saw my outfit." Aunt Laney ran her hands along the front of the tunic. I decided Aunt Laney became about as excited helping people sell artwork as she did about buying Ralph's tomatoes.

"Aunt Laney, where are you going to put all this stuff?" I said as we hauled all her purchases to the car.

"Oh, I'm not keeping it all. I've bought ahead for Christmas."

I held up the iron fish sculpture in my hand and hoped she didn't plan to send this rusty thing to Asheville. I'd hate to see Mama's face if she opened a box with this shabby sea creature in it come Christmas.

*

"We're glad to have Laney back today," Pastor Warren said on Sunday morning. Everyone clapped and turned toward Aunt Laney. Color rose in my cheeks again at being close to the center of attention. I caught a glimpse of a particularly dazzling smile in my peripheral vision, and turned to see the mail carrier, Archie Campbell. I found it nearly impossible not to smile back, so I did.

After church, Aunt Laney wanted to have a picnic, so Mavis came along to the house. We made sandwiches, took them over to Massengale Park, relaxed under the trees, and I practiced my gnat blowing until Mavis said it was too hot. Then we headed home.

"Anyone for a game of Scrabble?" Aunt Laney asked when we returned to her cottage.

She had to be kidding. I started to protest, but then Mavis chimed in.

"I'd love to play. It's been quite a while since I took you on in Scrabble, Laney."

That walk to the top of the lighthouse must have drained the oxygen supply from Mavis's brain. But, I got out the game anyway and set it up in the kitchen, trying mentally to prepare myself for the inevitable slaughter I faced. To my disadvantage, I'd forgotten the amount of time Mavis spent in a world full of words.

"L-o-g-o," I spelled vertically as I built on the word *frog* I used in my first turn. "That's five points."

"*Logography,*" Mavis said as she pulled her letters from her rack.

I felt beaten already. One, two, three, four, five, six tiles. Whew, one short of a fifty point bonus.

"Now that's twenty points times two for a double word score. Forty points," she said as she scribbled on the score pad.

Wordsmith Laney and now that library terror Mavis. I was sunk.

"Z-y-d-e-c-o," Aunt Laney spelled building on Mavis's *y*.

I almost fell out of my chair. "Can't be a word," I said protesting.

"Is," said Aunt Laney. She raised her eyebrow at me in a smug way.

I stomped off to the front room to retrieve the Webster's again. In misery I read the definition, "Zydeco: popular music of southern Louisiana that combines French dance melodies, elements of Caribbean music, and the blues, played by small groups featuring the guitar, the accordion, and a washboard."

I sulked back into the kitchen. "I want to know how you know that word," I said as I dropped in discouragement on my chair.

"One of the guitar players at the church, Alton, is from Louisiana, and used to play that kind of music."

"How many points?" I asked, not really wanting to know.

"That's twenty-two points including the double letter square, times three for the triple word square equals sixty-six points."

I threw up my hands. "How am I supposed to compete with you two dictionary brains?"

Aunt Laney smiled. "Your turn."

*

Monday morning came and there was no stopping Aunt Laney. The only thing I could do was help as much as I could. It had only been eleven days since Aunt Laney collapsed in the kitchen, and she was definitely sneaking around behind the doctor to do this, but she was determined to go to the marsh, so I loaded the car and made sure we had enough water like Mavis had told me.

We set up Aunt Laney's easel along the marsh road. Mavis had gone out and bought a little portable stool so at least Aunt Laney could sit.

"You know you don't have to stay out here. I'm perfectly fine by myself," Aunt Laney said as she picked up her paint palette.

Her stubbornness went beyond anything I'd ever seen. Well, anything I'd ever seen except in the mirror, I guess. I lounged on the bank and the rough grass prickled my bare legs. "I know, I know. But if you do need anything, I can fetch it. You haven't even been out of the hospital two weeks."

"I'm not going to need anything. Why don't you go on down to the Village and find Ben? You two take Harold out or something."

"Are you trying to get rid of me?"

Aunt Laney turned and smiled. "Of course not."

"I'll go down to the Village later. I think I'll sit here for a little while."

Aunt Laney shrugged. "Suit yourself."

I lay back on the ground and watched the seagulls flying above me, a few all white, some black headed, others gray winged. Two herons soared out toward the marsh. I scanned the sky to see where they went. Then I remembered what Mavis had told me.

"Do you need some water?"

"No, thank you. You know, I thought the idea was for me to be taking care of you, not the other way around."

Funny how things had turned out. "Strange, isn't it?"

"Very. I guess I never appreciated what it felt like to be under the weather for an extended time." Aunt Laney turned to me. "You know who this has made me think about, don't you?"

I knew whom all roads often seemed to lead to in her mind. "Let me guess. Sidney Lanier."

She laughed. "How'd you know?"

"One, because he's practically all you talk about sometimes. Two, because you said he had tuberculosis."

Aunt Laney pivoted back around to study her painting, and then she looked at me again. "Ah, so you have been paying attention. Yes, he had tuberculosis. Because of that, he often had to go places better suited to his health than Macon, Georgia, or Baltimore, Maryland."

"Like where?"

"Mobile, Alabama, Alleghany Springs, Virginia, Lookout Mountain, Tennessee, and of course, Brunswick, Georgia." She touched her brush to her palette. "Lanier only came to Brunswick because of the disease. It shows how God can bring something good out of something bad."

"Do you think God is going to bring something good out of your heart episode?"

"I have every reason to believe that. You know, Sidney Lanier had a hard life full of poverty and sickness, but he never gave up, he kept going." Aunt Laney faced her canvas and applied a bright yellow in long sweeping movements. After a few minutes, she continued her story. "Mr. Edward Mims wrote in his biography of Sidney Lanier that when Lanier wrote 'Sunset,' the first poem in the 'Hymns of the Marshes,' he had a 104 degree temperature."

"One hundred four degrees? I had a 103 degree temperature one time and I was so sick I couldn't lift my head off the pillow." I grew a little nauseous thinking of that time I had the flu.

"Amazing, isn't it. Writing something that beautiful with perspiration dripping down your face. Some people think that 'Sunrise' is his best poem. Of course, it's not. It's the 'Marshes of Glynn.'"

As Aunt Laney was speaking, a sprinkle of moist beads formed on her forehead. Her face took on a red glow "Speaking of perspiration, your face is awful hot looking."

She put her paintbrush aside and wiped her forehead with the back of her hand. "I guess I do feel a little warm."

"I think we'd better head back home."

"No, not yet. I'm only getting started."

Mavis was going to kill me. Aunt Laney kept painting. I tried to read a little of the *Lighthouse* book, but between swatting mosquitoes and looking up to check on her, I couldn't concentrate. Why couldn't I remember to put on insect repellent?

I found the repellent in Aunt Laney's tackle box, sprayed a little on me, and then settled back down and tried to read again. When I looked up, her face beamed cherry red. I had to say something else.

"I know you don't want to go back, but if you grow too hot out here, Mavis is going to have a fit." To my surprise, she gave in.

"Maybe you're right, but I didn't accomplish that much. What a shame, too. I was off to such a good start. Don't you think?"

I stood in front of her painting and studied it.

"Yes, it's good." The surprising truth was I meant it.

Chapter Twenty-One

Heartbreaking History

"What did I tell you? You've gone and overdone it. It's too hot for someone in your condition to be out there at that marsh this time of year," Mavis said when she dropped by after work. Aunt Laney's once red face had now turned ghostly pale and looked out of place next to her brightly striped pillowcase.

Aunt Laney rolled over in the bed toward Mavis. "What do you mean, 'my condition?'"

"You know exactly what I mean. Sylvester's just going to have to wait on these paintings."

"What am I going to tell him?"

Mavis put her hands on her hips. "You can tell him that his clients have lived this long without a Laney Hanberry original, they can live a little longer without one." She stood erect and took on the character of a dog bristling before a fight. "No, wait a minute I'll tell him myself. I'm going to that art gallery tomorrow and set him straight about all this."

"You're overreacting. I'm a little tired, that's all." Aunt Laney rolled over and faced the wall. Probably her way of saying she didn't want any more lectures. We left the bedroom and closed the door behind us.

"'What will I tell Sylvester?' she says. She acts likes the only thing that's important is fulfilling those commissions. She needs to take care of herself." Mavis collapsed exasperated in a kitchen chair.

I felt terrible about this. "I did the best I could."

"Oh, I'm sorry Mary Helen. I didn't mean it was your fault. I'm just venting. There was absolutely nothing you could do."

Mavis jumped up from her chair, went to the sink, and started drying pots in the dish rack. Rubbing the pots with the towel seemed to calm her a little. I was glad I'd agreed to meet Ben and Harold in the park, so I told Mavis about my plans and made a beeline for the front door and my bicycle.

When I wheeled into the park, Ben and Sylvester's playful poodle were already there. Harold was running and jumping as if he was the first dog ever to go to the park. Ben and I threw a tennis ball about a hundred times for him. He was great about retrieving it and bringing it back to us.

"You are such a good dog, Harold," Ben said taking the ball from the dog's mouth.

I rubbed the dog's black curly hair. "Did you know that Sylvester called Aunt Laney to tell her several clients want paintings from her? Mavis is mad."

"Why?"

"Because Aunt Laney went out to the marsh to paint today and got too hot."

"That sounds like Laney, but she'd have found a reason to go back out there even if Sylvester hadn't called."

"You're probably right."

I took the ball out of Ben's hand and threw it again for Harold. Quick as lightning, he retrieved it out from under some palmetto leaves and brought it back to me. "This is the best dog."

"I told you he was smart. It makes me want a dog even more. Poodles are great housedogs, because they don't shed. I'd like to have one like Harold."

Ben and I lounged on the grass and Harold collapsed beside us, his tongue hanging out of his mouth.

"Maybe you'll have a dog one day." I stroked Harold. "This is changing the subject, but do you know what you want to be? I mean, do you want to run the charter service like your dad?"

"I don't know. Maybe. I haven't thought about it much. What about you?"

"I want to be a writer."

"I've never known anybody who wanted to be a writer."

"Crazy, isn't it. I don't think I'm that good, but my teacher, Mrs. Harding, says I am. I guess it's just a dream."

"Maybe it'll come true." Ben reached over, took my hand, and squeezed it.

When Ben's hand touched mine, I felt a spark almost like static electricity in the winter. But unlike the winter flickers, this electrical charge did something to my heart.

"Maybe," I said as I studied his tousled blond hair, freckles, and blue eyes.

After a minute, Ben let go and stroked Harold. "You ready to go, boy. I have to get back to work." Ben turned to me. "Dad has a charter scheduled and I have to mind the store. Hey, my dad wanted me to ask if you and Laney can come for dinner tomorrow night?"

"I'll ask."

Ben rode off toward the Village, and Harold trotted along beside him. I watched as they disappeared out of sight. A new possibility emerged. Did I have a boyfriend? I'd never had one before, a few crushes here and there, but never a boyfriend.

As I pedaled to Aunt Laney's and pondered the implications of this development, a question surfaced. What happened to Ben's mom? Why didn't he ever talk about her? It's as if she never existed.

Mavis left as soon as I returned to Aunt Laney's. As I went into the kitchen for a glass of water, I heard Aunt Laney call from her bedroom, "Mary Helen."

I went to her door.

"Did you have a good time?"

"Yeah, great. Oh, and Ben and his dad want us to come over for dinner tomorrow night."

"Tomorrow night? That sounds fine."

I started to leave, but decided to ask her my question. "What happened to Ben's mom?"

Aunt Laney took a big breath and exhaled. "His mom. It's somewhat of a long story."

I perched on the side of her bed. She closed the book she was reading and put it on her nightstand.

"Ben's mom was lovely, so lovely that wherever she went heads turned. When Ben was about three, she became involved with a man who sold real estate here on the island. The next thing you know, she and that man went off to Atlanta. Ben's grandfather had just died, and Rob was already hurting. Rob wound up having a breakdown of some kind during that time and could hardly take care of his son. I'd been close to the family, because of my relationship with Ben's grandfather, so Ben stayed here a lot. We became close."

"Does Ben ever see his mom?"

"Rob has full custody, but still she could see him if she wanted. I don't guess Ben has seen his mom three times in ten years. She shows hardly any interest."

"That's horrible."

"Yes." Aunt Laney smoothed out the quilt covering her bed.

"Thanks for telling me."

"I thought maybe Ben would tell you."

"It never came up."

*

Aunt Laney didn't waste any time getting back out to the marsh.

At least she went early the next morning before the sun became unbearably hot. Since Aunt Laney had hung the eyeball painting in the kitchen, I usually finished breakfast quickly, so I had her supplies ready in no time and packed the car. After we reached the marsh, I unpacked and made sure she drank enough water. We arranged her easel and paints, and then I took my journal out of my backpack and spent time writing as I sat on the marsh bank. When I looked up from my writing, Aunt Laney seemed to be completely lost in the brush strokes she was making.

"Is that the next painting for Sylvester?"

She stopped and turned to me, but it seemed as if she had to collect her thoughts a minute before she answered, as if she had to remember which world she was in.

"It is," she finally said.

"It must be pleasing to make money doing what you enjoy."

"A real blessing."

A car blew by behind us, and as it did, we heard a horn. We turned to see who it was, and Sylvester threw up his hand from the driver's seat of an old silver Mercedes.

Aunt Laney and I waved after him.

"Mavis was pretty mad at him yesterday. I wonder if she's talked to him, yet." I tried to blow the gnats away like Ben had taught me. This was going to require practice.

"I wondered that, too. Mavis is a great friend, but she can be a tiger when she's crossed."

Aunt Laney wasn't exactly a pushover herself, but I didn't say it. "I guess we'll hear about it soon enough."

"I'm afraid you're right," Aunt Laney said just before she seemed to lose herself once more in the landscape before her.

I made a little progress at gnat blowing as I finally pushed a good blast of air out the right side of my mouth toward one of the tiny flying nuisances. How could a bug that little be so aggravating?

We stayed long enough for Aunt Laney to accomplish what she wanted, and then I loaded the car. Once we'd pulled away, Aunt Laney turned to me. "Why don't we drop by and see Ralph for a minute? I want to thank him in person. He was so good to me after I returned from the hospital." She evidently appreciated being smothered in vegetables.

When we pulled into "Ralph's Fresh Produce," something didn't seem right. And it wasn't. Ralph was gone. He usually put tarps over the produce when he had to leave for a few minutes, but all the fruits and vegetables were just sitting there in the open air. Aunt Laney turned off the engine, and I exited the car and went behind the stand to see if Molly was taking a nap back there. She wasn't, but on my return to the car, I saw dozens of photographs tacked to the back of his stand. They were all of the same two people, a teen-aged girl, and a woman about forty. I stopped for a minute to study the pictures of them—at the beach, working at the fruit stand, sitting on a sofa, standing by the lighthouse, the pier, and on and on.

"I didn't see Molly," I said to Aunt Laney when I took my seat in the car. "But, who are those people in the pictures he has tacked up on the stand?"

Aunt Laney closed her eyes, almost as if she were in pain. "Those people," she said, "are Ralph's wife and daughter."

I didn't think he had any family. At least I'd never seen them. "Have you ever met them?"

"Yes, a few years back."

"Why has it been so long since you've seen them?"

I thought that was a fair question. But after I asked it, Aunt Laney acted as if I'd shot her with a bullet. She rubbed her hands over the steering wheel as if she was trying to rub out the words I'd just spoken. Finally, she said, "Ralph has always had to make trips to pick up produce, like to Florida, or over in the southeast corner of Georgia. Sometimes, he has to spend the night. One winter night during a trip to Florida, an electric heater in their home shorted out, and the house burned to the ground. His wife and daughter didn't make it."

The sad stories were adding up like a bad triple word score—Sidney Lanier, Ben's mom, now this.

Aunt Laney continued as she reached over and patted my hand. "One day a couple of months after his family died, Molly just wandered up off the road to the stand. She was thin, her fur matted together. Ralph tried to ignore her for a day or two, but she wouldn't leave, so he finally broke down and started feeding her. She never left him after that. I know Ralph's a little gruff, so not everyone may see his tender side, but Molly's everything to him. I don't know what he'd have done without her."

I wanted to cry about Ralph's little girl and his wife. What a terrible tragedy to happen to him, but how wonderful about Molly showing up.

"Peculiar that he would take off in the middle of the day like this," she said. "Usually he makes his deliveries early in the morning or in the evening after he closes up."

Aunt Laney cranked the car, backed up, and then pulled the car into the road to go home.

When we reached the cottage, I expected her to be worn out, but she wasn't.

"To take our minds off of the situation, why don't we rearrange the front room like we did the bedroom?" she said as she studied the paintings on the walls. "That way I can hang up my gloxinia painting. I'm not sure I want to part with it just yet, maybe never. Oh, and I think we'll have to leave the birds and nest painting over the sofa because there's not another wall big enough to handle it."

Where was she getting this energy? I started taking down the other paintings and moving pottery and sculpture off shelves. I didn't touch the bookcase, as Mavis had left strict instructions that all books were to be left exactly as she had placed them. Soon, we'd emptied the shelves.

Aunt Laney rubbed her hands together. "Now, let's have some fun. Why don't you go grab a hammer out of the drawer by the sink in the kitchen, and while you're at it, bring the little picture hanging kit beside it. We'll need to put nails in different places."

I went to the kitchen to retrieve the hammer, and as I put my hands on it, I heard the crunch of gravel in the front yard. Whoever it was would have to sit in the kitchen because you could hardly walk in the front room. When I opened the door, Ralph was coming up the steps. He peered at me out of red-rimmed eyes. Aunt Laney joined me at the door.

"Ralph, come in," she said.

"Ain't got time right now," he said. "Lookin' for Molly. Y'all ain't seen her, have you?"

"Molly's missing?" Aunt Laney put her hand over her heart. "I'm sorry Ralph, we haven't. We did drop by your place a little while ago, but of course, you were both gone."

"I know, I been out lookin' for her."

"How'd she get lost?"

"I went over to the convenience store across the street for some gum. She was asleep behind my stand, so I reckoned I'd be over there and back before she ever woke up. But when I came back across the street, she was gone."

"Wait a minute, and let me get my purse," Aunt Laney said. "We'll help you look. Now tell us where you've already been."

Ralph listed the places he'd looked for Molly. How and why could something like this happen? It seemed like he should've already reached his pain quota in life. And Molly, did she wander off, or did some mean person steal her?

Aunt Laney slung her big satchel over her shoulder. "Okay, I think I have a plan. Why don't we all go out and meet back here in an hour. I'm going to call Rob and see if he can join us, as well."

"I sure do appreciate it," Ralph said.

Since Ralph had already searched toward the north, we went west. My trip to the top of the lighthouse helped me know exactly what area that was—toward the mainland. I imagined the panorama at the top of the lighthouse and poor Molly trying to find her way home in all that big space. Rob was already at the Village, so he searched south. We drove real slow and called Molly's name and asked people on the street if they'd seen her. We hunted as far as the causeway bridge and even asked one of the toll booth attendants if they'd seen a dog. We hoped as we drove back to Aunt Laney's that Rob or Ralph would have had more success than we did. But when we arrived, we found out the sad truth.

No one had seen even a trace of Molly.

Chapter Twenty-Two

A New Lead

"Ralph, you go on home, try to rest, and bring a picture by in the morning. I'll have Mavis make some flyers we can post around," Aunt Laney said.

He trudged off to his truck head down. He didn't have his signature baseball cap on and his hair stood out wildly at the sides as if he hadn't combed it in days. One overall suspender slipped off his shoulder, and he didn't even try to put it back up. I'd never seen anyone so low.

"We must do all we can to help Ralph find that dog," Aunt Laney said as she stood in the front door and watched him go. "I don't know if he can live without her."

She moved a pottery vase out of the green chair, collapsed in it, and surveyed the mess we'd made earlier. "I hate to say this, but I'm too tired to finish. Why don't you call Mavis at the library, tell her about Molly, and see if she doesn't want to do a little more interior decorating? She'll come over here in a huff, but she'll get over it. I'm going to bed."

Aunt Laney pulled herself out of the chair, trudged off toward her bedroom, and then stopped and turned to me. "Oh, and you better call Ben and Rob and tell them we're not coming over tonight. They'll understand."

I'd almost forgotten about our dinner invitation. I made the call, and a little later Mavis came by and helped me put all of the stuff we'd taken down back up on the walls. Amazingly, she didn't spout off too much about Aunt Laney getting so tired out, and she didn't say a word about her conversation with Sylvester.

"It sure is terrible about Molly. I'll come by in the morning and pick up her picture. Surely, on this little island somebody would've seen her."

"I hope so," I said as I put the last nail in the wall. "Is this about right?"

"Yes, that's perfect. I think Laney will be pleased. I know I am."

Mavis and I stood back and admired our handiwork. The array of artwork displayed against the purple walls spanned the gamut between enameled copper plates to hand woven tapestries, but somehow Mavis had brought cohesiveness to it. She had quite a knack for this sort of thing.

"You didn't say how your conversation went with Sylvester."

"It went fine."

"Did he understand?"

"Yes, I do think we came to an understanding."

With all that had been going on I realized I hadn't heard from Mama all day and it was almost ten according the clock on Aunt Laney's piano. Usually I waited for her to call me, because Mama didn't want me to run up Aunt Laney's phone bill.

"I need to call my mama, and see how she's doing," I said to Mavis.

I moved to the kitchen, picked up the phone, and dialed the number. When someone picked up, I didn't recognize the voice. "Oh, sorry, I've dialed the wrong number."

"Mary Helen?"

"Mama?"

"It's me." I felt a thud inside, like someone had dropped an anvil on the inside of my heart. Mama sounded like an old, sick person, not my young, pretty Mama. "Are you all right? You don't sound good."

"I'm tired, that's all. I'll be fine soon. I feel this way sometimes late in the evening. It takes time to get over the surgery."

Before I knew it I'd blurted out, "Why don't you let me come home? I could help you."

"No, Mary Helen. Now you agreed. I want you to stay there and have fun."

She would have never believed all that had happened here. But, I still didn't tell her, because it would have worried her more to know.

"Okay, but I sure miss you."

"I miss you, too, sweetie. What have you been doing?"

"Going to the marsh, eating at the Sandcastle, riding bikes with Ben." I left out the parts about seeing after a sick woman, re-decorating, and hunting for a lost dog.

"That sounds fun. We'll talk soon." Her voice trailed off to a weak whisper. "I love you with all my heart, Mary Helen."

"I love you, Mama," I said and hung up barely holding back a flood of emotion.

Mavis had come back in the kitchen to put the hammer in the drawer. She took one look at me, came over and gave me a hug. "She's so sick," I said as I sobbed on her shoulder.

Mavis didn't offer a word, because I guess there were no words to say.

*

The next morning, Ralph brought a picture of Molly. I examined the grainy image. It would be a stretch to reproduce it on a black and white copy machine. I knocked on Aunt Laney's bedroom door. She was sitting up reading.

"Aunt Laney, I'll save Mavis a trip and bike to the library with this picture. I want her to print those flyers as soon as possible. Then I'll see if I can get Ben to help me put them up around town."

"That's great. I'll be fine. You run along."

"Do you promise not to leave the house until I return?"

She put her book down and peered at me over the top of her reading glasses. Was she getting mad? Then she smiled and shook her head. "I promise," she said and went back to her reading.

*

"This isn't a good picture," Mavis said as she squinted and twisted her mouth at the fuzzy image of Molly I'd given her. I, however, was studying Mavis. What had she done?

"I know, but at least folks can kind of see what she looks like," I said trying to keep my concentration. "Maybe we can put a little description, too. Fluffy, almost white with beige spots, you know, like that. Maybe mention she has sweet eyes, too."

Mavis peered at me over the top of her reading glasses. "I'll come up with something," she muttered as she hurried off to the copy room. Mavis's hair appeared strange, as if she'd dyed it. Why would she do a crazy thing like that? And her clothes—it's like she'd met one of those people in the women's magazines and had them do a makeover. I liked her new long slim skirt and green silk blouse. But, it wasn't very Mavis-like. I think she even had on makeup.

I went over to the magazine rack, picked up a magazine for writers, and settled down to read it while Mavis made the copies. As I scanned the table of contents, I saw an article entitled, "The Power of Words" and turned to it.

Mavis took me by surprise when she put the flyer about Molly in front of my face.

"I didn't even hear you come over," I said looking up from the article.

"I noticed. I called your name twice and you never even twitched, so I had to walk all the way over here."

"Sorry, this article is so interesting. I'd never considered an author being able to change the world through words."

"Kingdoms have been subdued through words. Martin Luther said, 'If you want to change the world, pick up your pen.'"

I didn't know who Martin Luther was, but I liked what he'd said.

"Now, what do you think?" She waved the flyer in front of my nose.

Mavis had put all the pertinent information about Molly on the flyer, but the photo barely resembled a dog. "Is that the best you could do with the picture?"

"If you bring me a better picture, I'll give you a better looking flyer. But this is all I could do with that thing you dragged in here."

"You're right. Thanks. I'll run over to the charter service and see if Ben can help me. Oh, and could I have a copy of this article?"

"Sure," she said taking it from me and heading off to the copy room again.

When she came back, I had to ask, "Have you changed your hair?"

"Maybe I did have an appointment at Sarah's Cut and Curl early this morning. What do you think?" Not waiting for me to answer she went on. "And did you notice I have on a new outfit from Roberta's."

"I thought so," I said. "You look attractive."

Mavis nodded her thanks and went back to the circulation desk. I had to wonder what brought all this on.

*

"It's not a good picture," Ben commented as soon as I handed him the flyer.

I sighed. "No kidding," I said. "We've all figured that one out, but it's the only one Ralph had."

"Let's go then. I'll ride out Frederica, and you take the Village and Demere."

As Ben headed out the door, he turned to me. "You won't believe what Wallace's newest phrase is."

"What?" I asked.

"God be with you."

"How did he learn that?" I said in amazement.

"Archie the mailman," Ben said. "That's his contribution to Wallace's linguistic abilities."

We headed for our bikes, and as we snapped our kickstands, we simultaneously turned to each other and said, "God be with you," mounted our bikes and hit the road.

We both worked the whole morning putting up posters, and asking anyone we ran into if they'd seen Molly. When I finished, I rode over to Ralph's stand to see how he was doing.

I found him sitting on a crate behind the stand staring at the pictures of his family. He lifted his Bassett hound eyes to me. "I called everybody I know before I left the house this mornin'. Don't nobody know nothin' about her. I asked all my regular customers when they came by, too. Shoot, I asked all my customers that ain't regular."

"Ben and I have been out putting up flyers all over the island," I said hoping to be of comfort.

"I know. I saw Ben ride by while ago, and he waved one at me. Maybe it'll do some good. I sure hope so."

I left Ralph and went back to Aunt Laney's.

"How'd it go?" she asked as soon as I came through the door. She was dressed and sitting in the green chair and painting one of the wildest arrangements of flowers I'd ever seen.

"We got them all out," I said trying to figure out what she'd been thinking when she included dandelions in the mix. "Do you think she'll turn up?"

"I don't know." Aunt Laney dabbed lime green on the canvas, "but I've been praying about it all morning. Ralph needs that dog. Losing her takes him back to the loss of his family." She changed her brush and touched it to her palette.

"I know. I went by and he was staring at their pictures."

"Heartbreaking. It absolutely is." As if to accentuate her point, she stabbed the painting with her brush and left a red splash.

I stood for a moment longer scrutinizing the flowers and the canvas. As so often happened, I failed to see the correlation. Aunt Laney had her own way of seeing, which escaped me most of the time.

"I think I'll read for a while," I said and went in my room and closed the door. I was relieved to see Aunt Laney settled and painting inside which meant there wouldn't be the hassle of keeping her from going out. No sooner had I pulled the *Lighthouse* out, and stretched out on the bed to read, the phone rang. I was never going to finish this book. I knew Aunt Laney was involved in her painting, so I put my book on the bed and went to answer the phone.

"Hello," I said.

"I think I have a clue," an excited voice I recognized as Ben's said.

"A clue."

"Yeah, while I was putting up posters today."

"I'm waiting."

"Well, I decided to go on out toward the causeway, and I saw a man working in a church yard. I thought he might have been working outside the day Molly disappeared. I stopped and showed him the picture."

There was a pause.

"Ben, are you still there?" I said annoyed.

"I'm still here. I was building up the suspense."

"Forget the suspense. What happened?"

"The man said he was trimming shrubs and he remembered something. A truck came by with a dog similar to Molly in the back. He said he remembered because the dog was barking its head off as it passed."

"What kind of truck? Did he get the tag number?"

"No, none of that. He didn't remember anything about the truck, just the dog barking."

"That doesn't seem like much help."

"It does give us a bit of information we might not want to hear."

"What's that?"

"If somebody put her in the back of their truck, they could be in Florida right now. Molly may not even be on the island."

"You're right. I don't want to hear that."

"I know, but it's the truth."

"I don't think we should tell Ralph about this. He's so depressed. I think this bit of news might finish him off." Aunt Laney heard me say this and looked up from her painting. Her eyes searched mine for information as I talked to Ben.

127

"What are we going to do?" Ben asked. "We can't put posters up all the way to Florida, that's for sure."

"I don't know. We have to think of something, though."

When I hung up the phone, I had to bring Aunt Laney up to speed on what Ben had told me.

"He's right. Someone may have taken her off the island." Aunt Laney put her brush and palette down, rose up out of the chair and started rubbing her chin in a worrisome way. "What can we do?"

I hated to say what came out of my mouth next. "Maybe he should just move on. What about another dog?"

*

"Don't want no other dog. I want Molly," Ralph said the next day when I asked him.

"But Ralph, a new dog would help you."

"I'm not givin' up on Molly. I want her back," Ralph said with conviction, and then marched over and started stirring the boiled peanuts. He pulled a steaming ladle out, drained it and poured the peanuts in a bag.

"Here, take these to Laney," he said as he gave them to me.

I took the hint the subject was closed and accepted the bag of peanuts.

*

"That's about what I expected," Aunt Laney said when I told her what had happened.

Over the course of the next few days, Ralph received several calls about Molly from people who'd seen our posters. All of them were dead ends except one.

We pulled up to his stand to pick up some green beans late one afternoon to find him closing up the place.

"Sorry, I can't help you all. You'll have to come back tomorrow. I just ran home to check my answerin' machine and I got a call from a lady who seen the posters and thinks she has Molly at her house," Ralph said as he put tarps over his produce. "I'm closin' up and getting' on over there."

"Aunt Laney, can we go too? If it is Molly, I want to see her."

"Sure," she said, and we backed out to follow Ralph in his panel truck. We pulled into the driveway of a home in a wealthy neighborhood. The grand house in front of us was covered in what I'd learned from Aunt Laney was tabby, a mixture of cement and seashells that people on the island had used on the exterior of their homes since the first settlers came. We exited the car and followed Ralph up the walkway of the beautifully manicured front yard to the double entry doors. When he rang the bell, we could hear the ding-dong resonate through the house. As we waited, I admired two topiary trees on either side of the doors. Clipped footsteps approached.

"Hello," a neatly groomed older woman in a housekeeper's uniform said as she opened the door.

"We're here to see about the dog," Ralph said.

"The dog. Yes, come in," she said as she waved us to pass. She ushered us out of the spacious foyer into a beautifully appointed room filled with luxurious marble floors, fresh flowers, and a grand piano. A woman about my mama's age wearing pearls and an aqua dress sat writing at what appeared to be a French style desk. The desk caught my attention immediately because one day Ben and I had seen one in the antique store when we were riding our bicycles. I thought Mama would like it, so I stopped to ask the price. Definitely not in our budget.

"They're here about the dog, ma'am," the housekeeper said.

The lady looked up. "I'm sorry, I was so engrossed in my letter writing, I guess I blocked out the doorbell." She stood and came toward us in such a graceful way it almost seemed she was dancing. "I'm Kathleen Kirby. Such a pleasure to meet all of you." She extended her delicate hand to each of us, and I felt I might be touching the hand of royalty. Aunt Laney opened her mouth, I guess, to introduce us but Ralph interrupted.

"Where's the dog?" he said rudely.

"I know you're anxious to see her. Eleanor spoke with you on the phone, and from the conversation she relayed to me, we became hopeful that Muffin is your dog."

"Muffin?" Ralph questioned.

Mrs. Kirby laughed. "It's a name we gave her while she's here, so we wouldn't have to call her 'doggie' all the time. Come, let's see her."

She took us through a dining room, into a kitchen, and then out to a patio door. Even before she reached for the door handle, my heart leapt, because when I saw the dog, I knew it was Molly—the same long whitish fur with beige spots. I could hardly contain my excitement. As soon as the door opened, the dog bounded toward the kitchen and jumped up on Mrs. Kirby.

"That ain't Molly," Ralph said.

My heart, which had been soaring moments before, did a nosedive. Sure it was Molly. It had to be.

"Ralph, are you sure? There's sure a strong resemblance," Aunt Laney said.

"I tell you, it ain't her. Look at them spots. They's all in different places from Molly's."

I studied the spots. I still didn't understand.

"Plus, she don't even know me. She ran to the lady here, not me."

He had a point there. Ralph put his hand up to his head. His eyes reddened as if he might start crying.

"I'm so sorry," Mrs. Kirby said. "I was sure this was your dog."

"She seems a right smart like Molly, but she just ain't her." Ralph's shoulders drooped so much I thought both his overall straps might slip off.

"Ralph, this dog appears about the same age as Molly. I wonder if they're sisters," Aunt Laney said.

Ralph scratched his face through a stubby beard. "Molly was a stray. This dog sure enough might have come from the same litter." Ralph stooped to inspect the dog. He picked up one of her paws. "This dog's got rough places on her feet. Been on the road a long time."

"We washed her and combed the mats out of her hair to try to make her look better. Oh, my. If she's not your dog, whose dog is she?"

"Looks like to me she's your 'n," Ralph said.

"A dog?" Mrs. Kirby considered the thought. Muffin gazed at her adoringly.

Ralph, still down on the floor, took the dog's face in his hands and looked it in the eyes. "You done hit the jackpot in the dollar machine, girlie."

We all laughed, because it seemed she'd done just that.

"Well, thank you anyway," Aunt Laney said.

"I'm sorry it didn't work out," Mrs. Kirby responded as she looked back at Muffin.

As we headed for the front door, Mrs. Kirby touched Aunt Laney on the back of the shoulder. "Excuse me; I didn't get your name. You seem so familiar. I feel like I've met you before. Is that possible?"

"I don't know. I've lived on the island a long time. I'm Laney Hanberry."

Mrs. Kirby clapped her hands together. "Laney Hanberry, of course. Come this way."

Chapter Twenty-Three

Fever

We followed Mrs. Kirby into a room that glowed with a turquoise aura. On one wall, brilliantly colored saltwater fish swam in a huge aquarium. On the opposite wall between two windows hung the largest Aunt Laney original I'd ever seen. One of her Lanier pieces for sure, as it seemed to be a much larger version of the one with the nests displayed in Aunt Laney's front room. This refined lady had an Aunt Laney painting.

I read the familiar words woven in the painting:

> As the marsh-hen secretly builds on the watery sod,
> Behold I will build me a nest on the greatness of God.
> —Sidney Lanier

"It's one of my favorite pieces in the house. I bought it from the gallery in the Village a few years back." Mrs. Kirby seemed awestruck as she stood before the painting.

"I declare," Ralph said, looking it over. "It shore is a beauty."

"It is." Mrs. Kirby smiled at Aunt Laney.

A little color rose in Aunt Laney's cheeks. "Thank you. I'm glad we had the chance to meet. Always a joy to meet people who appreciate my work. This is from a series I did. I actually have a much smaller canvas from the series hanging in my own home. It's one of my favorites, too."

Mrs. Kirby clapped her hands together. "You must stay for dinner. It's only me here, and we always have too much food left over. Please stay."

"I can't," Ralph said his hands in his overalls. "Gotta get back. Maybe somebody else will call about Molly."

"What about you two?" Mrs. Kirby said.

Aunt Laney turned to me. "I guess we could. Oh, this is my niece, Mary Helen. She's staying with me this summer."

I nodded in agreement.

"We'd love to," Aunt Laney said as she turned to Mrs. Kirby.

"It's settled then, and pleased to meet you, Mary Helen." Mrs. Kirby tipped her head toward me.

After Mrs. Kirby and Aunt Laney talked a while longer, Eleanor ushered us into a formal dining room. Now, the Vanderbilts would have gone for this house. In fact, this room appeared as if it might fit right in at the Biltmore House. I counted the chairs around the table—twenty. Why, Mrs. Kirby could have seated my whole English class in here. We took our seats at one end of the table where Eleanor had already added place settings.

Though so far, I enjoyed visiting at the Kirby house, the dinner served to us that night was suspect from the beginning, because it started with shrimp cocktails. Of course, Aunt Laney lapped them up.

"Delicious," she said as she savored them. "Where did you buy such large shrimp?"

Aunt Laney was food obsessed. As she and Mrs. Kirby discussed the origin of the shrimp, my mind raced as to how I was going to dispose of them. Mrs. Kirby had left Muffin in the house, so I discreetly slipped a couple of the shrimp off my plate and under the table. Lying underneath the table on the other side, Muffin must have smelled them because I felt her tongue on my hand as she took them from me. Just a couple more, and they'd be gone. Now Mrs. Kirby was asking Aunt Laney about what projects she was working on. I slipped a couple of more shrimp off the table and Muffin took them immediately.

When Eleanor came to remove our plates to serve the main course, Aunt Laney turned to me, and noticed the shrimp were missing. "Why, Mary Helen, you have learned to like shrimp. Didn't you enjoy them?"

I gave her a big smile, but didn't answer.

"I'm sorry we're not serving anything more exotic than a chicken casserole for the entrée, but it is one of our favorites."

Casserole? There might be all kinds of weird stuff hiding out in a casserole. I'd have to tread carefully.

"We particularly like this recipe as it includes marinated artichoke hearts in the mix," Mrs. Kirby said.

Oh, what I'd give for a simple grilled cheese right now. As Eleanor served the plates, I realized there was no way I was going to slide this casserole under the table to Muffin. I'd have to eat at least some of it, and I was sure it'd be like eating my way through a minefield.

"Ralph seems devoted to finding his dog." Mrs. Kirby lifted a fork full of the chunky casserole to her mouth.

"Yes, he's quite attached to her," Aunt Laney said as she took her first bite.

I put a piece of what appeared to be chicken in my mouth, and got a big surprise. I chewed quickly and swallowed to make it go away. The vinegary taste must have been the marinade on the artichoke. To my disappointment, there wasn't even a consoling vegetable like corn on the cob to fall back on. Five stalks of asparagus lay in slimy repose on my plate. Weird upon weird.

"Does he have a family?" Mrs. Kirby was asking.

"No, he lost his family some time ago," Aunt Laney said, and then she told Mrs. Kirby the sad story of Ralph's family.

As Aunt Laney related Ralph's losses, Mrs. Kirby's eyes filled with tears, and she dabbed them with the corner of her napkin. At one point in the story, I thought she might have to leave the table.

"And after all of that, now he's lost his dog," she said. "I'm sorry that our Muffin wasn't Molly. My husband and I were never able to have children. He died a couple of years ago, so it's just Eleanor and me now. I know a little about what it means to lose someone, and it's hard. I do wish I could help him find his Molly."

"I think all that can be done is being done at this point," Aunt Laney said. Muffin must have slipped from the house out to the patio because a bark sounded from the back yard.

"She must see a squirrel. She always lets us know when one tries to come onto the property. She's very protective."

"Maybe Muffin was sent to you like Molly was sent to Ralph," Aunt Laney said.

Mrs. Kirby smiled. "Maybe she was."

Eleanor took our plates before she served dessert. Aunt Laney glared at me when she saw how much I'd left. What could I say? How I hoped for a dessert bearing a hint of familiarity. Chocolate cake would be good.

"We've saved the best for last," Mrs. Kirby said. "The pièce de résistance. Crème brûleé! It's Eleanor's specialty."

"My favorite," Aunt Laney said. "I don't eat it much, because of the fat, you know, but how I love it."

I stared at the dish in front of me, which bore a striking resemblance to egg custard. Our next-door neighbor back in Asheville used to make egg custard all the time, and I could smell it in the backyard when I was outside. I didn't like eggs. I could starve to death on this island. I took a deep breath, put my spoon in the concoction and brought it to my lips. I blinked as the creamy warm bite dissolved in my mouth. This stuff was good. I dished out a bigger bite, and then another, and in no time it was all gone, and I wished for more.

"I see you didn't have any trouble choking down the crème brûleé," Aunt Laney said dryly as she observed my empty dish

"Delicious," I said.

As we left, Mrs. Kirby took Aunt Laney's hands in hers. "If there's anything I can do to help find the dog, please call me," she said. "Anything at all."

*

After the posters had been out about four days, what few calls we did receive came to a halt. And as we passed signs, wilting of dew and rain on power poles and signposts, my hope started to wilt, too. We stopped by to see Ralph one day and buy a cantaloupe.

"Your face is red. Have you got a fever?" Aunt Laney asked him.

"Don't know." Ralph went over and stirred the peanuts.

"I'm telling you, Ralph, your face is flushed. I think you should see a doctor."

I had trouble seeing the red because of the whiskers he hadn't shaved in days.

"Don't need no doctor. I'm fine."

"Ralph, you've been through a lot. Let me call my doctor, Dr. Gunn. I bet he could see you today."

"Don't want to go to no doctor," he said as he picked out a big melon from his stand.

"This one looks purty good," he said holding it up to Aunt Laney.

"Don't change the subject. I've known you a long time. I can tell when you don't feel well. I'm making the call."

Aunt Laney could be a force of nature when she wanted to be. She went home, made the phone call to Dr. Gunn's office to secure an appointment for Ralph right away, and then went back to the fruit stand. She made him shut down the stand, and we helped put the tarps over the produce. Then she put him in her car. When we reached the doctor's office, Dr. Gunn said he had an infection and needed to go to bed. Ralph balked.

"Ain't never gone to bed sick in my whole life."

"You're going to go now," Aunt Laney waved for me to get in the car.

"Who'll watch my stand?"

"We will." Aunt Laney said.

My mouth dropped open. I couldn't tell a bean from a pea. Plus I thought I'd die if I had to stay at that hot stand all day. I was pretty sure Mavis would never let Aunt Laney do it either. In fact, I thought it was an interesting turn of events that Aunt Laney was now doing to Ralph the exact same thing Mavis had been doing to her.

"You ain't well yourself. How are you goin' to watch my stand?"

"I'm fine, and we'll figure it out. Leave it up to us."

Aunt Laney bought Ralph's medicine from the drug store, took him home from the doctor, and made sure he had plenty of soup, crackers, and juice.

"Too much fuss," Ralph said complaining about all the attention.

Aunt Laney made him climb in bed and told him to stay there.

"We'll be back to check on you later," she said.

After leaving Ralph, we got in the car, and I wanted to know what Aunt Laney was thinking.

"You know Mavis will never let you watch that stand," I said. "And I don't know a thing about produce." I couldn't even imagine what Mama would say if she knew I was staked out at a roadside shack.

"I know," she said. "But I think I have an idea that might work."

As soon as Aunt Laney returned home, she called Rob.

I was in my bedroom and couldn't hear what she was talking about, but in a few minutes she knocked on my door.

"It's all settled," she said. "Rob's going to be around next week at the charter service which means Ben can watch Ralph's stand."

I bet Ben was excited about that arrangement.

*

Sunday, after church, Ben joined us for what was unfortunately becoming a Sunday tradition, the dreaded Scrabble game.

"Wonderful, a foursome," Mavis said. "Scrabble is always more fun with four."

136

I bit my tongue as Aunt Laney lead off with q-u-a-g. Strange to me how she always got the q. For that, she raked in twenty-eight points with a double word score. I managed to spell g-r-i-t using the g from Aunt Laney's quag, and then jotted my tally on the score-pad—a pathetic five points.

As Ben studied his rack, Mavis said, "Yes, Mary Helen, we're proud of our Ben. Do you know he was the spelling bee champion for the whole county in the sixth grade?"

No one had bothered to share that tidbit of information with me, or else I would have been sure to have other plans for this Sunday afternoon. I braced myself for the inevitable.

Ben picked up a few letters and began to arrange them on the board. "*Muntjac*," he said.

I studied the word. I was sure I'd never heard it before. "What's that?" I asked.

Ben grinned. "You don't know? I thought everybody knew what a muntjac was."

What a game player. "No, I don't, and I don't think you do either because I don't think it's a word." I was about to wear a path out on the floor going for the Webster's dictionary all the time, and was tired of being the one to retrieve it every week, so I brought it back to the kitchen. "We'll keep this with the Scrabble board." I laid it on the table, opened it up, and found the word. "Muntjac: a small deer of the genus Muntiacus of southeastern Asia and the East Indies."

I raised my eyes to Ben suspiciously, and as if he could read my mind he said, "I go through a lot of *National Geographics*."

"What did you score?" I said as I closed the dictionary and reached for the pad.

"Hmm, three, four, five, six, and the eight from the j makes fourteen, fifteen, and three from the c makes eighteen, times a double word score. That's thirty-six."

As Ben gorged himself on Scrabble tiles to re-fill his rack, I studied the scores. Aunt Laney, twenty-eight; Mary Helen, five; Ben, thirty-six.

It seemed painfully apparent to me that I was out of my league, and I sure didn't know what to do about it. Mavis added four little letters to Aunt Laney's quag to make quagmire. She received twenty points for her efforts.

Mercifully, they didn't enforce the rule that you had to skip your turn after a challenge, so at least I was able to add a few paltry points on my turn.

137

The rest of the afternoon went much the same way. Aunt Laney, sixteen points; Mary Helen, six. Mavis, thirty-five points; Mary Helen, four. Ben, forty points; Mary Helen, six.

When the game ended, no one seemed to notice that the winner, Mavis, outscored me three to one. Ben came in second. "Thanks for inviting me," he said. "I don't have an opportunity to play that often. Scrabble is not Dad's game."

I knew how Rob felt. I needed to figure out a way to weasel out of this.

"You're welcome. Why don't you plan on joining us next Sunday, too," Aunt Laney offered.

"Thanks, I will." Ben left the table and I followed him out to the front porch.

"How'd you learn all those words?" I asked.

"I read the dictionary."

Must be island fever. "Read the dictionary?"

"Yeah, when I was preparing for Spelling bees, I read the dictionary."

Ben's social life must have been pretty sad through the years.

"A friend and I did it together. That made it more fun." Ben sat on the front steps.

"Who?" I asked as I joined him on the steps.

"Angela."

I hadn't seen that coming. "Why haven't I ever met her?"

"She moved to California after school this year. Her dad wanted to start a deep sea fishing business for tourists on the West Coast near Newport Beach, California."

"Do you miss her?"

Ben didn't speak for a few minutes, but only blew at a few gnats. Then, "I used to." Before I could ask another question, he said, "I guess I better get home. I'm excited about being at Ralph's place tomorrow."

Island fever again.

"Hey, if you want to come over, we could read the dictionary during the slow times." He swung a leg over his bike and perched on the seat.

"Sure," I said before I had time to think. What had my life come to? Read the dictionary at the fruit stand? I had to be moving up on the nerd index.

Chapter Twenty-Four

Insight

"Nothing to it," Ben said the next day when I biked over to Ralph's stand. "I went to see Mavis at the library, and she gave me several old *National Geographic* issues so I wouldn't get bored during slow times. Then I checked out a couple of books." Ben pulled a volume out from under the counter and showed me a double page spread of different kinds of vegetables. "This one has pictures of all the produce so I can study it and know what people are talking about when they come in. If it's not in this book, I have an even bigger one with absolutely everything in it for reference." Ben produced a large green tome and handed it to me.

"I don't need to see it. I trust you," I said.

Ben sat and tipped back in his chair. "This is sure a switch from just answering questions and shoveling out brochures all day."

I didn't exactly see his point, but decided to take a different route.

"Did you notice how Mavis looked when you saw her at the library?"

"Come to think of it, she did seem changed. What do you think it is?"

"First of all, she's done something extreme to her hair, plus she had on a new outfit when I saw her, and it wasn't a cardigan sweater which is what she usually wears. She told me once she had to wear a sweater because the library is always freezing. I don't know. I can't figure out what's going on."

"This is changing the subject, but Dad still wants you and Laney to come over for dinner. He said to check with you about Wednesday."

"I'll ask Aunt Laney. It'll probably be fine."

A mini van pulled up, and a young blonde woman in a bright floral sundress with two toddler girls approached the stand. Ben took care of her with amazing efficiency. After they left, he pulled a dictionary out from under the counter. "Now," he said, "come back here, have a seat on this crate and let's go over a few words."

*

Later that day, I biked home, went to my room and sprawled on my bed. After I pushed aside the jumble of words in my brain all beginning with *HA* like hachure and hadal, I began to see what a good attitude Ben had about being drafted into the produce stand business. It made me feel bad about mine. Plus, he was helping Ralph, and I was doing zero.

When I came out of my room later in the afternoon, Aunt Laney, was sitting on the red sofa sketching a frozen fish. It was lying on ice in a cooler.

"Gross, what are you doing?" I asked.

She gave me one of those forbearing smiles of hers. "Sketching, of course."

"But it's dead."

"How do you think I'd sketch a live fish?" She asked holding back a chuckle.

"Well, yes … uh, no … I don't know."

She held up the stiff sea creature by the tail. "When Rob makes an interesting catch, he freezes it for me. I sketch it, and then later we eat it. This way I can take as long as I want." She put the fish back on the ice and tapped it with the end of her paintbrush. "He's not going anywhere."

I hoped I could soon forget this Aunt Laney episode. "Speaking of Rob, he wants us to try and come for dinner on Wednesday night." I sure hoped we didn't eat that fish Aunt Laney was sketching. I didn't want to eat a food I'd ever looked in the eyeball.

"Sure," she said as she glanced up from her sketchbook. "I feel terrible I had to cancel on them the last time. Tell them I'm excited about it, and ask what I can bring."

Later, after I knew Ben was home, I called and let him know we were coming.

"Ben's Dad insists you not bring a thing," I said to Aunt Laney when I hung up the phone.

"Very well, then." Aunt Laney went back to studying what appeared to be an art magazine judging from the cover. She couldn't get enough of that business.

*

"It sure is gracious of you to have us," Aunt Laney said as we entered Ben's apartment. As I stepped through their front door, I expected it to smell like a fishing boat, but instead it smelled like ... I couldn't quite place it—cakes baking—vanilla. Yes, that's what it was—vanilla. As I looked right, a giant stuffed fish, his mouth gaping open, greeted me from the wall in the living room. I suppose I shouldn't have been surprised. On the far wall, I spotted the unmistakable style of Laney Hanberry. I proceeded past the fish to see it. I could tell right away it wasn't a Lanier piece, and I was beginning to scare myself at how good I'd become at identifying Aunt Laney's paintings.

"You found Laney's work," Rob said as he moved beside me.

"Yes." She'd done a seascape depicting a boat on the horizon. As usual, I didn't quite understand her sense of color. I didn't remember the ocean having that much yellow in it.

"That's my boat," Rob said beaming.

Aunt Laney moved up beside me. "I happened to be down at the pier one day, doing a little dabbling when Rob's boat pulled out and I did a quick sketch of it and finished it later."

"I sure was surprised when she gave it to me for my birthday that year. Best present I ever received." Rob reached over and hugged Aunt Laney. "Always good to be with an old friend. Of course I mean that in the best way."

"No offense taken," she said and smiled.

"Always pleasant to see you, too, Mary Helen," Rob said.

I nodded at Rob and heard a bird call. "Is Wallace here?"

"We're keeping him for the Kendalls who are on an out of town trip. He's in the kitchen."

When Rob and I went into the kitchen, there was the talkative parrot, high up on a perch in the corner. I reached out to stroke his tail feathers just as Ben entered the kitchen.

"There you are." Rob studied Ben a moment. "I wondered where you went."

"Just changing my clothes." Ben appeared a little sheepish.

"Pretty girl, pretty girl," Wallace chattered as I continued to caress him.

Aunt Laney came in with a picture in her hand. "Look at this," she said as she shoved the picture in front of me. "Have you ever seen a catch like that?"

But before I could say a word, Wallace called out, "That's a big one. That's a big one."

Everybody laughed and then Rob said, "I hope you folks are hungry. I always have trouble knowing how much food to prepare, so I think I may have overdone it a little." Rob strode over to the stove, pulled down the oven door, and then pulled out a platter mounded high with chicken pieces. "I heard Mary Helen wasn't big on seafood, so I cranked up the barbecue this afternoon and didn't know when to stop. I've tried to keep it warm. I hope it's not too dried out."

My mouth watered as I gazed at the steaming chicken. I hadn't had a meal like this since I'd come to the island. At last, food that didn't make me cringe.

"I have baked beans and potato salad, too."

My stomach did cartwheels of delight.

"Ben, why don't you set the table while I show Laney some more photos of our latest big catches?"

"I'll help him," I said. I didn't want to be stuck poring over dead fish pictures.

Ben handed me the plates to put on the table in the kitchen, and for a few minutes we worked making sure each place setting had the necessary elements. "Aunt Laney told me about your mom," I said as I put the last fork on the table then directed my gaze toward Ben.

Ben stiffened in a way I hadn't seen since that first day I met him. I saw his eyes redden. "So what?" he said.

"I just … I mean …" What did I mean? "I … I know how you feel."

Ben had a knife in his hand for the place setting in front of him. "You couldn't possibly know how I feel." The knife pointed directly at me.

"Yes, I do. My dad died. Your mom left. We're both without a parent."

He threw the knife in his hand on the table. "Your dad didn't have any choice about what happened to him. My mom chose to leave, and she continues to choose not to see me. You don't think those two things are the same, do you?"

"At least your mama's alive," I shot back, and then bit my lip. This meal was making me cringe after all.

"So let's get this show on the road," Ben's dad said as he entered the room. He paused for a moment and looked back and forth between Ben and me, but thankfully didn't say a word about it. I was certain the air crackled with the tension between us.

All through dinner, I kept stealing little glances at Ben. He hardly lifted his eyes from his food. I chewed methodically and swallowed. Each piece of chicken grew bigger and bigger in my mouth. Occasionally Wallace squawked, helping to break the strain only a little. Aunt Laney and Rob either didn't see or pretended not to notice what was going on between Ben and me.

"I always love the scent of vanilla when I come here," she said.

"Best remedy in the world to remove the fish scent on my hands," Rob said.

"I remember Marvin always smelled of vanilla." Aunt Laney went on to reminisce a little about Marvin, which she didn't do too often. Why in the world did she have to pick now to do it? All I wanted to do was get out of there.

"Ben, why don't you remove everyone's plates, and I'll serve dessert?" Rob said during a break in the conversation.

When he picked up my plate, I could feel the iciness emanating from his direction. As Ben and Rob had their backs turned, I leaned over and whispered to Aunt Laney who was sitting next to me that I wanted to go home. She appeared not to understand. "I want to go home," I said a little louder. Rob turned and gave a quick glance at us. Aunt Laney let out a sigh.

I passed on dessert even though it was banana pudding, my favorite. My stomach had sent me a message that is was refusing admission of any other food as it now was one great big knot. Ben took the pudding, but only picked at it. After Rob and Aunt Laney cleaned their pudding bowls, I nudged Aunt Laney again.

"Rob, this meal was delightful. I'm sorry we're going to have to cut our visit a little short." Aunt Laney lifted out of her chair to leave.

"Sorry to hear that. We'll do this again when you can stay longer."

"Next time, you come to our place."

We said our goodbyes and got in the car. Aunt Laney extended her hands to me. "I'm confused. What was wrong with you back there?"

"I think I made Ben mad."

"You didn't say anything to him about his mother, did you?"

"I told him I knew about her."

Aunt Laney turned to the driver's side window. "I assumed you would know that was a sensitive subject and if he didn't bring it up, you didn't need to bring it up. I'm afraid Ben thinks I've betrayed him."

"I don't think he's mad at you. He's mad at me because I compared him losing his mother to me losing my father. He said it wasn't the same. I told him at least his mama was alive."

Aunt Laney grew quiet. When we turned into her gravel driveway and stopped, she exited the car, paced up the front walkway, unlocked the door and went inside without one word. She never acted like that to me.

I went into my room, and shut the door. I missed Mama. The last few phone calls I had from her, she was beginning to sound stronger, not as tired as before. I left my room, went to the phone in the kitchen, and dialed our number.

"Oh, hi, Mary Helen. Good to hear your voice."

It was Amy. "Is Mama able to talk?"

"She went to bed early tonight. She was especially exhausted, but I'll be happy to wake her."

An elephant was standing on my chest. I wanted to say, "Yes, go wake her up. I need to talk to my mama. And do it now." But I didn't. I said, "No, no, that's okay. I'll call in the morning."

I felt like one of those lemon halves that I'd seen Laney crushing. It seemed a giant hand was squeezing and smashing my insides to pieces. I hung up the phone and shuffled, head down to my room. I heard Aunt Laney come out of her bedroom behind me.

"Is your mama all right?"

"She's fine, just tired, so she went to bed early."

"I'm glad she's fine." She paused. "Mary Helen, I'm sorry. I should have told you not to speak to Ben about his mom. I thought if you knew, it might help you understand Ben a little better. Maybe I shouldn't have. I guess I'm a little protective of him, because I know how much he's been through. I probably feel, because of my relationship with Marvin, like he's almost my grandchild."

What could I say? "I'm sorry if I caused trouble, but now I don't know what to do."

*

On Thursday morning when we went by to check on Ben, he wasn't there. Ralph was at his usual post behind the stand rearranging a bin of green peppers.

"I can't believe you're back out here in this weather after being so sick."

"I'm fine," Ralph said unconvincingly. He coughed. "Told Ben no need to come over here today. I'm perfectly able to take care of things myself."

"Heard any new information about Molly?" Aunt Laney asked.

"Not even a call yesterday."

Aunt Laney spent a few minutes reviewing the produce. Ralph drooped in his chair, and I went back to the car thinking about Ben's mom and my dad. I know my dad didn't choose to die, but it had sometimes felt like he did, as if he abandoned me—left me with Mama without even saying goodbye. Through the years, I'd tried not to think about it. All it did was make me sad.

Aunt Laney loaded a sack of large green peppers into the car, and since the top was up, their strong aroma filled the car.

"What are you going to do with those?" I asked after she plopped them in the back seat.

"Stuff them," she said. Visions of green pepper pillows popped into my head.

"Why would you do a thing like that?"

"To eat them."

Now, I was confused.

Aunt Laney went on. "It's a lot like a meatloaf mixture that you pack inside the peppers and bake in the oven. I know it's not one of the foods your mama told me you liked, but I thought you might want to try different dishes while you're here."

Was she kidding? I guess I needed to prepare for more of Aunt Laney's crazy cooking. Where was the macaroni and cheese? Where were the mashed potatoes?

"Why don't we go to the village and see Ben and iron out this situation?" she said with a smile.

"That's fine, but first I want to talk with you."

"Fine. We could go to the Village, sit in one of the gazebos by the ocean and chat. When we're finished, we can walk over and visit Ben."

"Okay."

We pulled under the cool live oaks at the Village, and Aunt Laney put the top down. We got out and strolled over to one of the gazebos by the lighthouse. The tide was high, and the breakers rolled in against the rocks piled high along the coast which I'd learned were to prevent erosion. When the waves hit, I could feel the spray.

I could see a shrimp boat not too far offshore, probably catching those big ones like I fed Muffin under the table. I took a seat under the gazebo and Aunt Laney positioned herself opposite me.

"What's on your mind, Mary Helen?"

I didn't exactly know how to say it. "I don't think Ben understands what I'm trying to say about my dad. In fact, I don't think I was even sure until I said it." I stood up and gazed after the shrimp boat. "It feels like my dad abandoned me. I know that doesn't make sense, but that's the way it feels. It's like he made a decision to die, and it didn't matter that he left me behind." I stopped a minute and studied Aunt Laney to try and gauge her reaction, but she had on her game face. I couldn't tell what she was thinking. This was the first time I'd ever told anyone how I felt. I'd never even told Leslie. I was glad Aunt Laney didn't interrupt, and she didn't try to argue with me. "That's why I never want to talk about him. I'm mad at him."

After I'd finished she remained silent for a while.

Finally, "Based on my experience with former students, the way you feel is normal for someone who's been through the death of a parent."

I could feel the tears welling in my eyes. "You mean I'm not weird and crazy?"

"Not at all. This is perfectly normal. It would have been better if you could have talked about it earlier."

"I didn't know how. I don't think I even understood why I've always felt mad at him.

I've never been able to say it before, but when Ben seemed to think I couldn't possibly understand how he felt, it all came rushing up to the top."

"I know it had to be hard for you to explain it to me after all these years. Thank you for trusting me with it."

I nodded.

She came over, and took my hands in hers. "Now let's go over and see Ben and talk this over."

Only, Ben wasn't at Dillard's Atlantic Charters.

"Ben's gone to visit a cousin in Valdosta," Rob said. "When Ralph called last night after you folks left and said he was coming back to the stand today, all of a sudden Ben decided he wanted to go visit one of his cousins. I was kind of surprised. He made the arrangements, and I met them halfway this morning. I think he plans on staying a week."

A week. My heart sank.

Chapter Twenty-Five

A Plan

"You two seem awfully low this morning," Mavis said when she saw us walking into the library.

Aunt Laney stopped short before she reached the circulation desk, and then crept along, as if she was approaching a snake. "What have you done to your hair?"

"What do you mean?" Mavis said and turned to a stack of books she was inspecting.

"You know what I mean. You've done something to the color."

"I touched it up a little," she said defensively.

"A little? Looks like to me you've stuck your head in a coal bucket."

Coal bucket? Mavis turned back to Aunt Laney and glared at her. "And I was feeling sorry for you today," she said.

"We've had a rough start." Aunt Laney shrugged, which made this day's lemon yellow version of the uniform fly out at the sides. She'd paired the tunic over a pair of leaf green pants, which gave her style an organic quality like a daffodil in bloom. Her look today contrasted seriously with my mood. "I'll tell you about it later," is all she said as she leaned against the circulation desk.

"I know what would make you feel better. Let's go over to the café and grab a burger."

"I don't care for a burger today," Aunt Laney said. "Besides, I have tomatoes at home I need to eat before they go bad."

Rats. More peanut butter for me, but thank God for George Washington Carver. If it hadn't been for him, I would've starved to death.

"We stopped to say hello."

"Hello to you, too," Mavis said as she stuck a date due pocket in the back of a book. "I hope whatever's eating you two gets better."

We turned and headed for the exit, and Aunt Laney glanced back at Mavis one last time. We loaded into the big yellow car, and made the trip home mostly in silence with one exception. "Mavis with dyed hair," Aunt Laney mumbled under her breath.

When we pulled into her driveway, it seemed she brightened a little. "Why don't we pack a lunch and go to the marsh?"

An alarm went off in my head. "Don't you think it's too close to noon?"

Aunt Laney checked her watch. "I guess you're right," she said sighing. "I hate to think about what Mavis would say if she found I went out there in this heat. There'd be no end to her shaking that jet-black head in disapproval. Plus, I guess I have to take my own advice since I've been giving Ralph such a hard time."

Saved.

"Maybe I'll go out tonight when it's a little cooler. I love the glow the setting sun gives to the marsh anyway."

With that settled, we both went inside. I went to my bedroom, and Aunt Laney took off for the kitchen. I took my journal from under the pillow, fumbled it and when it fell on the bed the article I'd found at the library dropped out of the back. I unfolded the photocopied pages, and "The Power of Words" title stared back at me. I reread most of the feature, and then an idea formed in my head, a plan to find Molly.

I popped out of my bedroom and found Aunt Laney in the kitchen making the promised tomato sandwiches for lunch. I strode over to the food cabinet, opened it, and pulled out the peanut butter.

"Still not going for tomato sandwiches?" Aunt Laney said waving one in the air.

"No, thank you." I took two slices of bread out of the package Aunt Laney was using, picked up a knife and started spreading the peanut butter. Should I share my plan? No, I'd wait until later when I'd had time to think it through.

She stopped slicing tomatoes a moment. "We probably need to go by and see how Ralph's doing after lunch."

"That's fine," I said as I cut my peanut butter sandwich in half.

"If we could only find that dog, it'd really boost his spirits."

Later after we left the produce stand Aunt Laney said, "He's coughing his head off. I don't like the looks of this. If he's not better by tomorrow, I'm going to have to take him back to the doctor."

On Friday, Ralph was even worse. Aunt Laney somehow managed to get Dr. Gunn on the phone, and he said to come on over.

*

Dr. Gunn listened carefully to Ralph's chest and then sent him along with a nurse into another room to get X-rays. We went back out into the waiting room, but in a few minutes the nurse called us back again. Dr. Gunn appeared. "Pneumonia, both lungs," he said as he held Ralph's chart in his hand. "I think we'd better put him in the hospital."

"That ain't necessary." Ralph sputtered, and then flew into a coughing fit.

"Yes, it is." Dr. Gunn's expression was stern. He turned to Aunt Laney. "I've already called and made arrangements for him to be admitted to the hospital in Brunswick. All you have to do is take him to Admissions, and they'll rush him on through. He needs to go immediately. If transportation is a problem, we'll call an ambulance."

"No, I can do it. Thank you," Aunt Laney said.

A nurse helped us get Ralph back in the car. He coughed the whole time. We drove across the causeway to Brunswick to the hospital, and I went in and found a nurse to help us get him inside. After the paperwork was filled out, they put Ralph in a wheelchair. He waved to us as a nurse whisked him away.

As Ralph disappeared down the corridor, Aunt Laney said, "I feel like he's giving up his will to live."

But Aunt Laney didn't know I had a plan, and I believed somehow my plan would work. I couldn't wait to get back to Aunt Laney's to put it into action.

As we crossed back over the causeway, I took in the marsh that stretched to the horizon and realized once more its vastness. I remembered the lines on Mavis's painting, "a world of marsh bordered by a world of sea." Somehow, I felt differently about the marsh from when I'd first seen it weeks before.

The phone was ringing as we came through the door back at Aunt Laney's. I picked it up. "Yes, Mrs. Kirby, good to speak with you again."

"Mary Helen, has Ralph found Molly yet?"

"No, he hasn't."

"I think I have an idea how we can find her. One of my husband's businesses was an outdoor sign company. We have someone else to manage it now, but I still own it. What about a billboard of her?"

"A billboard?"

Aunt Laney came and stood beside me.

"We'll use the one right out on the highway so that everyone who turns to come or go from the island will see it. Do you have a picture of her?"

"We do, but it's grainy. I don't think it would do well on a billboard."

There was a pause on the other end of the line. Aunt Laney mouthed, "What is it?"

"Doesn't Muffin resemble Molly except for the spots?" Mrs. Kirby asked.

"Yes, but …" I began.

"Why don't I take a picture of Muffin and use it? All we need is the head."

"Are you sure you want to do this?"

"Very sure. I probably should have asked for your aunt when I called, but I was so excited about my idea, I just poured it forth."

"Aunt Laney's standing right here." I handed the phone to her.

Aunt Laney listened for a few minutes. "Oh, that's generous of you Mrs. Kirby. This will mean so much to Ralph. We've had to admit him to the hospital with pneumonia. He's very sick, and I think mostly due to him giving up because of Molly's disappearance." She grew silent again apparently as Mrs. Kirby spoke, and then, "Yes, let me give you the information."

Aunt Laney rattled off all the same facts we'd put on the flyers, and then she hung up the phone. "Can you believe Mrs. Kirby?" she said.

"That's great." Next to a big expensive billboard, my plan now sounded stupid. "Ralph will be excited, won't he?" I said, trying not to appear disappointed.

Chapter Twenty-Six

Halcyon

Mavis stopped by that evening to help eat the stuffed peppers Aunt Laney had baked. Afterward, she went with us to the Marsh, and Aunt Laney filled her in on all that had happened.

"Y'all have had a hard day today." She paused for a minute and glared at Aunt Laney who'd stood up. "You sit down on that stool right this minute. You've already had enough excitement for a week just in the last few hours."

Aunt Laney turned. "I have to stretch my legs, Mavis. I'm not an invalid, you know."

"Let's keep it that way," Mavis said.

"Oh, no," Aunt Laney said as she collapsed on the chair.

Mavis twisted her mouth. "What's the 'oh, no' about?"

"Ralph's stand. I forgot all about it. We have to work out something to keep it going. We can't let all those fruits and vegetables rot over there. Ben went to Valdosta, and Rob told me on the phone that now Ben's gone to Florida for a couple of days with the relatives. He's out. Of course Rob's always busy on Saturdays." Aunt Laney turned to Mavis and me. "It looks like it's up to us."

I knew right away about that *us* business. She didn't mean to include herself as part of the *us*.

"Wait a minute, I had plans for my Saturday off," Mavis said.

Aunt Laney gave Mavis pleading eyes.

"Oh, all right, I guess I could use a little fresh air. Mary Helen and I can handle it."

She had to be kidding.

"Can't we, Mary Helen?"

I smiled weakly. "Sure." I remembered I thought I had a bad attitude when Ben was minding the stand, and now was my time to do something about it. I gave myself a pep talk inside. I could do this. A few fruits and vegetables wouldn't kill me. Besides, it was for Ralph.

As I put my clothes on early the next morning, I heard Mavis's Volvo hitting the driveway. I finished buttoning my shirt, picked up my backpack and headed out.

"Ready?" Mavis said as I got in the car.

"Yes," I said firmly.

Mavis had already made little signs for all the vegetables so I would know what's what, and then she showed me how to use Ralph's scale to measure everything. I knew from math at school how to add up the prices. I never guessed math would come in handy.

The customers started coming, and Mavis and I didn't even sit down until almost eleven. By then the sun was so hot, my shirt was soaked in the back. About that time, Aunt Laney pulled up and took a gallon pitcher and a cooler out of the backseat.

"I brought you folks lemonade and sandwiches."

Because of my thirst, I'd forgotten I was hungry.

She handed the cooler to me and I slid it behind the counter. When I looked up, my eyes fell right on a picture of Ralph's daughter.

"What was her name?" I asked Mavis as I pointed to the image.

"Ruth."

I studied the photo again. She seemed a little older than me. Ruth—that was a pleasing name. I think I would've liked her if she was anything like Ralph. If she hadn't died, I would have gotten to know her when I visited. And for a moment, I felt a loss, too. I missed Ruth, and I'd never even met her. An ache of something like grief pressed on my chest.

"Mary Helen, are you okay?" Mavis asked.

"Fine," I said and opened the cooler and handed out the sandwiches and chips.

"Have you folks been busy?" Aunt Laney said.

I took a bite of my peanut butter sandwich. Heaven.

"Have we?" Mavis munched on a potato chip. "Haven't even sat down."

"I was wondering if you could spare Mary Helen to go with me to see Ralph."

It seemed I was getting to be a hot commodity on this island. I don't know if I'd ever felt so useful.

"Well," Mavis said looking at me. "I guess she can go."

*

"Billboard," Ralph whispered. "I ain't never heard of such."

"Yes," Aunt Laney said, "right at the entrance to the island." She held Ralph's hand in hers as she sat by him. I stood at the foot of the bed.

For a moment a trace of a smile came across Ralph's face then disappeared again. His color was no longer red like it'd been in days past but now grayish white—a lot like Aunt Laney looked when she got too hot at the marsh. Just since yesterday, his condition seemed to be worse.

"Billboard of a dog," he mumbled, his eyes closed.

The nurse came in the room and nodded for us to leave. "We'll come back soon," Aunt Laney said and placed Ralph's hand gently by his side.

As we headed back to the island and came to the turn to go back over the causeway, Aunt Laney pointed to a billboard to her right. "I think that's the one Mrs. Kirby intends to use for Molly's ad," she said sounding pleased. "It's a prime location, don't you think?"

"Sure is," I said and blushed to think I could come up with a plan that would compare to that big advertising board.

We stopped by the produce stand and found Mavis putting tarps out.

"I think everybody came this morning," she said as she smoothed out the blue tarp over the cantaloupes. "I'm going home."

When we got back to Aunt Laney's, she plucked a few letters from the mailbox beside the front door. "This one's for you." She handed me a bright orange envelope.

I read the return address. Joy. "It's from Leslie! She must be feeling well enough to write." And with Ben mad and gone, and Molly missing, the letter couldn't have come at a better time.

I tore into my room and peeled open the flap. She wrote a lot about how sick she'd been, and how jealous she was of me being at the beach all summer.

If she only knew.

I hadn't written her about what had actually been going on, since her mother was reading the letters to her. Whatever her mama knew, my mama would know. But since she was obviously better and writing letters herself now, it might be worth the chance of spilling it all out and hoping that Leslie would actually read it with her own eyes. I was close to going home, and Mama was going to find out anyway.

So I ripped a few pages out of my tablet and spent two hours recording all that had happened. I stuffed the four pages covered back and front in an envelope Aunt Laney had, pressed a stamp on the corner, rode my bike to the post office, and mailed it. It was liberating to be able to do these things myself without asking somebody to take me.

The phone rang later that evening and Rob said he had a part-time person to help him and he didn't have any charters, so he could cover Ralph's stand for Monday. He didn't know what we'd do the rest of the week.

*

"Laney has requested special prayer for Ralph Tullos," Pastor Warren said Sunday morning at the end of the service. "I'm sure many of you know Ralph, as he's supplied us with the finest fruits and vegetables for many years." There were nods across the room. "It seems Ralph's dog, Molly, has disappeared, which has been a great disappointment to him. Now he's been admitted to the hospital with pneumonia. I visited him yesterday and found him much changed from the last time I saw him."

I saw Aunt Laney dab at her eyes with a handkerchief, which unbelievably, was tie dyed.

"Let's bow our heads in prayer," Pastor Warren said.

As Pastor Warren prayed, I heard the usual affirming "Thank you, Lords" and "Amens" go up from the crowd. When he concluded, the guitar players finished it off with a gentle song that I found quite beautiful, almost classical. Folks sang along and Pastor Warren sent us out with "In the name of the Father, and of the Son, and of the Holy Spirit." Like the words on the painting in Mavis's house, I wanted to spend time thinking about what Aunt Laney called the benediction.

That afternoon Aunt Laney, Mavis, and I gathered around the Scrabble board, and I tried to remember all the HA words I'd studied earlier in the week. I missed Ben, and my brain felt like a bowl of alphabet soup.

"Laney, these Scrabble games are the best thing we've done in years. Don't you know this helps our brain with being forgetful?"

"Who's forgetful?" All expression left Aunt Laney's face.

Must be one of the bad days the doctor said she might have.

"I didn't mean you are forgetful, I mean you could be, you know, getting older."

"Me getting older?" Aunt Laney stared Mavis down for a few seconds. "I'm not the one who felt the need to pay a visit to Miss Clairol. You go first," she said evenly.

Mavis shook her head and studied her rack. P-i-q-u-e, she spelled as she lay her tiles on the board. "How much is that?" she asked without looking at me.

I added three, four … ten for the q, so that's fourteen, fifteen, sixteen times a double word score is thirty-two. I wrote it on the pad.

Mavis looked up at Aunt Laney and raised her eyebrows. "Your turn."

"I believe I will," Aunt Laney said. I could hear the irritation in her voice.

She spelled her word using Mavis's q. "B-r-u-s-q-u-e."

Mavis cleared her throat.

"How many is that, Mary Helen?" Aunt Laney said, a sly smile creeping across her face.

I counted in my head twice to make sure I was correct. "Twenty-one," I said.

"Thank you, Mary Helen." Aunt Laney leaned back in her chair and crossed her arms.

What was going on? I could feel tension in the air, so I carefully picked up my tiles and put them on the board. "L-o-v-e," I spelled using the e from Mavis's pique. No one said a word.

"Nine points." I entered my score.

Mavis was up next and already had the tiles in her hand. "V-a-i-n," she spelled using the v from my love.

Aunt Laney didn't even wait for me to tally the score before she put two tiles down on the board. Using the r from brusque and the l from my love, she spelled rile.

The only benefit I could see from Aunt Laney and Mavis being mad at each other was that they spelled shorter words. I tallied the eight points from Mavis's vain and the six points from Aunt Laney's rile. I'd never seen anybody have a fight with Scrabble tiles.

Emotions simmered in the stuffy kitchen. Aunt Laney's air conditioner must have been as old as she was, because in the afternoons it barely kept up with the tropical July air. When you added the row between Mavis and Aunt Laney to the already hot air, well … I could hardly breathe. But as I studied the board, and then my rack, a stunning opportunity presented itself. I could hardly contain my excitement. I gathered the tiles from my rack and placed them on the board. "H-a-l-c-y-o-n."

Silence, but I didn't care. I could live without applause if I got a good score. "Fifteen times a double word score is thirty points and I actually used an HA word."

More silence, and then I heard Aunt Laney stifle a laugh, and Mavis giggle. Soon we all erupted into laughter.

"Thank God for HA words," Aunt Laney said.

"That's right, Mary Helen. You got the most points you've ever gotten," Mavis added.

So they had noticed.

"Where'd you learn that anyway?" Mavis asked.

"Ben and I read the dictionary together this week," I said. A pain shot through me. I lowered my head. "It means calm and peaceful."

"Read the dictionary together? That sounds serious," Aunt Laney said teasing.

I shrugged. "I don't know what difference it makes now."

Aunt Laney put her hand on my shoulder. "It's going to be okay, Mary Helen. Ben's coming back, and you'll get things ironed out."

"I sure hope so."

Chapter Twenty-Seven

Building a Nest

"When I went out to breakfast this morning, folks were talking about Molly's face being plastered all over that billboard across the causeway. I didn't have the heart to tell them it was a lookalike dog," Mavis said when she called on Monday. "Here it is the Fourth of July, and Mrs. Kirby had those men out there making time and a half putting up that billboard. I guess it helps if you're the owner of the company."

I'd forgotten all about it being the Fourth with so much going on. "I hope it helps," I said.

"Got to help. A lot of people come and go from this island especially on a holiday. I'll see y'all later. I have plans this morning."

Since when did Mavis have plans?

I resisted the urge to ask her what she was doing, said goodbye and hung up the phone. I heard Aunt Laney stirring around in her bedroom, and I knew she'd already eaten breakfast by the smell of coffee in the kitchen. I gathered a bowl, cereal, and milk and then sat with my back to the eyeball painting. I was glad I hadn't taken a bite yet, because I might have choked when Aunt Laney opened the bedroom door. I supposed in commemoration of the holiday, she had on navy blue pants, a red striped tunic, and three odd looking silver star shaped pins fastened to the bodice of her tunic. Guaranteed some artist friend of hers had made them.

"It's the Fourth of July," she announced prancing past me.

I didn't know whether to salute or not. "Where are you going?" I asked following her into the front room feeling as if I were in a parade.

"There's always a big celebration in the Village on the Fourth. Have you not eaten breakfast yet? I'm ready to go."

I knew as soon as she got out of her car at the village she was going to be the center of attention, especially in the get-up she had on today. I tried hard to think of some way to worm out. Nothing came to mind.

"Never mind about eating, we can get a bite downtown." She grabbed her big satchel.

I put the milk back in the refrigerator, retrieved my backpack out of my room and followed her. On the way, I filled Aunt Laney in about the billboard already being up.

"We won't miss any calls about Molly." Aunt Laney's silver stars sparkled in the sunlight. "That Mavis thinks of every detail, doesn't she? Letting us borrow her answering machine so we won't have to be glued to home base."

When we arrived at the Village, we stopped to see Rob for a minute, but he was busy taking care of a customer.

He handed the wannabe angler a receipt. "Thanks much. I hope the fishing will be good tomorrow." The man headed for the door smiling.

"Hi, Laney." He tipped his baseball cap. "Mary Helen. I guess you're here for the celebration in the Village."

Laney eased up to the counter. "We are, but I wondered if anything has been done about Ralph's stand."

"As a matter of fact, Archie Campbell, the mail carrier, has spread the word around town about Ralph's situation. Florence at the café has volunteered to watch his stand two days, and then Heather at the Sandcastle is taking over another."

"You're the best," Aunt Laney said, giving Rob a big smile. "God is answering my prayers. How wonderful that Ralph's stand is covered until Friday."

I liked the way God was responding to Aunt Laney's prayers. It sure worked for me.

"Don't have time to talk now," Florence said, blowing by us when we popped in the café. "I'm waiting on a party of ten in the back room, and a party of six in the front room, and every one of them is in a hurry."

We stayed a while for a band concert, talked to a few folks who'd seen Molly's billboard, ate barbeque, and then headed home.

When we checked the answering machine, we only had one message, which turned out to be a wrong number. We expected the phone to jangle incessantly because of the billboard. It didn't. We only received one more call on the Fourth and one call on the fifth. Both of them were about dogs found before Molly even disappeared. We should have put the date she went missing on the billboard, but we didn't think about that.

Kathleen Kirby called on Tuesday around noon hoping we had news, and Aunt Laney gave her the sad results. I could tell she didn't take it well.

"It was kind of you to do this," Aunt Laney said trying to be consoling to Mrs. Kirby. "We know that whoever took Molly may no longer be in the area, but we have to keep our hope alive. And yes, we'd love to have pictures of Muffin. We'll be in touch." Aunt Laney sighed when she hung up the phone.

When we visited Ralph that afternoon, he barely acknowledged us. His eyes flickered a little and then closed again.

Aunt Laney's eyes filled with tears.

"His condition is not good," the nurse said as we left the room. "I feel like he's given up."

"I wish we had good news about Molly. I know that would make a difference."

"I have no doubt that it would," the nurse said.

When we returned to the island, Aunt Laney decided she wanted to do a little painting at the marsh that evening. As we packed up her supplies, Aunt Laney seemed preoccupied, as if she'd left part of herself back with Ralph.

*

I was lying on the bank after lugging Aunt Laney's painting equipment to the marsh and setting up.

"Mary Helen," she whispered. "Do you see it?"

Why was she whispering? I sat up. "See what?" She had stopped dabbing the vibrant blue she was using for the sky.

"The marsh hen ... the clapper rail. Do you see it?" Aunt Laney pointed with her bright blue dipped paintbrush in the general direction of the creek. "Over there ... on that tuft of marsh grass."

I focused my eyes in the direction of her brush but still couldn't see it. There had to be at least twenty million tufts of marsh grass in front of me.

Aunt Laney motioned for me to stand, which I did. And there it was—the clapper rail, perched hen-like on a mound of gilded reeds about thirty feet out. Aunt Laney rummaged quietly in her tackle box, pulled out a pair of small binoculars and handed them to me. I trained them on the bird with brownish-gray feathers. I saw its long beak move, and heard a "kek-kek-kek" call which for some reason caused a smile to spread across my face. I handed the binoculars back to Aunt Laney.

She beamed back at me and put them up to her own eyes for a few minutes.

"Will it fly away?" I asked wondering if I might see it on the wing.

"Probably not, clapper rails don't often fly. She might swim a little, though."

As she said that, the clapper rail ambled from its tuft and hit the water. We watched for a few moments until it disappeared from sight in the thick grass. "Thanks for showing it to me," I said and stood for a moment hoping for its return.

"It'd be a shame to visit the marshes of Glynn without seeing the marsh hen."

Aunt Laney went back to her painting, as I sat and leaned back once more on the bank. I realized we'd reached a point in our relationship that I only experienced with Mama and Leslie. We could be quiet and not say a word, and it was okay. I never expected this. A question floated into my brain, and I rose up again.

"You like your life, don't you, Aunt Laney?" I asked.

Aunt Laney nodded. "I do. I've been blessed to realize deep desires—the things God planted in my heart. What do you want to do with your life?" she asked.

My conversation with Ben weeks before came to mind. "I'd love to write, but I don't think I'll ever be good enough to make a living at it. My teacher last year said I showed real potential. I think she was being kind. Plus, as we've played Scrabble every week, you all know many more words than I do. You and Mavis even had an argument during the game with words I'd never heard. I guess I don't have a broad vocabulary."

"But look what a little studying did for you," Aunt Laney said. "You came up with a great word and settled an argument." She turned to me, a smile forming, and she got an expression on her face I'd often seen.

"Go ahead. I know you're about to pop to tell me more about Sidney Lanier."

"As a matter of fact I am. He had the same struggle as you."

Aunt Laney moved back to her painting. "I told you what a wonderful flute player he was, but he aspired to be involved in the literary world as well." She wiped her brush on a multi colored rag. "Of course, after the war times were hard, people were hungry. So a literary career seemed out of the question. One of his friends from up North begged him to travel with him to study in Germany which had long been one of Lanier's goals, but he didn't feel he could leave with the South being in such tatters."

I swatted a mosquito off my shoulder. "What did he do?" Why couldn't I remember to use insect repellent? I rummaged through Aunt Laney's tackle box, found her can, shook it and learned there was only a little left. I had to remember to use the can at home from now on.

Aunt Laney waited for me to spray myself, and then she put her brush down and occupied the stool I'd set up for her. "For a while, he tutored on a large plantation, but that involved teaching a crushing number of classes a day. It began to take a toll. He had to go to the coast again for his health, this time to Mobile."

"That's in Alabama, right?"

"Yes, on the Gulf Coast. He stayed for a while then moved up to Montgomery where his grandfather owned a hotel." Aunt Laney shook her head. "Can you believe he worked as a desk clerk? This brilliant musician, this man who would write one of the few great American poems worked as a desk clerk. But, no matter how menial the job he always executed it with great care."

Aunt Laney paused for a while. A family on bicycles passed behind us along the marsh road. As they turned and disappeared down Ocean Boulevard, Aunt Laney stood up and started painting again while continuing her story. The wind picked up her patriotic tunic and blew it behind her making her appear as a flag waving in the breeze. "He tried to stay in touch with the literary world by reading journals, and even had his first poems published in one called *The Round Table.*

I stood up for a moment to stretch my legs while Aunt Laney continued. "While in Montgomery he wrote a book called *Tiger Lilies*, published by a New York company. It received mixed reviews. It was not time for his literary career to take hold, as he still couldn't make a living at it. He went back to teaching, this time in a classroom."

I sprawled on the prickly grass and tried to make myself comfortable. I also kept forgetting to bring a blanket with me when we came.

"Eventually Lanier returned to Macon, and worked for his dad in his law office. At that time, one could learn law by studying under someone rather than having to have a degree. By this time Lanier had married and had a family to support. He and his wife, Mary, were so proud of their first born, Charley."

"It doesn't seem like he's ever going to be a poet."

"He did have a hard time, and many people would have probably given up the dream. After working at law for some time, he had to make another trip for his health, this time to San Antonio. After his stay there, he determined once and for all to pursue his passions—music and poetry."

"Finally," I said thinking we'd never reach this part.

"He secured a position playing flute with the Peabody Orchestra in Baltimore and that same summer *Lippincott's Magazine* published one of his poems. That was the beginning of many published poems, but he still couldn't generate enough income to support his family."

"It doesn't seem right that someone so talented was not appreciated. So sad."

"Yes, and it gets sadder. It was about this time his discouragement grew to such a level that he wrote, 'Altogether, it seems as if there wasn't any place for me in this world, and if it were not for Mary, I should certainly quit it, in mortification at being so useless."

"How'd you remember all that?"

"I memorized it a long time ago to remind myself that even Sidney Lanier almost gave up."

I was right about Aunt Laney staying up nights memorizing his writing, but why was that particular quote easy for her to recall. It seemed unlikely, but had Aunt Laney been discouraged in her own life? And what about Sidney Lanier? It was incredible the man that Aunt Laney loved and admired so much wrote lines filled with such despair. I almost couldn't take it in. I picked up my journal and the chestnut pen I'd brought and held them in my hands. Aunt Laney must have read my face.

"It breaks your heart, doesn't it?" She paused for a minute. "But the good news is he didn't give up, and you can't ever give up your dream either. You have to keep trying. If that's what you're convinced you're supposed to do, then keep at it. I read somewhere that Lanier sought with a passion the purpose to which God had called him."

I put my journal and the pen in my backpack and looked up at Aunt Laney. I wanted to remember what she was saying to me.

"Somehow, he managed to keep going, and only a couple of years later he was appointed as a lecturer in English literature at Johns Hopkins University. He realized his breakthrough during this time, and he was most productive. He penned 'The Marshes of Glynn' during these years."

Aunt Laney paused holding her brush above the surface of the canvas. "But sadly, he didn't have long to live." She dropped her brush to her side. "Did I tell you he spent his last summer in Asheville?"

"My Asheville?"

"He accepted a commission to write a railroad guide of the area, just as the doctors sent him to the mountains again for his health. It seemed a perfect arrangement. But his health rapidly declined, and he died a few miles from Asheville in the fall."

Aunt Laney paused as if trying to decide whether to say what came next. "He was only thirty-nine years old."

Dead at thirty-nine. My heart ached. "Mama's only a year older than him. That's so young to die."

"Yes, very young. Imagine what he might have accomplished had he lived longer. But it was not to be." Aunt Laney wiped her paintbrush and started to gather up her belongings. "Well, I guess we better get back before Warden Mavis starts calling to see where we are."

"Aunt Laney?"

"Yes."

"Thanks."

"You're welcome, my dear, you're very welcome."

"I'll help you pack up, and then I think I'll stay here for a while. You take the car and go on back. I'll walk. It's not far."

After we'd loaded the car, I watched Aunt Laney drive off. I plopped back down on the bank. Sidney Lanier's struggle, Ralph, Molly, Aunt Laney, and the nest painting all mixed in my mind. Something like determination rose up inside of me. What did I have to lose? Stupid or not, I was going to do it. With that settled, I set out for Aunt Laney's house.

"Do you have any good stationery at your house that I could use?" I said to Aunt Laney who was in the kitchen making lemonade when I returned.

She took her eyes off squeezing lemons and glanced at me. "I'm sure I can find some. Are you writing a letter?"

"Yes, I think I will." Aunt Laney didn't query me again, and I was glad because I didn't want to answer any more questions.

Chapter Twenty-Eight

What Good Has Come

"I think you'll find what you're searching for in this drawer," Aunt Laney said as she pointed to the second drawer of the chest in the purple room. I pulled it out and immediately found ivory linen stationery.

"Are you sure you don't mind if I use this?" I said holding it up.

"Somebody gave it to me years ago. I'm not much of a letter writer, just like my sister. Take it. It'll go to waste here."

Perfect. I went to my room and set to work on my project. I picked up the chestnut pen and wrote a couple of drafts in my journal before I penned it on the stationery in my best handwriting. What I anticipated I could do in one afternoon actually took that whole afternoon and evening.

Early the next morning, I put the letter in an envelope along with one of the pictures Mrs. Kirby sent to us, told Aunt Laney I needed to go to the Village, and pedaled to a newspaper stand in front of Dressner's. I bought a newspaper and found the name I was looking for. On my already stamped envelope, I wrote Elton Cook, Editor, Brunswick Times, Gateway Street, Brunswick, Georgia. I dropped the letter in a mailbox near the library and then rode back to Aunt Laney's house. Then I waited.

I was impressed that Aunt Laney never asked me what I was up to. Maybe she sensed it was something I had to do myself.

Sylvester dropped by to see how the paintings were coming along.

"I'm making progress," Aunt Laney said, emerging from her bedroom to talk to him.

"When may I expect a finished work?"

"Sylvester, you know I don't paint under pressure, so you might as well accept that."

"Very well," he said, exhaling as his bow tie bobbed wildly. "The calls, you know."

"Didn't Mavis talk to you about this?" Aunt Laney said.

"Mavis? Yes, we've talked."

"Well then," Aunt Laney said.

The expression on Sylvester's face seemed as if he was puzzled, but I sure didn't want to get in the middle of this. Sylvester left and Aunt Laney went back to whatever she was doing, but that conversation seemed strange to me.

I waited a couple of days for the newspaper to receive my letter before I bought another one to check if my letter was in it. Once more, I woke up early, dressed, and biked to the paper stand. I was so excited I couldn't wait until I returned home to find out. Right there on the sidewalk in the Village I turned to the "letters to the editor" page and searched for my letter. It wasn't there. Disappointment overwhelmed me. Maybe they chose not to run it. Discouraged, I mounted my bicycle and slowly pedaled home. After all, I was just a kid.

When I reached Aunt Laney's, she met me at the door. "Where have you been?" she said.

"I went to the Village to buy a newspaper."

"Let me see it." She took it from my hand. "Oh, my goodness," she said as she studied the front page.

"What?"

"This." She turned the paper around for me to see.

There at the bottom of the front page was a picture of lookalike Molly and my letter.

I took the newspaper from her and stared at the article. I felt like I did that time I won the golden egg at the Easter egg hunt. "I can't believe it. They printed it, and on the front page." It never occurred to me to check the front page when I'd bought the paper. The headline on the article read Help Find a Beloved Companion. They didn't even edit my story. Aunt Laney read it aloud:

"Dear Mr. Cook,

"I am Miss Laney Hanberry's fourteen-year-old niece from Asheville, North Carolina, and am visiting my aunt this summer on St. Simons Island. You may know Mr. Ralph

165

Tullos, the proprietor of Ralph's Fresh Produce on St. Simons Island. For many years, he has supplied a great number in the coastal area with the best fruits and vegetables available. Now, Ralph needs your help.

Molly, his beloved dog and companion, is missing. Molly's no ordinary dog. She appeared weeks after Ralph's wife and daughter were tragically killed in a house fire and has been his constant companion since that time. Since June 21, Ralph has been searching for his missing dog. His health has deteriorated to the point he can no longer look for her.

Would you help find this special dog and bring back a halcyon time in Ralph's life? There is reason to believe she may have even been taken off the island. Please contact Miss Hanberry with any information.

"Yours truly,
"Mary Helen Reynolds

"Editor's note: I've bought my tomatoes from Ralph for many years and have met his dog, Molly. As a community, let's make a special effort to help Ralph find his dog.
Ralph, our prayers are with you. In addition, aren't we all impressed with Miss Reynolds's vocabulary? Not many fourteen-year-olds know the word 'halcyon.'"

Beside the letter was Mrs. Kirby's picture of Muffin which was almost a mirror image of Molly. Aunt Laney took a tissue out of her pocket and dabbed her eyes. "This is lovely, Mary Helen. I'm so proud of you. The phone has rung five times since you left this morning with people calling to say they saw the letter. Think how many people are reading this right now."

"Really?"

"Really," she said.

The next morning, the eyeball-painting man called from Jacksonville and told Aunt Laney he saw my letter in the Jacksonville paper. He said that evidently one of the wire services had picked it up, and the Jacksonville paper ran it. Later, one of Sylvester's clients from Atlanta, who'd bought one of Aunt Laney's paintings, called to say it was in the Atlanta paper.

I couldn't believe it. I went to my bedroom, picked up the chestnut pen, held it, and sat staring into space. In my mind, I saw the map at the Sandcastle with all the pins. People were reading my letter in many of those pin places. People were reading my letter in places I could see from the top of the lighthouse. And the boats in the channel were coming and going to places where people were reading my letter.

At six that evening, Mama called. I answered the phone. "Mary Helen," Mama said in a voice that was stronger than I'd heard in a long time. "I saw your letter on the front page of the Asheville paper. It's the sweetest piece I've ever read in the news. I'm so proud of you." She was crying on the phone, and it got me crying too. "Why didn't you tell me about this?"

"I didn't want to worry you with all the sadness of it."

Mama waited a moment before she answered. "How thoughtful of you. I can't believe my little girl has done something like this. I guess you're not such a little girl anymore."

"No, Mama, I'm not," I said, as I wiped my eyes.

"Have you heard from the article?"

"Not yet."

"I guess it might take time. How's Ralph doing?"

"He's very sick. The doctor told Aunt Laney last night that he doesn't know if Ralph will make it."

At seven, there was a knock on the door. When I peeked through the curtains, Ben stood on the front porch. He held up a newspaper that said *Valdosta Herald* at the top. There was Molly again on the front page.

"Seems like you've made it as a writer," he said when I opened the door.

I stepped out on the porch and put my arms around him. "I'm glad you're back."

"Yeah, I'm glad I'm back too. I guess we need to talk."

I pulled away from him. "Yes, we do.'"

"You know, my dad talked to Florence, and she said everybody she saw at the produce stand this week wanted to talk about Ralph and his dog. I think a few people came by to talk and bought some vegetables just 'cause they were there. He's made a lot of money. There was even one of his farmers over in Valdosta who saw the article and wanted to donate his produce to the stand because he knew Ralph was in the hospital. Can you believe people can be so giving? How'd you get the idea to write that letter anyway?"

"When I went to the library for Mavis to make the fliers about Molly, I read a magazine while she ran off the copies. There was an article on the power of words. I had Mavis make a copy, and when I got home, I stuck it in the back of my journal. It fell out the day you left for Valdosta. I wanted to help too. So I came up with the idea of the letter, but I gave up on it after Mrs. Kirby put up the billboard. A letter seemed stupid beside something big like that, but then Aunt Laney told me a story about Sidney Lanier's struggles that helped me get the courage to do it."

"I'm glad you did. I can't wait for school to start so I can tell everybody I know you." Ben laughed. "I have to go now, but are y'all playing Scrabble tomorrow?"

"We usually do."

"Maybe we can talk before the game."

"Sure."

Ben turned to go and then spun around again. "Halcyon?"

"I guess dictionary reading pays off."

"In more ways than one," Ben said, a glint in his eyes.

He turned, mounted his bike on the gravel drive, and rode away.

*

"All of us at Glynn Fellowship are proud of you, Mary Helen," Pastor Warren said as I left church on Sunday.

"Thank you."

"Have you had any promising contacts so far?"

"Not yet."

"We're praying."

The phone continued to ring at Aunt Laney's house that Sunday. People from all over the country had somehow managed to find Aunt Laney's phone number and called about dogs they thought might be Molly. But as we talked to them, we ruled the dogs out, one by one. All of it was exciting, but I knew it wouldn't matter unless we found Molly. Ralph was dying, and he needed his dog. We were going to have to take turns during the Scrabble game to answer the phone.

As Ben helped me set up the Scrabble board, I said, "I'm sorry about what happened at your house at dinner that night."

"Yeah, me too."

168

"I want to try to explain. I've never told anyone this until I told Aunt Laney the other day. I don't think I even understood myself until that night.

"All my life, I've had this feeling of abandonment. I've never verbalized it, just carried it around with me like a basket, and in this basket was a nameless feeling of being left behind. My mama has always been there for me, so I couldn't figure it out.

"I guess when Aunt Laney told me about your mama, I started to think about where that feeling came from again. Then I drew a line to my dad. Maybe it's that feeling that made me angry about coming here. I didn't want to be separated from Mama."

As I explained about how I felt, I saw understanding in Ben's eyes.

He said, "When I went to Valdosta, my cousin Margaret asked me what was wrong. I guess she could tell I was mad. Anyway, when I told her, she said she had a friend whose dad had died, and she felt just like you explained. I guess up until then, it didn't make sense that somebody could feel abandonment from a death. Like a person had a choice, or something. I guess I started to see from some viewpoint other than mine. Anyway, it helped me to come back. And I'm trying hard to understand."

"I hope you don't feel Aunt Laney betrayed a confidence. I asked her what happened to your mom, and …"

"I know, I know. It's all right."

"If you don't want me to ever mention your mom again, I won't. I know it's not exactly the same as losing my dad, because I can't even imagine my mama leaving me. It has to be hard."

"I have to try and not feel sorry for myself and walk around with a great big chip on my shoulder like I did the other night."

"I guess I knocked the chip off, huh?"

"Yeah, but maybe I needed it knocked off. Anyway, I'll try to not be hotheaded about it in the future."

"Everybody ready to go?" Mavis said, as she breezed into the room.

"Ready," Aunt Laney said, emerging from her bedroom. Aunt Laney didn't say it with her usual enthusiasm. I knew Ralph's situation was weighing heavily on her mind. I hoped she and Mavis didn't get into it like they did last Sunday.

We gathered round, and everyone drew a letter. When we turned them over, Mavis had drawn a b, which was closest to the beginning of the alphabet, so she was first. We put our tiles back in the box and drew the seven for our racks.

"Mavis, you shot out like a cannonball after church. Where were you going?" Aunt Laney said as she arranged her tiles on her rack.

"Oh, I was just meeting someone for lunch," Mavis said evasively.

"Who?"

"Can't a person have a private life?"

"Sure a person can, but you've never had one before."

"Always a first time," Mavis said as she put her letters on the board. "C-l-o-s-e-d," she spelled.

Uh-oh, here we go again. "Eighteen points," I said, writing her score and watching Aunt Laney's reaction at the same time.

"S-a-s-s-y," Aunt Laney spelled as she put her tiles on the board.

I'd never seen anyone use that many esses before. Mavis twisted her mouth to the side. Ben stifled a snicker.

I wrote eleven points on the pad. Aunt Laney didn't even ask about her score.

Ben went next. Using the c from Mavis's closed, he spelled aloud, "C-o-e-v-a-l."

I stared at the word and then at Ben. He knew I'd never gotten anywhere challenging words, but then maybe he was hoping to make up a word and slither away with it, thinking I'd given up. I reached for the Webster's and flipped to "coeval: originating or existing during the same period of time."

"So where did you learn that?"

"The wooly mammoth was coeval with the brontosaurus."

"More *National Geographic?*"

"Right."

Even though he used that hard word, he only tallied thirteen points.

I gave some careful attention to the situation as Aunt Laney and Mavis simmered on the other side of the table. I could feel Aunt Laney's foot tapping on the floor. She always did that when she became aggravated.

I picked up my tiles and wished for a drum roll as I lay them down. "Y-a-p-o-k."

Ben's eyes widened. "How do you know what a yapok is?"

"I don't know what a yapok is," Aunt Laney said, leaning forward and seeming to forget she was aggravated at Mavis. I passed the dictionary to her.

She turned to the Ys. "'Yapok: an aquatic marsupial mammal, Chironectes minimus of tropical America, with dense fur, webbed hind feet, and a long tail.' See, a picture."

We all studied the little pen and ink drawing. It sort of looked like a raccoon and a possum combo.

"So how did you know what it was?" Ben asked.

"I was bored one night while you were gone to Valdosta, so I studied the Ys."

Once more, dictionary reading saved the day as Mavis and Aunt Laney both burst into peals of laughter.

The phone rang and I got up to answer it. I listened for a few minutes and then said, "No, Molly is a female dog's name. I know we didn't specify it, we just thought everyone would know. Thank you for calling." I hung the phone up and shrugged at the Scrabble bunch.

More laughter.

Mavis said, "That reminds me of a joke Archie Campbell told me this week about dogs. Why did the dog run in circles?" She paused for effect. "It was too hard to run in squares." Mavis leaned back in her chair and howled.

What was going on with Mavis? Something had sure brought a transformation.

*

By Monday, the calls had subsided and life returned to normal. Well, as normal as things ever got at Aunt Laney's house. With the normalcy came a growing fear we'd never find Molly.

I talked to Mama late in the afternoon.

"I'm having my first chemo treatment tomorrow," she said.

"Are you feeling pretty well?"

"Yes, I'm ready to face this."

Mama was the first thought I had the next morning when I woke up. I went into the kitchen where Aunt Laney was drinking coffee and reading her Bible.

"Mama's supposed to have her first treatment today," I said, in case she'd forgotten, and then I retrieved my box of cereal from the cabinet and put it on the table.

Aunt Laney looked up from her reading. "I remember. I've been praying for her. I hope she does well."

"Yeah, me too."

"When is it?"

"This afternoon at two. Until then, I might go over to the produce stand and talk to Ben." I ate my cereal and tried not to make visual contact

171

with the eyeball painting. Aunt Laney had already taken the chair next to the wall.

After I ate, I went to my room and dressed. It was especially hot this morning, and I was already damp with perspiration due to Aunt Laney's aging air-conditioning system. I put on my coolest white shirt and denim shorts.

When I rode up to the stand, Ben was handing an older gray-haired man some change. "Thank you," Ben said.

"Thank you, young man, and you tell Ralph we're praying for him to get well and to come back soon."

"Did you know him?" I said after the man left.

"No, but he sure knew Ralph. So many people have come by and said they're praying for him."

"Pastor Warren talked about praying yesterday. Aunt Laney prays a lot at meals, and sometimes I can tell she's praying when I come into the kitchen in the morning. Do you think it helps?"

Ben picked up a fuzzy peach in his hand and then turned to me. "Yes I do. Want one?" he said, offering it to me. "First of the Georgia peaches to come in. Ralph's regular supplier came by, and my dad had already told me to make sure we had some, so I bought them myself."

"A regular businessman," I said. I took the peach and bit into it. It was good. The juice dribbled down my chin. I wiped it away with my hand. "Mama's having her first chemo treatment this afternoon."

"Is she upset about it?"

"She didn't seem to be. She always tries to be brave for me. I'm a little nervous about it though."

"You could always do that prayer thing," Ben said.

"I could at that."

When I returned home that afternoon, I noticed Mavis's car in the driveway. Odd at this time of day. I opened the door and found Aunt Laney ringing her hands and Mavis pacing back and forth. The instant they saw me, Aunt Laney froze in her chair, and Mavis stopped her pacing and said, "I was about to start searching for you."

"Looking for me. Why?" I said. My mind raced through the possibilities.

"Amy called about your mama. She had an allergic reaction to the drug in the chemotherapy. They've had to take her to the hospital and put her in intensive care." Mavis paused for several seconds and averted her gaze to the floor. Then she lifted her eyes to me. "It's serious."

I fell back into the green chair, and almost immediately, Mavis was holding me in her arms. Then another set of hands held my head and kissed it. I knew it was Aunt Laney.

"It's going to be all right," Mavis said.

"She promised me she wouldn't die," I said through sobs.

"Mary Helen, I'm sure she'll do all in her power to keep that promise. And we'll pray, we'll definitely pray," Aunt Laney whispered.

I shot up from the chair. "Pray. Everybody talks about prayer. But I don't see what good it's doing. You had a heart attack, Ralph is dying, Mama is dying, and Molly is gone. What good has come out of prayer? I didn't want to come here to begin with, and all it's been is one bad thing after another."

I stormed out to my bedroom and slammed the door.

Chapter Twenty-Nine

Eyes of Faith

I crashed across the bed as the anger and fear surged through me. My head hurt so badly, it felt like it might come off my shoulders. Since I used up all the pages in the journal I'd brought, I reached for the one Aunt Laney had given me when I first came. I sat up and wrote robotically. "Mama's in intensive care. She had a reaction to the chemo." I had to log what was happening right then. "Don't die, Mama." The pen felt slippery in my clammy hands and my throat hurt from the cry that hung there. She'd promised she wouldn't die. I remember the feeling of doubt I had when she made that promise. I stared at the words in my journal. Sidney Lanier was thirty-nine when he died. At forty, Mama was older.

I could hear Aunt Laney and Mavis out in the front room praying for Mama. I pulled my dad's letter from the bedside table and reread it. Then I read the letter from my grandmother. I held the chestnut pen to my lips and lay back on the pillows. I didn't think I was crying, but I had to keep wiping my face. The tears rolled out by themselves, like something deep inside was pushing them up past the gatekeepers of my tear ducts.

Only weeks before, Mama had lain on this very bed. I tried to recapture the picture of her in my mind. The image helped me see just how alive she was. I'd touched her chest as it rose and fell with every breath. "Oh, Mama, keep breathing, keep breathing."

Then, strangely, I started remembering Aunt Laney again, on the floor, blood around her head, blood on my clothes, and then a new memory surfaced. I saw Mama, and she was in the front seat of a car, not a car I ever knew we had. She was crying and staring horrified at someone in the driver's seat. In the driver's seat, a man slumped against the steering wheel, with blood on his head and the seat. I looked at my clothes, and the blood from the man had spilled all over my dress. I tried to rub crimson fluid from my hands onto the car seat.

"Stewart!" Mama screamed.

The man was my dad.

I began to shake and wasn't even conscious of making the piercing cry that brought Aunt Laney and Mavis running.

"I was there," I cried. "I was there when my dad was killed. I was in the car."

The two women flew toward the bed and wrapped me in their arms. For a long time, no one uttered a word. I could feel Aunt Laney sobbing too.

"Help her, Lord," Mavis said.

Aunt Laney wiped my face with her tunic, and whispered, "Mary Helen, I didn't realize until you and your mom came that you had no memory of the accident. I guess the shock of your mama going to the hospital has triggered this."

"Why didn't someone tell me?" I said, sobbing. "I thought he was in the car by himself."

"Your mama had as much as she could deal with managing her own pain. Maybe she wasn't up to talking about it." Aunt Laney stroked my head. "Or she hoped it would all just disappear in your subconscious."

"That's why after you fell, I started remembering blood on my clothes."

"I didn't know about that," Aunt Laney said, "but yes, I guess it is. Seeing me with blood on my head must have started the process."

"Poor Dad," I said. Mavis squeezed my hand.

"Mary Helen, the doctors said when the other car smashed his door, he had a severe head trauma. He died instantly. You and your mama miraculously only had cuts and bruises."

I started to fall back, but Aunt Laney and Mavis went with me, and we all simultaneously collapsed against the pillows on the bed, me in the middle like sandwich meat. "I can't believe I didn't remember all these years."

"Sometimes that happens with children. They edit out what's too painful, and it helps them manage a difficult event like that."

Aunt Laney prayed in hushed tones, and strangely, that seemed comforting to me. But then I thought about Mama being so sick and the shaking resumed.

Mavis rose up and held my face in her hands. "Tell me," she said.

I pulled up on my elbows. "I was thinking about Mama. I don't know if she's going to make it."

"Do you remember that last story I told you about Sidney Lanier?" Aunt Laney said.

I turned to her. "I guess."

"About how he almost gave up, but he didn't. He was sick and discouraged, but he kept going. It was right after that he did his most wonderful work." She paused. "We can't give up either, Mary Helen. We have to keep hoping, for your mama who's too sick to hope and for Ralph, who also doesn't have the energy to keep believing."

"How do I do that when everything seems so bad?" It seemed an impossible task.

"I believe God is the source of all of our hope. I turn to Him in prayer. In fact, I'm going to pray about this memory you have of your dad and ask God to heal that hurt."

"But it doesn't seem as if the prayers are helping."

"That's where faith comes in. Seeing with eyes of faith. St. Paul said, '...faith is being sure of what we hope for and certain of what we do not see.' God is at work Mary Helen, even if we don't understand right now." Aunt Laney patted me on the leg. "Listen, Rob has a charter in the morning, but he's trying to work it out for someone else to go. He's coming over here bright and early to take you back to Asheville."

Eyes of faith. Believing what we can't see. I grew sleepy, and I don't know when, but sometime I fell asleep. When I woke up it was dark, I was by myself, and the phone was ringing.

I heard Aunt Laney talking.

I jumped out of bed and bounded to the kitchen in a moment though I wasn't sure I wanted to know what was going on. Aunt Laney handed the phone to me.

"Mary Helen?"

"Mama?" The tears started again.

"Honey, I'm fine. The doctors say I'm stable now. It's going to be okay."

Relief washed over me. I glanced at Aunt Laney, and she was crying too. "Oh, Mama, I was so scared."

"I'm sorry, Mary Helen, but I'm fine now. Aunt Laney tells me you had a ride back to Asheville this morning, but there's no need. Stay there a little longer, and then we'll have a grand reunion when you return home."

After telling Mama I loved her, I hung up the phone and fell into Aunt Laney's arms. This time I cried for joy.

When I turned to go back to my bedroom, Mavis woke from sleeping in the green chair.

"What ... what's happening? Did I hear the phone ring?" She rubbed her eyes and then extended her hands.

I put my arms around her. "Mama's okay. She's okay. I talked to her."

She pulled me into the chair. "I'm glad, so very glad."

Aunt Laney came and stood beside us.

"Mama said not to come home just yet. She's fine. We probably need to call Rob," I said.

"I know. I'll do that in a minute. You go back to bed, get some sleep, and then we'll all go to the Sandcastle in a few hours and have breakfast."

Mavis had to go to work, but when Aunt Laney and I loaded in her big Cadillac convertible and put a tape of Beach Boys music in the tape player, the events of the night before started to drift away.

When we reached the Sandcastle, we found a parking space right in front and stepped up on the porch in time to see one of the beggar birds steal a piece of toast off of a gray-haired lady's plate. She did not take it lightly. She set after that bird swinging her pocketbook and yelling. She had to be at least ninety.

We went into the Sandcastle and took a seat, almost bowed over with laughter.

"You folks all right?" Heather said as she came to the table. She eyed us suspiciously, as if laughing too much could get you into trouble.

"We're just high on life," Aunt Laney said as she winked at me.

And we were. As I ate my Belgian waffle, a sense of resolution to the longtime feeling of abandonment seeped into my consciousness. Knowing where the sense of abandonment came from didn't make it go away, but it helped to understand. Maybe I'd talk to Mama about it when I returned home.

When we arrived back at Aunt Laney's after breakfast, with Mama's crisis behind me, I started thinking about Ralph again.

I plopped beside Aunt Laney on the red sofa. "I feel bad for Ralph. If after all this, Molly can't be found, I don't know what else anybody can do."

A quiet moment passed.

"Eyes of faith?" I said.

"Eyes of faith. Let's pray again," Aunt Laney said.

She dropped to her knees beside the sofa.

I didn't know what else to do but kneel on the floor beside her.

"Lord," she prayed, "we have done all we can do. You know our need. Please help Ralph get Molly back. We commit this matter to you in Jesus' name. Amen."

Aunt Laney stood up, went straight to the kitchen, and started fixing crab cakes for lunch with some meat Rob had brought by. We'd been so busy visiting Ralph and answering the phone that Aunt Laney had hardly been to the marsh for crabs.

There was a knock on the door. I peeked through the window and saw it was Sylvester. I opened the door.

"Well, if it isn't our famous author," Sylvester said as his bow tie bobbed.

Harold jumped up on me. "Hi, boy, it's good to see you."

"Is Laney available?"

"Come in and have a seat."

"I'll do that." Sylvester came in and reclined in the green chair. Harold sat obediently beside him, looking as if he were posing for a painting himself.

I let Aunt Laney know about Sylvester, and she went into the room wiping her hands on a kitchen towel.

"Came to retrieve the new painting," Sylvester said.

"It's in my bedroom. Mary Helen, could you bring it in?" Aunt Laney said to me.

I went and brought back the newest Laney Hanberry and leaned it against the sofa. I had to admit the marsh-scape was extraordinary.

Sylvester folded one arm across his chest and put the other hand on his cheek. "Oh, my," he said. "I must say, Laney, this is one of your best." He then proceeded to examine the canvas.

"It's been a challenge with all that's been going on to finish it. Mavis and Mary Helen never let me out of their sight." Aunt Laney winked at me.

"Yes, this is fine work. I'll contact my client immediately. When can I expect another?"

"I've already started, but you know I don't paint under pressure. I paint because I love it."

"I understand. It's the clients. They're anxious for their paintings."

The phone rang and Aunt Laney turned to answer. I heard her muffled talking.

I knelt and started to pet Harold. He rolled over on his back to allow me to scratch his stomach.

"My, you do have a way with animals, don't you?" Sylvester said.

I smiled as Aunt Laney came back into the room wearing a puzzled expression.

"I think we may have a lead. A woman up in Darien thinks she may have spotted Molly in the yard of one of their neighbors. Her description fits perfectly, and the dog appeared about the same time Molly disappeared."

"What do we do?" I said.

"Can I be of assistance?" Sylvester asked.

"We have to go to Darien to check out the story."

"I'll drive. Let's go." Sylvester waved for us to pass in front of him to the front door.

"Are you sure? This will take a chunk out of your day—two hours at least … and it may all be for nothing," Aunt Laney said.

"It will be my pleasure," Sylvester said in his genteel way.

"I'll get my purse, and put the crab meat in the refrigerator," Aunt Laney said and moved faster than I'd seen her go since I came to this island.

We had to travel about thirty minutes across the causeway and north up the Interstate. Thankfully, the caller had given Aunt Laney easy directions to her house. Aunt Laney's talk about eyes of faith kept floating across my mind. Could this be the answer to the prayers?

When we stepped out of the Mercedes at the address of the caller, we trekked up a gravel walkway and knocked on the front door.

"Are you Mrs. Carter?" Aunt Laney said to the middle-aged woman who answered.

"I am," she said.

"We're here about the dog."

I'll bet Mrs. Carter thought we were a strange bunch: a man in a bow tie with a Standard poodle, a woman in a tunic wildly emblazoned with sunflowers, and a teenage girl in shorts.

She took us through the house to the backyard. "I'm sorry I've been so long in calling. I was up in Savannah for a few days helping my daughter, who's just had a baby. I was going through the newspapers that my other neighbor had saved for me while I was gone and saw this article about

Molly. The picture sure looked a lot like the dog that showed up here a few weeks back."

When I stepped through the kitchen door, I was afraid to hope because I'd been wrong before, but the dog next door matched Molly exactly.

"Molly," I cried and raced over.

Molly perked up her ears and dashed to the fence whimpering and crying.

"It's her!" I cried. "It's her!" I rubbed her snout through the chain link. "Her spots are in all the right places."

Aunt Laney turned to Sylvester. "What should we do?"

"Call the local authorities, of course," he said. "Do you have a copy of the newspaper article?"

"Not with me," Aunt Laney said.

"I do," Mrs. Carter said. "I saved it because I thought we might need it. The folks next door aren't there right now, but they'll be home from work soon."

The police arrived shortly, and we showed them the newspaper article. Then we demonstrated that Molly came to me when I called her. The police had not been there ten minutes before a man pulled in the driveway of the house next door.

"They never have been good neighbors," Mrs. Carter said. "They don't recycle or anything, and they play their music way too loud."

The police talked to the man, showed them the article, asked questions, and eventually the truth came out. His two teenage sons had brought the dog home one day, saying they'd found it abandoned on the side of the Interstate. No way could Molly have gotten there in the time Ralph was gone. When the sons came home, the police talked to them, and they confessed they'd seen the dog at the produce stand, thought she'd make a good pet, and decided to take her.

After they'd obtained all the information they needed, the police let us put Molly in the car and take her with us. They took the two sons to the police station.

Molly jumped in with Harold, and I squeezed between them on the back seat. I could hardly believe it.

Molly was going home.

Chapter Thirty

The Greatness of God

"Girl, is that you?" Ralph's eyelids flittered open as Molly lay on his hospital bed licking his face. "Is it really you?" he whispered as a nurse helped Molly move closer to him. Ralph lifted a weak hand and stroked her head.

Molly's presence in his room was strictly against the rules, but Dr. Gunn knew how important she was to his recovery and asked all the hospital personnel involved to turn their heads when she went by. It didn't hurt that he was also the chief of staff.

"I reckoned I'd never see you again," Ralph said as tears streamed down his face.

Pretty much everybody in the room was crying by that point. Dr. Gunn even acted as if he had a speck in his eye.

"How'd you find her?" Ralph whispered, scanning from face to face searching for an answer.

Aunt Laney pointed at me. "Mary Helen wrote a letter to the editor of the Brunswick paper, and he ran it on the front page along with a lookalike picture of Molly."

"I have a copy of it somewhere," Ralph's nurse said and left the room.

"Someone saw the dog and called us," Aunt Laney said. "It's that simple, but it would have never happened without Mary Helen."

"I sure do thank you, missy." He held Molly's face in his hands and gazed at her. "How're we ever going to thank the gal who found you, Molly?" Ralph lay back on the pillow, his eyes twitching from side to side—a little of the old Ralph showing through. "I know, free tomaters for life!"

I didn't know what to say, especially to the tomato part, but Aunt Laney started laughing, and then pretty much everybody joined in. Even Ralph managed a giggle and then a huge cough. About that time the nurse came in with the newspaper article.

"I saw this in the paper and saved it, but we all believed it best to wait for developments before we showed it to you."

Ralph admired the picture on the page. "Somebody hand me my glasses there on that table." Sylvester handed the glasses to Ralph. As Ralph began reading the letter, the tears started again. "No, ma'am, I don't know how I'll ever thank you, 'cause havin' Molly back is about the best thing that's happened to me in a long time." He barely said the words before he collapsed against his pillow.

"Speaking of dogs, I think I'd better be going." Sylvester checked his watch. "Since I never leave Harold in the car because of heat, we've left him in the charge of a parking attendant downstairs who was kind enough to dog sit for us. But he's likely to have more to do than watch Harold."

"That means we have to go too, because Sylvester took us to retrieve Molly." Aunt Laney moved toward Ralph.

Ralph weakly extended his hand to Sylvester, "Much obliged for your part in all of this."

"My pleasure," Sylvester said, shaking Ralph's hand.

Aunt Laney gave Ralph a peck on the forehead, "Ben said you're having great days at the stand, and a farmer in Valdosta even donated produce to help out."

"I can't get over how big-hearted folks have been." Ralph gave Molly one last hug and lay back against his pillows. "See you soon, girl."

I moved over to help put Molly back on the floor. I snapped a leash on her collar and then reached over and gave Ralph a hug. I started to pull away but he held me and gazed at me with tear-filled eyes. "I meant what I said, missy. Someday I'll think of a way to thank you."

"No thanks needed, Ralph. It was thanks enough to find Molly." I gave Molly a pat on the head.

"She'll stay with us until you feel like coming home," Aunt Laney said as she gave Ralph a hug.

Stepping from the hospital into the warmth of a July evening, I felt a satisfaction unlike I'd ever known before, a fulfillment beyond any I'd ever imagined.

As we crossed back over the causeway to the island, I scanned a marsh lit by the glow of a setting sun and remembered Aunt Laney's simple prayer earlier that day. "Build me a nest on the greatness of God," her nest painting said. It seemed something great had happened that day, and it was definitely bigger than I or any letter I'd written.

It was all I could do to wait until Mama called that evening so I could tell her all about Molly coming home.

I could hear sniffling on the other end of the phone, as if she was crying. "This is such a wonderful thing you helped to do. I'm proud of you."

Later, Molly perched on my bed, her ears perked up, peering at me with what seemed to be grateful eyes. It was a little hard to concentrate with all the excitement of the day.

"You're glad to be home, aren't you, girl? Hopefully in a few days you'll really be home, because I think Ralph is going to be fine now." Molly leaned over and gave me an approving lick on my arm, and I petted her fluffy sides.

I was in the kitchen the next afternoon looking for a drink, because I was hot and thirsty. I opened the refrigerator and spotted a pitcher of lemonade Aunt Laney had made the night before. Just then, Aunt Laney came into the kitchen from out back. She'd been cleaning her trap from our crabbing and painting trip to the marsh that morning.

"I think I'll call Mavis," she said as she stepped to the phone.

I took out the lemonade pitcher, opened the cupboard, and took down a glass.

"Mavis, how about coming over tonight to help us celebrate Molly's return?" Aunt Laney said into the receiver and then waited for a response. "What do you mean you already have plans? So what are you up to? Why do you have to be so clandestine?"

Aunt Laney had her back to me and twirled the telephone cord with her finger.

"This is all very cryptic, Mavis, but have it your way. Maybe another night." She hung up the phone.

I reached into the freezer, took out an ice-cube tray, and dropped the ice in my glass. "Would you like some?" I said to Aunt Laney and pointed to the lemonade pitcher.

"No, thanks," she said, a quizzical expression on her face. "Did you hear that? Mavis has other plans. What's this about plans all of a sudden?"

She settled on one of the dinette chairs. "Do you think I've made her mad?"

"I'm sure you haven't. Maybe she does have other plans. A date or something." I took a sip of lemonade.

"Mavis, a date? Are you kidding? She hasn't had a date since … since forever. But come to think of it, she has dyed her hair and has been dressing spiffier than usual."

"I thought she just bought a few new clothes and decided to touch up the gray."

"Mavis is a tightwad. If she's bought new clothes, there has to be a reason for it. So there could be a man involved. But who? Who could she be interested in?"

"Beats me," I said as I drained the lemonade from the glass.

"Maybe one of the men who comes to the library."

"No, couldn't be. She talks about old Mr. Mayberry who comes in and tries to flirt with her. She says he always has a toothpick in his mouth. She can't stand that." I rinsed my glass and put it in the dish drainer by the sink. "Gotta go," I said.

"Where?"

"I have a date," I said with a smile.

"Very funny. Fine, go on and leave me to solve this by myself."

"I will." I left the kitchen, grabbed my backpack from my bedroom, and headed outside to my bicycle.

*

Molly trotted along beside me on my bicycle, and Ben started running toward us as soon as we came into his view.

"You found Molly! You found Molly!" he shouted while running.

As soon as I drew close, I threw my bicycle down and we hugged. Molly jumped on us and licked us. I pulled away. "How'd you find out?"

"If you stuck around a little bit longer, you'd find out this is a small island. Sylvester called Dad from his car phone after he dropped you folks off yesterday, and then Laney called, and then Florence, and then … I don't know who else. The phone rang off the hook at the charter service. Dad said he just about had to let the customers help themselves." Ben paused a moment and grew more solemn. "I heard your mom got really sick too," Ben said. "I'm glad she's better."

We sauntered over to a grassy area and found a place to sit. "It was scary, but she pulled through."

"I'm glad." Ben had brought Harold along for an outing, so we threw the ball for him a while and marveled at how much more skilled he had gotten at retrieving in the few short sessions we'd had with him. Molly had no interest in fetching. She collapsed at our feet.

"How have you liked working at Ralph's stand?" I said as Ben continued to throw the greenish-yellow tennis ball. I lay back on the cool grass.

"I like it. I've learned a lot."

"It's been a big help to Ralph. You know, he's had an amazing recovery in the last couple of days since Molly came back. Dr. Gunn called it a miracle."

"Dad told me. I'm kind of jealous you're keeping Molly until Ralph comes home."

Harold came back and nudged me with his snout. I sat up and took the ball out of his mouth as Molly nipped at my hand. "It's been great. She sleeps on my bed at night. Hey, are you going to Mrs. Kirby's party for Ralph?" I threw the ball again. Molly suddenly found fetching an appealing option and outran Harold for the ball.

"Are you kidding? I definitely want to be there for Ralph, plus I want to see that saltwater aquarium she has."

"We don't know the exact date yet, but we think the doctor is going to let Ralph go home by Wednesday, so she's kind of planning it for this weekend."

"It's kind of her."

"She wanted to help him, and she was disappointed about the billboard results, so she's doing this." I paused a minute, not really wanting to say the next words. "You know I'm leaving in a couple of weeks. Amy's driving down and spending the night so she can take me back."

Molly brought the ball to Ben. "Yeah, I know." He took the ball and held it in his hand.

I summoned my courage. "I never imagined I'd feel this way, but I'm going to miss this place. I'm going to miss you."

"I'm gonna miss you, too." Ben took his hand and placed it on top of mine. I turned my hand over, and we held tight. "I guess I realized during the dictionary reading that I like you more than a friend. Then while I was in Valdosta, I missed you so much."

"I know what you mean. It was a sickening feeling when I found out you were gone for a week, like somebody knocked the air out of me."

"Hey, maybe you could visit again, next summer. You and your mom ..."

"Maybe I could." The idea brought me hope. "And maybe"—I looked at Ben—"you and your dad could come visit us in Asheville sometime. Sometime during the winter. That'd be great wouldn't it? Maybe at Christmas."

Neither one of us spoke, and I realized in the moments that passed between us that I could add another person to my list of people with whom I could be quiet.

Harold licked me in the face. "I'll miss you, boy, and Aunt Laney, Mavis, Ralph ..." Molly loped over to me and fell across my lap. "And you too, girl."

*

Later that night, when I was saying goodnight to Aunt Laney, I remembered something. "Aunt Laney, I have to leave pretty soon, and I almost forgot to ask you about the line in Sidney Lanier's letter. The one about chestnut trees. Remember?"

Aunt Laney put aside the book she was reading. "That's right, I didn't ever finish that story. I'm glad you remembered. Come sit here." She smoothed out a place on the quilt covering her bed.

I crossed over and perched on the edge of her bed.

"Remember I told you how Mr. Lanier had to come to Brunswick for his health and stayed with the Johnston family?"

"Sure, I remember. You said he was inspired to write 'The Marshes of Glynn' while in Brunswick."

"That's right. It seems he wrote that poem while sitting under a chestnut tree." Aunt Laney turned her eyes to the fading light flickering through the window. "After he returned home, he wrote Mr. Johnston and signed it by saying, 'Give my love to the chestnut trees.'" Aunt Laney rearranged her pillows.

"So he loved the chestnut trees because he wrote his best poem under one?"

"Right. I think he felt like the beauty of that tree helped him do his best work." She stopped for a moment and in her eyes I saw she'd gone far away. "My mama and grandmamma were like chestnut trees to me."

"How do you mean?"

"By the arching limbs of their beautiful lives, they helped me find that I wanted to teach literature and paint." Aunt Laney reached for the volume of Sidney Lanier poems on her bedside. "My mama even helped me by

186

naming me Lanier. If I ever had a daughter, I was going to name her Lanier too." A flicker of grief crossed her eyes. "Does this make any sense?"

I nodded in agreement. "It makes perfect sense."

"But as important as all that is, it's not the most important gift my mama gave me."

I waited as Aunt Laney paused once more.

"Someone once said that Sidney Lanier was the most Christ-like man they'd ever known. I could say that of my mama too. She made me want to know Christ."

A tear slipped down my cheek as I considered Aunt Laney building her "nest on the greatness of God." I understood now. She settled back in her bed and closed her eyes. I slipped out the door and went into the front room. I stood before the nest painting a while and then went to my bedroom.

Chapter Thirty-One

F-o-r-e-v-e-r

The foamy waves lapped at my toes as I sat on the glittering sand of East Beach. The sandcastle Ben and I had built stood as a monument to two hours of digging, putting sand in plastic buckets, and dumping them out. I'd never built a sandcastle before. What would have seemed a stupid thing to do when I first arrived on the island now appeared glorious.

"Not too bad," Ben said as he seemed to stand back to take in the full effect. "I hate to say it, but the tide's going to grab our creation pretty soon."

"After all that work? I thought the tide was going out."

"Uh uh. Coming in." Ben started gathering our tools together. "Haven't you noticed the waves edging closer?"

"Not really. You know, I've not come to the beach much this summer because of Aunt Laney's heart business and Molly's disappearance. This is fun, but it sure is hot." I stood up, brushed sand from my legs, and went back to my beach towel and stretched out. "Your grandfather making the chestnut pen for Aunt Laney is a pretty neat story."

"Yeah." He nodded. "It really is." Ben dropped to his towel and leaned back.

I caught a glimpse of a boat coming into the channel, so I sat up to watch, "Man, that's a big ship."

Ben peered out to sea. "Sure is. It's been a while since I saw a freighter that large come through." We watched the massive gray ship in silence for a while as it cruised along and then we lay back down. Sounds of gulls overhead and children's laughter drifted in the hot breeze. A few moments went by, and I heard a scream. I bolted up and a giant wave smacked me right in the face. I struggled to get my bearings as the water rose around me. I glanced up and down the beach and saw people grabbing children, sending bags and purses airborne toward the dunes.

"My backpack," I cried as I spit out water.

"I don't see it," Ben shouted back.

"The pen, the pen's in the backpack."

The water receded quickly, and we, like everyone else on East Beach, began trying to gather our gear together. I looked out to sea and saw colors bobbing in the distance. I desperately hoped none of the items was my backpack. Our castle-building tools were gone. Ben's body board was gone. Our beach towels were buried, and our exquisite castle had been transformed into a wet blob weeping rivulets of water down its sides. As I stooped to dig out my dripping beach towel, I moaned, "Ben, what will I tell Aunt Laney if I lost the chestnut pen?"

"The pen's not lost yet," Ben said. "Let's walk down the beach. The current's moving south, so maybe we'll find it if we walk toward the Village."

"What happened? Why did that huge wave come in all of a sudden?"

"Yeah, like a tsunami. Remember that ship? I've seen it happen before. When a big ship comes into the channel, It sometimes causes an unexpected surge like that. I don't know why I didn't think about it. Dad once lost a camera."

Beach people poked around in the sand for their belongings. We tried to maneuver around half-buried beach chairs and cooler lids.

"I'll die if I've lost that pen," I said.

"Don't do that." Ben gave me one of his freckle-faced smiles and extended his upturned palm to me. I took it, and we continued on hand-in-hand.

We traveled as far as the lighthouse and decided we'd gone far enough. We turned and started back. I tried hard not to give in to despair about losing the pen, but the image of Aunt Laney's disappointed face kept coming to my mind. "I'm remembering what Aunt Laney said about 'eyes of faith.' It's not exactly easy. It's a lot easier to give up."

Ben gave me a smile. "Yeah."

We plodded back up the beach, searching the edge of the dunes for any sign of red. We had to be careful, because we couldn't climb on the dunes. Sea turtles nested there, and we didn't want to destroy any eggs. In our search we came up with a red plastic cup, a bandana, and the bottom to a woman's red swimsuit.

I held up the sandy swimsuit. "I hope the person was already out of it before the big wave came."

Even in the face of the impending disaster of the pen, we both laughed.

We trudged on, and as we came in sight of the place we had started, I spied a bit of red in some sea grass. "There," I cried. I sprinted toward the dunes and pulled my red backpack out of the sand. "It's hardly wet." I opened it up and there was the pen, nestled in the bottom of the pack. I collapsed on the sand. "I'm so relieved."

Ben patted me on the back. "Me too."

*

We'd barely stepped through the door before Aunt Laney called out to us.

"Rob called and wanted to know how you two were." She came from the kitchen, wiping her hands on a towel. "He said there was a big surge at the beach today because of a ship coming in."

"There was. We lost the sandcastle tools and the body board, but otherwise we're fine." I didn't mention the almost-lost pen. Aunt Laney's summer had already been exciting enough.

"You might want to call your dad to let him know you're okay," Aunt Laney said to Ben as she put the dishtowel back in the kitchen.

"Sure," he said, and went to the phone.

While Ben made the phone call, I took the Scrabble board out. "Aunt Laney, do you want to play Scrabble?"

"Not this evening. I have to put the final strokes on a painting. I appreciate Sylvester acting as my agent, but I don't like the pressure of having people waiting on me."

"Do you think Mavis would want to play?"

"She told me at church this morning that she had a prior commitment this afternoon. I sure wish I knew what she was up to."

"I guess it's just Ben and me then."

After Ben hung up the phone, he headed over to the kitchen table, sat down, and we drew for who started first. He won.

"Have you read any good dictionary words lately?" he said.

"Not really."

Ben went first with e-v-e-r.

Not such a great word for Ben, but he still scored fourteen points.

The best I could do was use Ben's r and make r-o-s-e. I scored only six.

Ben added f-o-r to his e-v-e-r to make f-o-r-e-v-e-r and received seventeen points.

I used the s in r-o-s-e to make s-u-n. I only added three to my tally.

Ben paused a minute before he laid down his tiles. His blue eyes met mine. He used the v in f-o-r-e-v-e-r and spelled aloud, "l-o-v-e." I started to enter his seven point score and then looked back at the horizontal f-o-r-e-v-e-r and the vertical l-o-v-e. Tears welled in my eyes. Then I studied my rack, picked up three letters, and added them to the n in s-u-n.

I'd heard it often at Aunt Laney's church. "A-M-E-N," I spelled aloud.

Ben smiled.

Aunt Laney came to the kitchen from her bedroom. "Who's winning?" she said.

"We both are," I said, as I refilled my rack with tiles.

*

That night as I read before going to sleep, a sound of movement from the purple room distracted me. Musical notes began to sound from the piano. Aunt Laney was playing "Into the Woods," in such an uncharacteristically soft way, if I hadn't known otherwise, I never would have guessed the music was coming from her. The haunting minor melody filled my bedroom and subsided after a few minutes. Footsteps padded past my door. Aunt Laney's bedroom door closed and her box springs sounded their familiar squeak as she lay down.

Chapter Thirty-Two

Indebted to the Lot of You

"Sure is kindhearted of you, Mrs. Kirby," Ralph said as he rested in his wheelchair on Kathleen Kirby's patio and watched Molly and Muffin play on her clipped green lawn. "I do believe them dogs is sisters. Look out there at how they're gettin' along."

"I think you may be right, Ralph," Mrs. Kirby said, beaming.

I took another sip of my lemonade, went inside, and found Ben and Rob mesmerized by the saltwater aquarium.

"Wow," Ben said, his eyes like saucers. He pointed to an orange and white striped fish. "Do you know what that is? A clown fish."

"Mary Helen, come in here a minute, please," Aunt Laney called, interrupting.

I moved into the hallway. She nodded to her left as she offered me a meatball appetizer. "What do you know about that?" she whispered.

I turned my eyes in the direction of her nod and saw Mavis and Sylvester holding hands. No way. "I don't know anything." And I didn't.

"Imagine, we've been friends for such a long time, and I didn't have an inkling those two were seeing each other," Aunt Laney said, and then she laughed. "Can you imagine a more unlikely couple? So that's what all the plans and lunches have been about. She was going to straighten him out on my behalf. It appears she might have been sidetracked. Mavis Trueblood and Sylvester Myers. Who would have guessed?"

I think I was in shock. Mavis was in a red dress tonight, and Sylvester wore a matching red bowtie.

"All right, can I have everyone's attention?" Mrs. Kirby said as she tapped on a glass with a knife. "Could you make your way into the foyer?"

We did as we were told. I couldn't believe how many people were there. Mrs. Kirby must have invited the whole town. Aunt Laney said after the billboard and newspaper article, everyone on the island felt like Ralph was a relative, or at least some kind of celebrity. I pushed past the crowd and took a perch on the bottom step of the curved staircase in the marble foyer.

"Ralph wanted me to make sure I thanked everyone who helped watch his stand, sent him letters, and brought him flowers while he was in the hospital. He especially wants to thank Dr. Gunn and his fine staff who took such excellent care of him."

Mrs. Kirby turned to me, "He gives special thanks to you, Mary Helen, for writing the letter that eventually led to Molly being found."

I bit my lip because I felt like I might cry. Ralph nodded at me and said, "I ain't much on makin' speeches, but like Mrs. Kirby said, I'm indebted to the lot of you for all you've done. Thank you."

"Ralph, I have a little gift for you," Aunt Laney said. "Sort of a welcome home gift for you and Molly." Aunt Laney pulled a package off the credenza in the foyer and handed it to Ralph.

"Present? Why, I declare." He started to pull open the paper. "Reckon what it is, Molly?" he said, looking at the dog gazing happily at him. When he finally pulled the paper away, we all saw the back of a framed canvas. Ralph's eyes crinkled and a big smile erupted. "It's Molly, it's my Molly."

Ralph turned the canvas around, and sure enough, Aunt Laney had rendered an absolutely striking likeness of Molly.

"When did you find time to paint her?" I leaned over and asked.

"I worked all along while we were waiting to find her," Aunt Laney said.

"I'm gonna hang it over my mantelpiece," Ralph said and then paused a moment. "Wait a minute, I ain't got no mantelpiece."

The place erupted into laughter.

"Glad you like it," Aunt Laney said, giggling so hard I had that paramedic sensation again.

We all clapped, and Molly and Muffin barked their agreement. Out of the corner of my eye, I could see Sylvester and Mavis slipping out the front door. I elbowed Aunt Laney. Her eyes grew wide; she gasped and put her hand to her mouth in shock. We both resumed laughing.

*

I nestled the copy of *Moby Dick* in the bottom of my suitcase next to a stack of underwear. I put the Eugenia Price book in my backpack, hoping that I'd at last be able to read it on my way back home. Wrapped in some T-shirts for protection, I placed the blue vase beside *Moby Dick*. Scanning the room to see if I'd left anything, I pulled my journal out from under the pillow. My dad's and my grandmother's letters were safely tucked inside, along with the newspaper clipping of my article about Molly. Aunt Laney had laminated it so I could show my friends who hadn't read the story back in Asheville. I'd already returned the chestnut pen to Aunt Laney and thanked her for letting me use it and for telling me the story. Then there was the Polaroid of Wallace perched on my head that Ben took when I first came.

A Polaroid. Of course. I hurried from my bedroom and dialed Ben. "Didn't you say you had a Polaroid camera like the one at the bait shop?"

"Sure," he said.

"Would you bring it when you come tomorrow?"

"I'll buy a new package of film."

Chapter Thirty-Three

Give My Love to the Chestnut Trees

"Mary Helen, it's about time to go," Amy said as she rested in the green chair, her purse in her lap.

"I know." I stood from the red sofa. Amy had been good enough to drive to St. Simons to get me and take me back to Asheville. She'd spent the night, but I knew we needed to get on the road so we wouldn't arrive in Asheville too late.

"Before we leave, I want to take a picture of everyone. Ben has brought his Polaroid. Amy, do you mind?" I handed the camera to her.

"Not a bit." She took the camera and peered through the viewfinder. "Now everyone, line up in front the painting there. Yes, that's about right. Now smile."

Aunt Laney, Mavis, Ben, Ralph, Sylvester, Harold, Molly and I all tried to line up. There didn't seem to be enough room. Amy kept moving us around.

"Won't work," Amy said. "I can't fit you all in, and somebody has to make those dogs sit still. They're both writhing. Why don't we go outside for a minute and see if we can't do it there?"

Everybody filed outside and stood on the porch and steps.

"That's better," Amy said as she aimed the camera at us. "Now I can see everyone."

She took three shots and handed them to me.

"Hey, I want one," Mavis said.

"Me, too," Ralph said.

Amy wound up using Ben's entire package of film so that everyone could have a copy, and then she tapped her watch. "Now we must go." She handed the camera back to Ben.

I turned to Aunt Laney. "Thanks, Aunt Laney, for everything. I'm glad I came." I reached out to embrace her, and then Mavis stood beside me and put her arms around me too.

"You come back next summer and stay a while and bring your mama," Aunt Laney said.

"I will."

Next Ben gave me an awkward hug. "I have something for you." He turned to a bag sitting beside the steps and pulled out a Scrabble game. I took it from him and tried not to cry. Ben said, "We'll talk on the phone and write. Next summer for sure, okay? Oh, and send me pictures of snow if we don't make it for Christmas."

"Next summer."

"I enjoyed our little adventure finding Molly." Sylvester shook my hand.

Harold jumped on me, and I gave him a hug. Molly got jealous and pawed at me, wanting her share of attention.

Ralph wrapped his arms around me. "Missy, you saved my life."

I smiled and wiped away tears.

Once more, I turned to Aunt Laney and our eyes met. She reached out to me and held me tight, and this time I didn't try to wiggle free like I did the first time we'd met.

"I'm really going to miss you," I said.

"Thank you for letting me share my stories with you. I hope I didn't bore you too much."

I pulled away, wiped my eyes again, and picked up my suitcase.

Aunt Laney extended a paper bag to me. "I packed a few snacks for you folks."

I took it, and Amy and I headed for the car.

*

The trip back over the causeway was bittersweet; two opposite feelings again. The longing to see Mama and be home again was great inside me. I could almost smell the evergreens of the mountains, but I also wanted to run back to Aunt Laney's house, and sit in front of the eyeball painting while she ate her crab cakes. I wanted to go down to the village and visit with Wallace and Ben. I wished I could take Ralph, Molly, Mavis, Harold, and Sylvester with me. I wanted to bike again with Ben and feel the breeze through my hair and smell the scent of the marsh. I wanted to sit at the marsh border, watch Aunt Laney paint, feel the prickly grass, and listen to her stories about Sidney Lanier.

As we crossed over the wide expanse of the marsh, I rolled down the window and inhaled deeply. I gazed behind me and followed the waving marsh until it seemed to touch the sky. I tried as hard as I could to take a Polaroid with my mind, so I could remember this place when I was lying in my bed at night deep in the North Carolina mountains.

*

"Mary Helen, why don't you pull out the bag Aunt Laney sent? I'm getting a little hungry," Amy said.

We'd been on the road a few hours, and my stomach was beginning to growl, too.

I reached for the bag in the back seat, opened it, and pulled out a sandwich. Then I saw a strange object in the bag. I reached in and pulled out the chestnut pen.

"How did that get in there?" she said.

"Aunt Laney, I guess."

"What an unusual pen. I wonder where it came from and why she put it in the bag."

"It's a long story."

"And we still have a long way to go," Amy said.

*

"Mary Helen," Mama cried as I came into the house.

I dropped my backpack and flew into her arms. "Mama, it's good to be home." I pulled away and visually examined her. Her usual brown shoulder length hair had been cut to a bob. "What happened to your hair?"

Mama patted her head. "My hair fell out, but don't you think this wig is charming? I've always wanted to wear my hair short like this but never had the courage. Now when my hair grows back I can wear it like this anytime."

I knew Mama was trying to find something positive to say. Her eyes void of eyelashes and eyebrows were ringed with dark circles. Her cotton print sundress hung on her. "How are you feeling?" I said.

197

"I'm sleeping better now. Overall, I think I'm doing much better. Wouldn't you say, Amy?"

"Definitely. Much better," Amy said as she dropped the last of my bags on the living room floor.

"So tell me everything about your stay with Aunt Laney," Mama said.

I glanced at Amy, who'd been brought up to speed during her stay at Aunt Laney's and on the way home.

"It's too long a story to start tonight. Let's all get some rest, and you can tell it in the morning," Amy said.

Mama put her arm around me. "It's good to have you home."

The next morning after breakfast, Mama said she could wait no longer to find out what happened during the summer. So I began my story.

"Oh, my," she said much later. "You've had quite an adventure this summer."

"I don't think she's the girl you left in St. Simons two months ago," Amy said.

"I guess not." It seemed to me that Mama breathed a sigh of relief, as if a burden she'd been carrying a long time had been lifted.

"Do you need anything, Mama?" I said as I left the table.

"Not a thing, but thanks for asking."

I spent all day catching up with friends, and Leslie came over and helped me unpack.

"No way," she said after I'd filled in the gaps from my letters. "I didn't even get to go to camp. It's not fair." She threw herself on my bed and propped up on my pillows. Her dark hair contrasted even more with her pale skin than it normally did.

"You had a great summer," she said.

"I did, but I sure didn't expect to. Strange how things work out sometimes. Did I tell you about Ben?"

"Yes, you mentioned him." Leslie smiled.

A grin spread across my face.

Leslie's eyes narrowed. "Okay, spill it. I want to know every detail. Remember, I was sick most of the summer, so I need a little excitement."

I plopped on the bed beside her and started from the very beginning, when I first met Ben outside the bait shop.

"That's so sweet. Do you think you'll ever see him again?"

"I hope I'll see him next summer."

"Next summer? You're going back?"

"Maybe we all can go back. Maybe you can come with me and Mama to visit Aunt Laney."

"That would definitely be an improvement over Camp Whitestone and mono." Leslie paused as a thoughtful look crossed her face. "Yes, I think I'd like to visit Aunt Laney a lot."

*

I lay on the peony bed writing in my journal that evening. The letter from my dad fell out, and as I picked it up, I realized there was something I needed to do. So I went to my desk, and lifted a couple of sheets of stationery and an envelope from the top drawer. I went back to my bed, thought a few minutes about how to compose the letter, and then began to write the words endued with the blessing of another generation:

Dear Aunt Laney,

It was hard to come back to Asheville after being on St. Simons with you. Just like my dad, I dreamed about the marsh for days after I got back. It's so difficult to explain to anyone else why I love it so much …

*

"So when did you become such a big Scrabble player?" Mama asked, raising what would have been her eyebrows as I set up the Scrabble board on her bed. It had been a week since I returned from Aunt Laney's, and I was actually beginning to miss playing with these tiles. Mama felt a little tired that evening, so Amy and I set up in the bedroom. It was a bit of a problem, though, because everybody had to be careful not to shake the bed or we'd have alphabet jumble.

"After Aunt Laney had her heart episode, we started playing Scrabble on Sundays. I didn't like it at first, but I guess it grows on you." I gave Mama and Amy their racks, and then we drew for who went first. I drew a c, so that put me leading off.

I smiled as I put down my letters on the board. "H-o-m-e," I spelled. I looked up and smiled at Mama, and her eyes seemed to crinkle with pleasure.

"*Home*," she said as she reached over and touched my arm. I logged my eighteen points. I loved double word scores.

Amy spelled h-a-v-e. Mama spelled t-r-e-a-t-s. Mama was proud of the ten points she received for it. I didn't want to disillusion her by sharing a few of the scores I'd seen folks accumulate.

I led off the second round with the word e-v-e-n. Amy arranged six letters to form s-t-e-a-m-s, and Mama finished with e-x-t-r-a. I was kind of missing words like s-p-r-a-c-h-g-e-f-ü-h-l, c-o-e-v-a-l, and y-a-p-ok.

I spelled s-h-e-e-t, Amy put down g-r-a-n-d, Mama pulled out tiles for w-i-t, although it hardly registered with me, because when Amy spelled g-r-a-n-d, I saw an enormous opportunity.

"Mary Helen, did you tally my score?" Mama said interrupting my thoughts.

"Oh yes, w-i-t, that's eight points. I wrote down the score."

"Not bad for three letters," Mama said.

I studied and rechecked my letters to make sure that I was right before I put my tiles down.

"Your turn," Mama said to me.

A grin crept across my face. I started adding my letters to Amy's g-r-a-n-d, bridging the gap to a t on the end of s-h-e-e-t, which I'd spelled earlier. With confidence I spelled, "G-r-a-n-d-i-l-o-q-u-e-n-t."

"*Grandiloquent?*" Mama said. "Where in the world did you learn a word like that, and what does it mean?"

"Ben and I studied the GRs together the last week I was in St. Simons. One of the meanings Webster's gives it is 'using high-sounding language.'"

"When did you get to be so *grandiloquent?*" Amy said, laughing.

Mama even joined in the merriment until I told them the rule about fifty extra points if you used all your letters in one turn.

"Are you sure?" Amy said, the smile sliding from her face. "I've never heard that before."

"I'm sure. Aunt Laney did it, plus it says so right here on the box. See?" I held the box up for Amy to read.

She studied it a few minutes. "You're right. How many is that anyway?"

I started to count. "Six for grand, plus eighteen for the rest of the letters. That's twenty-four. Oh, wait. The word covers two triple word scores. I have to check the rules." I picked up the box lid and read. "Here, 'If a word is formed that covers two premium word squares, the score is doubled and then re-doubled (four times letter count), or tripled and re-tripled (nine times the letter count) as the case may be.' Wow. Nine times the letter count. Let me multiply that out."

I turned the score pad over and multiplied nine times twenty-four. That equaled two hundred and sixteen plus fifty points for using all my letters. I couldn't believe it.

"Two hundred and sixty six points," I said, beaming. "Wait until I write Aunt Laney and Ben about this."

Amy stared at me, unbelieving, and then put her rack on the bed. "Do you have Monopoly?" she said.

I sure knew how she felt. "Don't worry, Amy, you need to study the dictionary a little bit."

"Sure," she said dryly.

The phone rang on Mama's bedside table, and I answered it.

"Hello, is this Mary Helen?"

"Yes."

It sounded like Mavis. "This is Mavis. Honey, I have some bad news."

"Oh no."

"It's Laney. She collapsed again this morning. I'm afraid she didn't make it this time."

A cry exploded inside of me. "She didn't make it. Do you mean she's dead?" I tried to breathe. Amy came to me and put her arm around my shoulders.

"Mary Helen, when she collapsed the first time I talked to the doctor, and he said her heart was worn out. She wasn't a candidate for a heart transplant, and he didn't know how long she had."

I couldn't believe this. I shook with sobs and choked out, "I didn't know."

"I decided not to tell you. Laney knew her time was short. She told me after you left it was about the best summer of her life because of you. She received the thank-you letter you wrote just a couple of days before she died. It sure did mean a lot to her."

I wiped my face with a tissue Amy handed to me. Then I felt Mama's hands on me. She'd crawled out of bed and put her head on my shoulder and her arms around my waist.

Mavis went on. "She told me that if anything happened to her she wanted you to have the gloxinia painting and the nest painting that hung over the sofa. I'll send them out soon. Her will specified that the rest of her estate would be divided between the church and the art foundation in the county, so that every child who wants to, even the ones who can't afford it, can have an art-filled life."

"Thank you," I managed to say as I collapsed on the floor taking Mama and Amy with me.

"And Mary Helen?"

"Yes?"

"She died at the marsh."

I smiled through my tears, remembering Aunt Laney's wish that she die gazing at the marsh she loved so much.

Mavis continued, "Everyone here sends their love to you. Don't worry about coming to the funeral. Laney always wanted a short service. 'No fanfare,' she used to say."

"All right." I pulled another tissue out of a box on Mama's table.

"Goodbye, honey," Mavis said.

"Goodbye," I said as I stood up and put the phone back on Mama's table. I helped Mama off the floor and saw she'd been crying too. We stood for a minute with our arms wrapped around each other. After a moment, I pulled away from her.

"Thank you for sending me there. I would've hated to have missed Aunt Laney."

"You're welcome, my dear. You're welcome."

I turned and went upstairs to my room, picked up the chestnut pen lying on my bedside table, and closed my fingers around it. I sat with my journal and wrote a prayer through my tears, "Dear Lord, thank you for the wonderful gift of the chestnut tree in my life, Grace Lanier Hanberry."

Chapter Thirty-Four

Beloved Marsh

"So you see, the pen can never be replaced," I say to the cyclist.

"I'm so sorry." Tears stream down her face.

I pat her on the back. "I'm sorry too, but it was an accident after all. There's nothing to be done about it. "

"But what ever happened to your mom and Ben and ..."

A silver SUV pulls up and distracts us both from our conversation.

"Mama, Mama."

I bend and hug the two little girls who've sprung from the car. Then I get a lavish licking from our poodle.

I turn back to the cyclist. "After all this time you've spent listening to my story, I'm sorry, I don't even know your name."

"Melissa. My name is Melissa."

"Melissa, these are my girls, Laura and Lanier. And this is my mother, Laura Campbell," I say as I gesture toward Mama, who's exited the vehicle and is walking toward us.

The cyclist glances quickly toward me and then back to the girls and Mama. "I'm glad to meet all of you," she says and embraces them. "Campbell?" she says as she looks back at me.

"Yes, Mama found she loved Archie Campbell's jokes and dazzling smile too, when she met him here the next summer after Aunt Laney died. She married him three months later, and we moved here."

"He keeps me laughing," Mama says.

"I've heard," Melissa responds.

"Hey, I thought we were all ready to go eat brunch at the Sandcastle," a husky voice says from the other side of the car.

"And Melissa, this is my husband, Ben," I say as he strides toward us. "Ben, this is Melissa. We met by accident this morning." I smile at her and see her tears are pouring. Mama pulls a tissue out of her pocket and hands it to her.

"Ben, I've heard so much about you," Melissa says as she dabs her eyes.

"Oh, well, now that's scary. I hope we can still be friends."

"I think we already are," she says.

"Well, since we're such good friends, why don't you join us for brunch? We have a bike rack on the back of the car."

"Yes, you should since you've heard our stories," I say in agreement.

Sylvester nudges my leg. I shoo him away. "We'll help you load the bike."

The dog persists with his cold wet nose on my leg. I look down annoyed. "Sylvester, what is it?" Then I see why he's nudging me. "Oh, Sylvester," I stoop and take the chestnut pen from his wet snout and give him a big hug. "Good dog, very good dog. I thought it was gone forever in the marsh."

Melissa starts to sob.

"What's been going on here?" Ben asks.

"We'll tell you over brunch." I put my arm around Melissa, and we all start walking to the car. "It's okay," I say to Melissa, and she starts to calm.

"Hey, I can't believe I almost forgot to tell you. An advance copy of your next book came today," Ben says as we climbed the marsh bank.

"Book? So you're a writer?" Melissa says between sniffles.

"Yes."

She slaps her hand to her forehead. "Oh my goodness. I've just realized who you are. *The Mystery of the Marsh*. That book changed my life. I can't believe it. I almost killed Mary Helen Reynolds."

"I use my maiden name for my pen name."

"Here, Sylvester, get in the car," Ben calls.

Sylvester bounds up from the marsh, jumps in the car, and splashes everyone with marsh water. As Ben loads Melissa's bike on the rack, I open the door for Melissa. She pauses. "What's this?" she asks pointing to a sign on the car door.

"Oh, that's an advertisement for Ben's businesses. He inherited Dillard's Atlantic Charters from his dad, of course."

"Right, but this says Ralph's Fresh Produce Markets as well."

"That's right. Ben manages Ralph's Fresh Produce Markets all over this part of the state. Ralph left the business to me. He wasn't kidding about giving me tomatoes for life."

Melissa erupts into laughter, and everyone starts to pile into the car. A loud catcall pierces the air.

"Pretty girl, pretty girl."

Melissa's eyes widen. "Is that … ?"

"Melissa, I'd like you to meet Wallace, our African grey parrot."

"He's in the car?" Melissa peers into the back seat.

"He's an old guy now, but when the Kendall's moved to Miami they gave him to Ben, and he goes with us everywhere," I said. "He obviously likes you."

Melissa nods as she takes a seat.

Ben walks around the driver's side of the car and puts his hand on the handle. "Hey, this is great, we have enough for a foursome in Scrabble later."

"I can't believe you want to play again, especially since I beat you so badly the other night," I say.

"I've been studying the dictionary." He winks at me.

Just before I take my seat in the car, I turn to my beloved marsh once more, and I can almost hear her voice saying:

> By so many roots as the marsh-grass sends in the sod
> I will heartily lay me a-hold on the greatness of God:
> Oh, like to the greatness of God is the greatness within
> The range of the marshes, the liberal marshes of
> Glynn.

Author's Note

Each of us has a few Chestnut trees in our lives who've helped us become the people we are today.

As Aunt Laney said, some have already been swept up into the arms of the Father. We must wait until we see them in heaven to thank them.

But others are our daily companions. Still others, we've lost touch with due to distance or time. Wouldn't today be a wonderful day to sit down, like Mary Helen, and her father before her, to write a note or two to express our gratefulness?

Who knows what God might do through our gratitude?

B. V.

Recipes

Mary Helen encountered another culture when she first came to St. Simons Island, and much of the island's culture was defined by its food. At first she resisted any departure from the familiar favorites of her childhood, but in the years that followed, she found the foods she most resisted often became her lifelong favorites. To that end, Mary Helen felt it wasn't enough to share about the chestnut pen, Aunt Laney, Ralph, Ben, and Sidney Lanier. She wanted to pass on the cuisine, which she has enjoyed for many years with her friends and family and which has helped shape the memories her own children will carry into their lives.

Tomato Sandwiches

Tomato sandwiches are a staple in summer kitchens south of the Mason-Dixon Line. Everyone has their own version—some with crusts, some without. Some on the traditional white bread—some on the artisan breads so popular today.

Aunt Laney's Tomato Sandwiches

Aunt Laney's take on tomato sandwiches always included the heirloom Brandywine tomato often found growing in the field of an organic or heirloom farm or purchased from Ralph's Fresh Produce. Ralph is the one who originally told Aunt Laney about the tomato, and Laney found he never steered her wrong with his recommendations.

Brandywine Tomatoes
Mayonnaise
White Bread
Salt and Pepper

Slice tomatoes to desired thickness. Spread mayonnaise on bread, and then layer tomatoes. Sprinkle with salt and pepper, cover with another slice of bread, and enjoy.

Alice's Tomato Sandwiches

Though Aunt Laney's version of the tomato sandwich is a favorite, Mary Helen also found another way of preparing them that she came to love just as much—but with a slight twist. She, too, found the Brandywine tomato the best for this sandwich. She received this recipe from her friend Alice Mills, who along with her husband, Tim, own Mills's Heirloom Farm in North Georgia.

> Brandywine tomatoes
> Sliced Provolone cheese
> Olive oil
> Salt and Pepper
> Whole Grain Bread (toasted if you like)

Spread a little olive oil on a slice of whole grain bread. Slice tomatoes and arrange on the bread. Cover with a piece of provolone cheese and another slice of bread.

Fried Okra

Aunt Laney always said the secret to fried okra is to have the oil hot before you put in the okra.

> Fresh Okra
> Canola Oil
> Cornmeal
> Flour

Wash the okra, drain but don't dry, and then cut it into slices about 1/8 to ¼ inch thick. Put two cups cornmeal and ½-cup flour in a plastic gallon size bag. Put 1 cup of okra in the bag and shake until okra is evenly coated. Spoon into hot oil, and cook until golden brown. Repeat.

Stuffed Peppers

Ben loves the way Mary Helen prepares stuffed peppers. Of course if it hadn't been for that summer Mary Helen spent on the island with Aunt Laney, she might have never come to appreciate this dinner favorite.

> 1 pound of lean ground beef
> ½ cup oatmeal
> ½ cup chopped onion
> 4 green peppers
> ½ cup ketchup

Wash and core green peppers. Mix oatmeal, onion, ketchup, and ground beef together. Stuff into peppers and bake at 350 degrees for 30 minutes.

Mrs. Kirby's Chicken Casserole

This is the casserole Mrs. Kirby served the night Mary Helen and Aunt Laney had dinner with her. Of course she didn't prepare it—Eleanor did—but Mrs. Kirby insists this is her recipe.

> 4 boned chicken breasts
> 1 can cream of chicken soup
> 1 sixteen ounce carton sour cream
> 2 small jars artichoke hearts (drained)
> 1 package frozen broccoli
> Cheese or wheat cracker crumbs

Preheat oven to 350 degrees. Boil chicken until thoroughly cooked. Chop and mix with all other ingredients except crackers. Put in a 13 by 9 inch pan. Top with buttered wheat or cheese cracker crumbs. Bake until bubbly.

Stewed Squash

Mary Helen initially turned up her nose at this dish, but now she can't wait for Ben to bring in the first tender squash of the summer to Ralph's Fresh Produce Markets.

> 5 or 6 yellow squash
> 1 small Vidalia onion
> Salt and pepper.

Slice squash and cover with water in a pan. Add chopped onion, salt, and pepper. Cook until tender over medium heat.

Crab Cakes

Sorry, but Aunt Laney never gave anyone her crab cake recipe. However, there are several coastal restaurants in the St. Simons area that serve outstanding crab cakes.

The Marshes of Glynn

Glooms of the live-oaks, beautiful-braided and woven
With intricate shades of the vines that myriad-cloven
    Clamber the forks of the multiform boughs,—
        Emerald twilights,—
        Virginal shy lights,
Wrought of the leaves to allure to the whisper of vows,
When lovers pace timidly down through the green colonnades
Of the dim sweet woods, of the dear dark woods,
    Of the heavenly woods and glades,
That run to the radiant marginal sand-beach within
    The wide sea-marshes of Glynn;—

Beautiful glooms, soft dusks in the noon-day fire,—
Wildwood privacies, closets of lone desire,
Chamber from chamber parted with wavering arras of leaves,—
Cells for the passionate pleasure of prayer to the soul that grieves,
Pure with a sense of the passing of saints through the wood,
Cool for the dutiful weighing of ill with good;—

O braided dusks of the oak and woven shades of the vine,
While the riotous noon-day sun of the June-day long did shine
Ye held me fast in your heart and I held you fast in mine;
But now when the noon is no more, and riot is rest,
And the sun is a-wait at the ponderous gate of the West,
And the slant yellow beam down the wood-aisle doth seem
Like a lane into heaven that leads from a dream,—
Ay, now, when my soul all day hath drunken the soul of the oak,
And my heart is at ease from men, and the wearisome sound of the stroke
    Of the scythe of time and the trowel of trade is low,
        And belief overmasters doubt, and I know that I know,

And my spirit is grown to a lordly great compass within,
That the length and the breadth and the sweep of the marshes of Glynn
Will work me no fear like the fear they have wrought me of yore
When length was fatigue, and when breadth was but bitterness sore,
And when terror and shrinking and dreary unnamable pain
Drew over me out of the merciless miles of the plain,—

Oh, now, unafraid, I am fain to face
The vast sweet visage of space.
To the edge of the wood I am drawn, I am drawn,
Where the gray beach glimmering runs, as a belt of the dawn,
     For a mete and a mark
        To the forest-dark:—
          So:
Affable live-oak, leaning low,—
Thus—with your favor—soft, with a reverent hand,
(Not lightly touching your person, Lord of the land!)
Bending your beauty aside, with a step I stand
On the firm-packed sand
         Free
By a world of marsh that borders a world of sea.
     Sinuous southward and sinuous northward the shimmering band
      Of the sand-beach fastens the fringe of the marsh to the folds of
       the land.
Inward and outward to northward and southward the beach-lines linger
     and curl
As a silver-wrought garment that clings to and follows the firm sweet limbs
     of a girl.
Vanishing, swerving, evermore curving again into sight,
Softly the sand-beach wavers away to a dim gray looping of light.
And what if behind me to westward the wall of the woods stands high?
The world lies east: how ample, the marsh and the sea and the sky!
A league and a league of marsh-grass, waist-high, broad in the blade,
Green, and all of a height, and unflecked with a light or a shade,
Stretch leisurely off, in a pleasant plain,
To the terminal blue of the main.

Oh, what is abroad in the marsh and the terminal sea?
     Somehow my soul seems suddenly free

From the weighing of fate and the sad discussion of sin,
By the length and the breadth and the sweep of the marshes of Glynn.

Ye marshes, how candid and simple and nothing-withholding and free
Ye publish yourselves to the sky and offer yourselves to the sea!
Tolerant plains, that suffer the sea and the rains and the sun,
Ye spread and span like the catholic man who hath mightily won
God out of knowledge and good out of infinite pain
And sight out of blindness and purity out of a stain.

As the marsh-hen secretly builds on the watery sod,
Behold I will build me a nest on the greatness of God:
I will fly in the greatness of God as the marsh-hen flies
In the freedom that fills all the space 'twixt the marsh and the skies:
By so many roots as the marsh-grass sends in the sod
I will heartily lay me a-hold on the greatness of God:
Oh, like to the greatness of God is the greatness within
The range of the marshes, the liberal marshes of Glynn.

And the sea lends large, as the marsh: lo, out of his plenty the sea
Pours fast: full soon the time of the flood-tide must be:
Look how the grace of the sea doth go
About and about through the intricate channels that flow
        Here and there,
                Everywhere,
Till his waters have flooded the uttermost creeks and the low-lying lanes,
And the marsh is meshed with a million veins,
That like as with rosy and silvery essences flow
        In the rose-and-silver evening glow.
           Farewell, my lord Sun!
The creeks overflow: a thousand rivulets run
'Twixt the roots of the sod; the blades of the marsh-grass stir;
Passeth a hurrying sound of wings that westward whirr;
Passeth, and all is still; and the currents cease to run;
And the sea and the marsh are one.

How still the plains of the waters be!
The tide is in his ecstasy.
The tide is at his highest height:
        And it is night.

And now from the Vast of the Lord will the waters of sleep
Roll in on the souls of men,
But who will reveal to our waking ken
The forms that swim and the shapes that creep
        Under the waters of sleep?
And I would I could know what swimmeth below when the tide comes in
On the length and the breadth of the marvellous marshes of Glynn.

Sidney Lanier—Baltimore, 1878

Acknowledgements

My many thanks ...

To my husband, Jerry, who read and reread the story from conception to final draft and encouraged me in the long days of waiting. I love you more ...

To my precious children, Aaron and Bethany, who I know have made sacrifices because of my writing and helped by reading the story aloud. My love for you both only grows with each passing year. To Mari, Brent, Walker and Sara Alden for your love and encouragement. Thank you Brent for the web help. To my sister and best friend, Tammy Todd, who through countless conversations wouldn't let me give up on the dream, and to her husband, Foy Todd, for sharing her with me. To my nephew Christopher, with whom I share a passion for the music of life. To my dad, Steve Chitwood and his wife, Irene, for a lifetime of love and the phone calls that help anchor my days. To Marni Dodd and Mandy Dorsett Perry, my dear almost daughters; and to my Aunt Nell Dooley for doing great things in her latter days.

To a group of faithful, praying women on my email list. You've been such a blessing. To these people, not only for their prayers but for proofreading: Nancy Fajardo; Evelyn Voris; and especially Lilyan Hanberry West, who once saved my life. A special thanks to Dr. Joel Cook for his proofreading and his medical advice to my characters. And to Elizabeth Ludwig, who was such a help early in the process.

To the people of Gateway Church, who were our family for twenty-five years, among them Jerri Ziegler; Amy Williams; Claudia Woodruff; Lilyan West; Cathy Coburn Harris; and Marion Bond West Acuff, who Sunday after Sunday for several years helped me call things that were yet to be as though they were. Thanks to Dr. Gene Acuff for the nourishment, Cheryl Cook for a special painting, Rev. Rick and Mary Lucy Bonfim for Brazil; also to Andy and Julia Hines, Alton and Freida Thornton (Freida,

215

your Christian fiction insights have been so helpful), and Tom and Terese Crane for your faithful support.

To our new family at Ray's Church for your warm embrace and much love.

To the men of the Athens YMCA Bible study, for long years of steadfast prayers on my behalf. To an amazing group of my husband's pastor friends, whom I affectionately call "The Cronies": Howard Conine, Lee McNeil, Mark Northcutt, Morris Sapp, and Scott Shepherd. Your friendship to our family has been life giving. To Dr. Warren and Jane Lathem, Rev. Grady and Doris Wigley, Dr. Gary and Diane Whetstone for your spiritual guidance. To Bishop Mike Watson for carefully tending the sheep in his flock. To faithful friends Joseph and Joye Slife, Jim and Joy Meunier, Rev. Dan and Brenda Dixon, Rev. Tom and Melissa Tanner, Elizabeth Wolfe, Griffin and Betty Moody, Carolyn Cathey, Dick and Marilyn Williamson, Dr. Cody and Janie Gunn, Rev. Bob and Carole Murphy and our friends old and new at St. James. To Jane Kilgo and Sandy Blount, companions on this journey for many years. To sister J. for traveling half a lifetime with me. Someday …

To Jim Talley, the talented woodworking artist who created the chestnut pen that inspired the one in this story.

To my agent, Les Stobbe—truly a legend in Christian publishing.

To my many writing mentors—Jan Karon, who years ago took the time to write and encourage me personally. To Gayle Roper, Susan King, and Deborah Raney for their wonderful teaching and exhortations. To Yvonne Lehman, founder of the Blue Ridge Mountain Christian Writer's Conference, from which so many good writing related events in my life have sprung, including my involvement with the Gideon Conference and Rodney and Lori Marrett. To Rusty Whitener, who offered words of hope when my spirit sagged, and to his wife, Rebecca, for her prayers. To my high-school English teacher, Connie Harding, who read the poems of a budding teenage writer and took them seriously. To Bettie Sellers, my college professor and notable Georgia poet. To Harriette Austin, who has influenced me more than she can ever know. To Terry Kay, who gives hours of his precious time to unknown writers like me.

To the American Christian Fiction Writers and the Christian Writers Guild, who have taught me much.

To my writing friends at the East Metro Atlanta Christian Writers, who sponsored the contest that provided the door for this book to be in print, and especially to their director and president, Colleen Jackson and

Joyce Fincher. You've made a difference in the lives of so many writers, including mine.

To Westbow/Thomas Nelson, who generously awarded this book package as the prize for the above contest. Along with the books, you gave fulfilled dreams, as well. A special thank you to Monica whose editorial encouragement has meant so much.

To the readers of my blog, *One Ringing Bell, http://bev-oneringingbell. blogspot.com,* you've been such blessings.

To the late Edward Mims, who provided much historical background through his book *A Biography of the Poet, Sidney Lanier.* To the folks at the St. Simons Library and St. Simons Island Bait and Tackle for help with research. Special thanks to Nancy Thomason at Beachview books for a great suggestion.

To one of the greatest American poets to ever hold a pen, Sidney Lanier. As a tribute to your enduring work, many a Georgia schoolchild will continue to carry your words in their hearts.

To friends long departed, Becky Bramlett Carter and Debbie Benton Parrish, whose lights will never dim in my life. In memory of my still loved and missed neighbors, Margaret and Mell Edwards. And to our beloved Dr. Jim Kilgo, whose inspiring words helped carry me to this place.

To my mother who never saw but now leads the cheers from heaven.

Most of all, I give thanks to the God I love and serve, who planted this story in my heart and helped me hear the voice of a fourteen-year-old girl named Mary Helen.

Ad majorem Dei gloriam

"To the greater glory of God"

About the Author

Beverly Varnado's *Give My Love to the Chestnut Trees* was one of ten semifinalists in the 2010 Christian Writers Guild Operation First Novel contest. Also in 2010, she won a writing competition with the East Metro Atlanta Christian Writers and was awarded a book deal with Westbow, a division of Thomas Nelson. In 2009, Varnado's script for this story was a finalist for the Kairos Prize, and in 2008 and 2009, it was a finalist at the Gideon Film Festival.

Beverly's nonfiction has appeared in several publications, including *The Upper Room Magazine*, ChristianDevotions.US, and a Focus on the Family publication. Her work garnered two honorable mentions in the 2007 Writer's Digest Competition.

She makes her home in Athens, Georgia, with her husband, Jerry, their children, Aaron and Bethany, and an ever-changing number of cats, dogs, fish, and occasional reptiles. A lifelong church musician, worship leader, and songwriter, she also sings with the Athens Symphony Chorus.

Visit her on her blog, bev-oneringingbell.blogspot.com or her website www.BeverlyVarnado.com

The screenplay for Give My Love to the Chestnut Trees is under option with Dave Moody of Elevating Entertainment. Find out more at http://greenlightgroupe.com

CPSIA information can be obtained at www.ICGtesting.com
Printed in the USA
LVOW061344051011

249217LV00002B/4/P